SIDELINE

INFRACTION

EMILY SILVER

TRAVELIN' HOOSIER BOOKS

Copyright © 2022 by Emily Silver

All rights reserved.

This is a work of fiction. Names, characters, places and incidents are either the product of the author's imagination or are use fictitiously. Any resemblance to actual persons, living or dead, businesses, companies, events or locations is entirely coincidental.

No part of this book may be reproduced in any form or by any electronic or mechanical means, including information storage and retrieval systems, without written permission from the author, except for the use of brief quotations in a book review. For more information, please email the author at authoremilysilver@gmail.com.

Cover Design by Kari March Designs

Editing by Happily Editing Anns

www.authoremilysilver.com

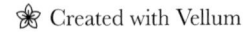

❦ Created with Vellum

Flag on the Play

SIDELINE INFRACTION

Definition: A player is outside of the team box, a coach is outside the coaches' box (along the sideline in front of the team box), or too many coaches are in the coaches' box

Chapter One
ALEX

"Black Fifty-two. Black Fifty-two. Set, hike!" The ball snaps and hits my fingers at the perfect angle. Scanning the field, Colin is right where I expect him to be. Backpedaling, I launch the ball twenty yards down the field.

It's the perfect spiral, landing right in Colin's waiting hands. He's a blur as he races into the end zone.

"Fuck yeah! That was perfect, Young!" Our center, Kelly, claps me on the helmet.

"It was a beauty, right?" I laugh as I jog toward the sidelines.

Even after being in the league for six years, watching the perfect pass hit its target is a feeling that doesn't get old.

"Damn, Alex. You're making us look bad out there." Knox is at the sidelines, swigging water.

It's the first week of training camp and spirits are high. We're excited to be back this year. After a tough loss in the playoffs, everyone is ready to go far this season.

"Maybe if you actually knew how to block, you

could've stopped me," Colin jests as he comes back to the sideline.

"Fuck off, man. You wouldn't know what hit you if I landed a block."

Chugging water, I listen to these two go back and forth. It's the thing I miss most during off-season.

Sure, there are workouts and team activities, but it doesn't beat this. Getting to play and train together.

I live for this.

"Maybe you should work on your block, Fisher. Could use some more power," Frankie states, matter-of-factly, as she walks toward the defense.

"Dude. What did we say about getting off her bad side?" I swat at his pads. "She's going to bench you if you're not careful."

He dumps his water over his head, cooling off in the late-summer heat. "I could figure out world peace, and she would probably still find a reason to be mad at me."

"Good thing she's not taking it out on me. I don't know if I could do another full workout like you do." Knocking back the rest of my water, I throw my water bottle to the bench and head back onto the field.

Knox flips us off as we all run back to the huddle. "Alright, boys. Quit gossiping. Time to run through some more plays."

Fuck, I love football.

"ANYONE UP FOR A DRINK TONIGHT?" Pulling the T-shirt over my head, I look up to see four sets of eyes staring back at me. Like they've already had this discussion and couldn't figure out who would break it to me.

"Sorry, man. Noah is still colicky, so I'm heading home to help out." Jackson gives me a chagrined smile. Being a new dad, if he's not at practice, he's at home. That kid has him wrapped around his little finger.

"I'm hopefully seeing Audrey tonight." Logan has a dopey look on his face.

"You're still seeing her?" I ask, grabbing my bag out of my locker.

"I mean, she hasn't dumped me yet."

"How a beautiful woman like that wants to be with your ugly mug, I will never know." Knox ruffles Logan's hair as he tries to shove him off.

"What about you two?" I wave a finger between Knox and Colin.

Knox shakes his head. "Can't. I have plans to kick my grandma's ass in bridge."

"What happened to Bingo?" Colin asks.

"Bingo got a little too intense. They were told they couldn't allow it after a bloody nose."

Colin bursts out laughing. "Fuck. I love Darlene. I need to go visit her."

"Take Peyton. She'll love her." Knox points in his direction.

"No way. Darlene will give her all sorts of ways to gang up on me."

I roll my eyes. "Please. As if she needs to find a reason." I elbow Colin. "You up for a drink?"

Digging around in his locker, Colin pulls out our trusty bottle of bourbon and two plastic cups. "How about we head out to the field and have a drink?"

I take the proffered cup. "Sounds good to me."

This late in the afternoon, the practice field is deserted. The sun has slowly made its way closer to the mountains, but the heat of the day hasn't loosened its stranglehold.

"Don't feel like being alone tonight?" Colin asks, dropping down on top of the Mountain Lion logo in the center of the field.

"Nah. Too much energy with our first preseason game coming up." I don't want to tell him the real reason I don't want to go home.

"Tampa Bay will be a good team this year. Think they're going all the way?"

I shake my head. "Not if we can help it."

"God, we're so close. If we lose to Vegas again, I'm going to be pissed."

"We're the better team, by far."

Colin sips his drink, leaning back on his elbows, taking in the field. "And yet, we still can't make it to the big game."

"It's going to happen for us. I can feel it."

It's a question that has plagued the Mountain Lions for the last few years. We have the team and the talent. But we can't seem to get past that one final hurdle.

Every sports analyst out there asks if we have the talent to go far. If *I* have the talent to win the big game.

I hate that I get singled out. It's a team sport, but the weight falls on my shoulders. If I have an off game and we lose, the blame is placed at my feet.

Just like us losing in the first round of the playoffs last year.

"Who let you two out here unsupervised?" Peyton strides toward us. Colin's entire face lights up at seeing her.

"I thought you went home." Grabbing her hand, he pulls her down next to him and lays one on her.

I shift my gaze to the mountains in the distance.

This. This was why I didn't want to go home.

The suffocating quiet of being alone. I don't have someone to go home to. And now, with the guys partnering off, the amount of alone time during the season is increasing. There's only so much film a man can study before he starts to lose his mind.

And I fucking hate it.

"How was practice today?"

"Colin made a great catch. Think we're looking good." I down the rest of my drink and add a bit more, not wanting to get wasted out on the field.

"You should've seen his pass, Rocky. It was a thing of beauty."

Peyton smiles at me. "I know it was. We have the best quarterback-receiver duo in the league."

"You have to say that because you're dating this guy." I wave off her compliment.

"You clearly don't know me very well if you think I wouldn't call him out." Peyton quirks a brow at me.

"It's true, man." Colin nods in agreement. "Who else will tell me what I do wrong other than her?"

I shrug a shoulder. "What about your receivers' coach?"

"Please. They're too nice about it. I need some harsher feedback."

Peyton punches his shoulder. "Excuse me. I'm not harsh."

"I just like how you dole it out." He wiggles his eyebrows in her direction.

"I'd say get a room, but I think you actually would."

"You're missing out, Alex." Colin doesn't look at me as he says it.

Ever since he got back together with Peyton, Colin has turned into a complete sap. I never thought I'd see the day where I saw him fall in love, but these two could not be more perfect for each other.

"Maybe Darlene could set you up." Peyton turns to me

with a grin that matches Colin's. She's equally as happy with him. And considering Colin is my closest friend on the team, Peyton and I have become friends over the last few months.

"I don't think Darlene could find someone to meet my tastes."

Colin and Peyton dissolve into their own conversation about my perfect woman.

Except they are so far off the mark, it's not even funny.

Because my perfect person isn't a woman.

It's the reason I keep my private life so private. Why I limit myself to hookups only in the off-season in places where no one knows who I am.

Because if anyone found out that I am gay, my future in the NFL would be gone in the blink of an eye.

And that's not something I'm ready to give up.

I let them speculate as I sip my drink, hating that I'm lying to them. But it's the only way I can keep moving forward.

To my goal of winning a Super Bowl.

A man will come later.

I hope.

Chapter Two
CARTER

"Mr. Brooks. Can I have a word with you?" Mrs. Phillips pops her head into the classroom.

"Ooh. Someone's in trouble," I hear from the back of the classroom.

"Alright. Keep working on the assignment and I'll be back in a minute." I wave the students off as I meet my department head in the hallway.

"Sorry to disrupt the class, but just wanted to check in with the semester project for your class. I'll be out on leave in a few days, and want to be sure I have everything lined up for my sub." She rubs her oversized pregnant belly.

"I've got a few ideas lined up."

I love teaching. It's one of my passions. But this is the part I hate. Having to meet certain standards and making sure those get reported up the food chain.

"Make sure to have it to me by Friday, please." She pats me on the arm as she waddles down the hallway.

I've been trying to come up with a project that will make my AP Statistics students excited to learn. I keep coming up empty.

Opening the door, my ears are hit with words I'd never expect to hear in this city.

"The Mountain Lions suck."

"Whoa, you can't say that!"

"But it's true."

"You suck!"

"Lame comeback."

Oh for fuck's sake.

"Guys, what's going on over here?" Every set of eyes in the classroom is now on the two students bickering about our football team.

"Austin said the Mountain Lions suck!" Gabe answers in a rush.

"It's because they do, Mr. Brooks." Austin gives me a hard look, daring me to argue.

"And why do you say that?" Crossing my arms, I wait for his answer.

"Based on their win-loss ratio the last few years and the team's overall stats, they should have won at least one Super Bowl by now."

"Did you look at the statistics for the teams that have won?"

Austin nods vigorously. "Yes. Their stats aren't as good. Denver has the best team. Why aren't they winning?"

"Is this what you wanted us to find out when you gave us this assignment?" Gabe asks.

I huff out a laugh. "To say that the Mountain Lions suck? Not in those terms, no."

Gabe smacks Austin on the arm. "See? You can't keep saying that."

"I can if it's true."

"Then why did you give us this assignment?" someone shouts from the back of the classroom.

The joys of being a high school teacher.

Half the time, it is like pulling teeth getting the students to listen to me. The other half? They are buried in their phones on the latest social media craze.

Numbers? Numbers I understand.

The woes of high schoolers these days? Not so much.

"The idea was to see the practical uses of statistics in everyday life," I tell them. "Everyone knows football."

"I don't really like football, Mr. Brooks," Lucy says, her voice quiet from the front of the room. Students like her are the easy ones—always doing their homework and never complaining.

"You're not missing much, Lucy. As a Mountain Lions fan, I can statistically say, they suck. You should cheer for Vegas," Austin pipes up.

"Dude! That's even worse than saying the Mountain Lions suck," Gabe hisses. "Nobody likes Vegas."

"Can you stop saying they suck?" I ask Austin.

"I'm only following the assignment."

An idea comes to mind. One that would satisfy the semester project and give these guys a unique experience. "Want to see your statistics in action?"

"What do you mean, Mr. Brooks?"

"Instead of just looking at the statistics, why don't we go to the football team and see the statistics in person?"

"Please." Austin laughs. "The high school team actually does suck. We wouldn't learn anything there."

I shake my head. "Not the high school team. And you shouldn't say they suck either. Mr. Charles would make you run laps for that." I give him a knowing smile. "I'm talking about the Mountain Lions."

Austin's face visibly pales. "Wh-what? You don't have access to the team."

"Dude. Mr. Brooks's dad is the coach, duh." Gabe

slaps him on the shoulder. "You really need to pay attention more."

"Oh shit," I hear him mumble under his breath.

"I'm sure the team would love to hear your thoughts on why, as you say, they suck."

"Okay, I'll stop saying they suck," Austin says, throwing his hands up.

"Young would eat you alive." Gabe laughs. "He's the best quarterback we've ever had!"

"It's not like I'm joining the team."

"Okay, everyone. Notebooks out." I cut them off before they can descend into another argument. "This semester, we are going to be looking at the practical applications of statistics and how they can be used to predict a football team's win-loss ratio."

My eyes find Gabe and Austin. Gabe is whisper-shouting at Austin, who still looks ghostly pale.

"I will see if I can arrange a day to meet the Mountain Lions, maybe even talk to some of the staff on how they use statistics to help with the team."

There are a few whoops and hollers and some groans from others.

"Maybe we can meet the cheerleaders," Gabe whispers.

"Doubt they'd be interested in a skinny sophomore kid," Austin snickers.

Just another day in the life of a high school teacher.

Chapter Three
ALEX

"Think you can get past me today?" Knox slaps Logan on his pads.

"I'm going to barrel right over you." Logan pushes him off.

"In your dreams, kid. In your dreams."

"I'm going to break that tackle and run eighty yards into the end zone for the touchdown."

Knox laughs in Logan's face. "Now I know you're dreaming."

"Fuck off, man."

Colin pulls Logan and Knox apart as Jackson runs into the locker room.

"You're late, Fields." I tap my watch in his direction.

"Try telling a six-month-old that in the middle of a cry fest."

Jackson looks more exhausted than ever, but I've never seen him happier.

"When do we get to meet the little guy?" Knox asks.

"As soon as he stops screaming at the top of his lungs?"

"Colic hasn't gotten any better?" I pull my practice jersey over my head.

"No. And now that the season will be starting, I'll be around less. I'm exhausted, but I'm trying to be there for Tenley every minute I can."

"Need help from us?" Colin asks, leaning against the lockers.

Jackson shakes his head, scrubbing a hand down his face. "I appreciate it, but we're good. The grandparents are helping out."

"Thank God. Because I wouldn't know the first thing about helping with a baby." Logan breathes a sigh of relief.

"That's because you're still a baby yourself." Knox laughs.

"Fuck you, man!"

"You're too young to be using that language," Colin further goads him.

"You guys are the worst."

I laugh as they give each other grief. Looking around the locker room, it's hard to believe this is the start of my seventh year. Everything about this place has become like a second home to me throughout my career.

The wooden lockers with name plates. The city skyline that paints the wall. The Mountain Lion logo on the floor.

And being a captain for this team means more than anything. Leading this group of guys means the world to me. More than anything else I might have going on in my life.

"Alright men, listen up!"

The locker room quiets at Coach Brooks's words. When Coach talks, everyone listens.

"We've been looking good out there. Some mistakes we can clean up, but overall, good team play." He shifts his gaze to where I'm standing at my locker. "Today we have some special guests coming in during practice. Captains, I want you to show them hospitality. Answer any questions they might have."

"Who are they, Coach?" I ask.

"A high school statistics class. They're learning about the practical applications of math."

"And football is practical?" Knox asks.

Coach stares back at him. "I'll let them answer that question for you."

"First Frankie giving you a hard time at practice, and now coach?" I slap him on the shoulder as I grab my helmet from my locker. "Someone's going to get it later."

"Now cut the chitchat and get out on the field. We've got a lot of work to do if we want to go far in the playoffs this year! Let's all have a great day of practice," Coach barks out at us.

Running out of the locker room, I am temporarily blinded by the bright sun shining on the practice field. It's a scorcher of a day, but will make for a good day of practice.

Knox jogs off toward the opposite end of the field as the defense starts their drills. Jackson heads off in another direction as Colin and I meet with our offensive coordinator.

"Alright boys, we've got some new plays we want to run with you."

"What are you thinking?"

"I thought a lot about the holes in our offensive plays after the loss in the playoffs last year."

"Probably one that could have been avoided," a voice quietly states from behind our coach. A group of kids is standing around.

"Dude! He totally heard you."

"I'm sorry, who are you guys?" I ask.

Both kids stare back at me, mouths gaping open. "I'm Gabe, and this is Austin."

"And what do you mean one that could have been avoided?" I cross my arms, giving him my best stare down, one meant to intimidate opposing defenses.

"Uhh…"

"C'mon. Tell me."

"This oughta be good," his friend whispers.

"Well, whenever you threw the ball to James, he'd only get five or six yards."

"Okay." Colin and I glance at each other before looking back to him.

"He's the top receiver for the team, so it makes sense."

"Hey, thanks kid." Colin nods at the teen.

The kid is now beaming at Colin acknowledging him. "But whenever you threw to your tight end, he'd break out for ten or more yards. No matter what corrections you made, the defense was always all over Colin."

"You want to try it?"

His face visibly pales. "Me?"

"Yeah. I know it looks easy and everything on TV, but when you're staring down linebackers like Fisher, it's not easy."

"C'mon, Austin. Do it!" The other kid eggs him on.

"Okay. But I don't know how good I'll be."

"I'll show you how to catch," Colin jogs over to him as someone appears behind them.

"What did you guys get yourselves into?"

Shifting my attention, I'm met with the most beautiful pair of dark blue eyes. Whoever this person is, he's sexy in the classic movie star kind of way. Sharp, defined features and blond hair that sweeps perfectly over his forehead. He looks like a real-life version of Superman—if Superman were blond. Right down to the dark-rimmed glasses.

"Sorry, they aren't being too much trouble, are they?"

His voice breaks me from my perusal. Thank God I'm already hot from the weight room earlier, or the flush in my cheeks would give away just how much I'm checking this person out.

"Well, I was told we could've avoided the loss in the playoffs because I wasn't throwing the ball to the right person. So he's going to put his money where his mouth is."

The mystery man swears under his breath. "Honestly, that's probably the nicest way he could've phrased that."

"And what would a bad way look like?"

"To be honest?" I nod my head. "He said the Mountain Lions suck."

"Whoa now."

He laughs. "Like I said, that was a nice way. He means well. He knows statistics like you wouldn't believe, so it's easy for him to read the numbers and not take anything else into account."

"Okay. So are you in charge of all of them then?" Looking around the field, I see there are groups of students everywhere.

"I am." He extends a hand in my direction. "Carter Brooks. I'm their math teacher."

I take his hand and instantly regret it. Because the shock of electricity that zings up my arm is very inconvenient. "Alex Young."

"I know who you are." He drops my hand. "I'd have to be living under a rock not to know who you are in this city."

I shrug my shoulders. "It'd be impolite if I didn't introduce myself. So, how'd you get the team to let your class come down here?"

"With a last name of Brooks, it was kind of easy.

Promote it as a learning opportunity and the team gets some good press."

"Brooks…I'm guessing you're related to the coach?"

"He's my dad."

Holy shit. As if my reaction to him wasn't bad enough, now I find out he's Coach's son. I glance around the field. No one is paying us the slightest bit of attention. Everyone is working on plays or talking with the kids.

"And you didn't grow up to be a football player?"

"I'm a math teacher. I think you can put together that I was very much not an athlete growing up."

I have to force myself not to rake my eyes over his body. "I bet you broke your dad's heart."

He laughs, a beautiful sound that hits me in my gut. "I think he knew the first time I tried to throw a football that it wasn't in my future."

"Maybe you just didn't have me showing you how to do it."

Fuck. And now I'm flirting with this guy.

"Alex, you ready?" Colin shouts from the sidelines. He's given the kid his gloves, as I send a nod his way.

"Let's do it."

"Try not to embarrass him too badly, okay?" Carter asks. "I don't want to have to deal with the kids giving him crap over it."

"Hey, if he can't put his money where his mouth is, maybe he shouldn't be talking smack."

"God. All you football players are exactly the same."

"Hey. We're not all the same."

"Care to prove me wrong?" Carter gives me a challenging look, one I like a little too much.

I should not be having these reactions to him. I should put him in the off-limits box and focus my attention on football.

Sideline Infraction

Like I always do.

Except, for the first time in a long time, I don't want to. That zap of electricity I felt is something I haven't felt in a long time.

One might even consider my lifestyle one of a monk.

So I do the dangerous thing.

"Let me prove this kid wrong, and then I'll do the same for you."

I don't miss the way his face heats up, and now I want to impress him even more.

"Alright, let's do this, kid," I shout toward the sideline. Grabbing a ball from one of the assistants, I call the play. The kid takes off running down the sideline, Colin on his heels as a defender.

I launch the ball, putting a little less spin on it than I normally would. He makes a dive for it, but the ball sails just past his fingertips.

"I knew you couldn't do it!" His friend laughs from the sideline.

I can still feel Carter's eyes on me as I jog over to the students.

"You're up, kid."

The quarterback coach is grumbling on the bench, but I ignore it. Colin and I work with each of the kids, tossing and catching balls, showing them the plays that they were critiquing us on.

It's fun. We set up a quick game with some of the defense and get them all involved. I feel Carter's eyes track me as we mess around. He's staying firmly on the sideline, not budging.

Turns out, it was a pretty great day of practice overall.

CARTER

"I DON'T THINK I've ever seen you so interested in a practice before." Dad's voice startles me from behind where I've found a spot to watch the happenings on the field.

"Just observing my students." I turn to face the man who I'm a spitting image of.

"I think the last time I saw you on a football field was when I was still playing."

"There's no way it's been that long," I scoff.

Having grown up around football, you would think I'd be more accustomed to being on the field. But one dickhead ruined the sport for me. Even supporting my dad became hard because of the players.

"Pretty sure it was when we lost in the playoffs. Very last game of my career."

I try to remember the last time. "But if that's true, I would've been seven. I've been around after that."

Dad throws his hands up in defense. "I'm not judging why. Your old man is just saying it's nice to see you where he works."

Alex has taken over the game, coaching my gang of unruly students. "Young looks good out there with the kids. Maybe he'll be gunning for your job in a few years."

Dad laughs. "Careful, kid. You're starting to sound like your mom."

"How?"

"That woman would have me retiring tomorrow if it were up to her."

"So why do you still do it? I'd be terrified of Mom."

Dad claps me on the shoulder. "Because she knows

how much I love it. She would get sick of having me at the house all the time."

My eyes drift back to Alex again. He shook my hand, but it felt like he scrambled my brain. I could feel those brown eyes on mine the moment we touched. The way his brown hair flopped into his eyes? He was sexy without even trying.

Damn football players.

I've dated a few guys over the years, but no one was ever *the one*. They didn't like the nerdy math teacher that was my very persona.

This time, my gaze locks with Alex. I don't know how long we stare at each other. It could be a second, maybe one thousand, but all of a sudden, the air feels thick.

Like that brief zap I felt isn't totally one-sided.

"Earth to Carter. You still here?"

I shake the fog from my brain, breaking the contact with the man I'm familiar with but don't actually know.

"Sorry."

"I was saying, your mom wants you to come to the team cookout with her and Marley."

I groan. "I thought I had a free pass to miss these kinds of things."

My parents know my tumultuous past with football players, so they never require me to make an appearance at team events.

He laughs. "Marley wants to go and wants you to come. Besides, we've never done anything like this, so family support would be nice."

"Marley really knows how to screw up my life."

"I'm sure she would say the same about her little brother."

A whistle blows on the other end of the field, and

another coach jogs up to my dad. "Ready to start the last round of drills, Coach?"

He nods. "Round 'em up." He turns his attention back to me. "See you at the cookout."

"Sure thing, Dad. Thanks for letting us come do this."

"Call it a perk of the job." He smiles at me as the students start gathering around the sideline. We stay for the rest of practice, the kids eating it up.

And while I wish I could admit that I was happy for them, I can't seem to fight the pull #18 is having on me.

Damn football players and their good looks.

Chapter Four

CARTER

"Why did you have to drag me along to the cookout? I have a ton of papers to grade," I bemoan, not for the first time.

"Are you already giving your students pop quizzes?" Marley asks, turning into the team's facilities.

"Hey, they should know better than to have their phones out during class."

"Sheesh, what a hard-ass," Marley mumbles to herself. "If I didn't know any better, I would say it was because of the event tonight."

I moan, rubbing the back of my neck. I'm not sure who this new staffer is who decided to put together a kick-off cookout, but I'm dreading it.

I'm better with numbers than people. Or the feelings that came along with meeting the team last week. Well, not the team.

One player in particular. A certain brown-haired quarterback with biceps that I imagined holding me down while he pounded into me.

Crap. These are exactly the kind of thoughts I don't want to be having.

"So sue me if I don't feel like having to make nice with a bunch of football players tonight."

"God, Carter, that was almost ten years ago. When are you going to move on?"

"Why couldn't Dad have coached baseball? I have no issues with them. Plus, they have great asses." I ignore her comment.

"Still players."

Opening the door, I take a deep breath of fresh mountain air. It doesn't do much to soothe my nerves.

Because if I'm being completely honest with myself, I hate the reaction I had to the quarterback.

I'm a terrible son, if I'm being frank, for not actually paying that close attention to the team my dad coaches. But you wouldn't either if you were humiliated by a football player during your formative years. And because my dad is wonderful like that, he never forced the issue.

Yet, I still offered the team up on a silver platter to my students. Knowingly walked into the lion's den after staying away for so many years.

Years of building up my own walls to anyone that didn't perfectly suit my needs. Sure, I got grief about it from my sister and friends, but it helped.

But one afternoon around Alex Young? I was ready to throw away years of progress. All because of one damn smile.

It was a really good smile though.

One that had no right to be making me feel things.

Knowing I'd be seeing him again tonight was causing all sorts of nerves to pop up.

"Hey kids. I'm glad to see you both here." Dad smiles at us as my sister and I walk out onto the field.

Sideline Infraction

Food trucks line one side of the field by the parking lot, while games are set up for the kids. Dozens of people are running around. I try to keep my eyes focused on the people directly in front of me. But my traitorous eyes keep straying.

"He can't stay locked away from football forever," Marley says, giving me a fierce look.

"I was okay trying," I grumble.

"I know this isn't your scene, son, but I appreciate you coming." Dad gives me a smile that mirrors my own. "Why don't you go grab a drink? It'll help you relax, and Marley, come with me."

Nodding at my dad, I walk toward a table filled with buckets of ice. Grabbing a Coke, I crack it open and take a hearty gulp.

"Hey, I was hoping to see you here."

Spinning on my heel, I'm greeted by that smile again.

"Oh, hey."

Sunglasses hide dark-brown eyes. His thick hair looks good enough to run my hands through it.

Shit. Stop thinking about him like that, Carter.

Football player.

Off-limits.

"How's your project going with your students?"

"Students?"

"The ones you brought to practice the other day? They are yours, right? You didn't kidnap them and bring them to watch a football team's practice against their will, did you?"

I shake the fog from my brain. "Oh, right, the project. Still remains to be seen. We'll be working on it over the course of the semester. Give them a chance to see how you guys do during the regular season."

"What got you into teaching math?" Alex grabs a can

of Coke next to me and takes a long pull. I force my eyes away from him and watching his Adam's apple bob. "I couldn't solve a math problem to save my life."

"Math was easy for me. I liked the complexity of the problems to escape my own."

"That sounds rather dire." Alex shifts, pushing his sunglasses up into his hair. God, he's even sexier than I remember. Freckles dot his face, no doubt from being out in the sun during the season.

"I don't mean it to. But I was always better with numbers than people."

"Seems to me like you're pretty good with both."

This pulls a smile out of me. "You have to be good with the kids, otherwise they'll never listen."

"Sometimes I feel like working with my offensive line is like working with a bunch of teenagers. Get them going on something, and it's hard to pull their attention back."

"It doesn't seem like it would be too hard to focus on you."

"That's nice of you to say."

"Oh shit, did I say that out loud?" I don't know what it is about this man, but he's turning me into a puddle of Jell-O. Normally, I'm calm, cool, and collected.

But around this guy?

It's like I'm a teenage boy ogling his crush for the very first time.

"I can pretend you didn't if it makes you feel any better."

"This is why I didn't want to come tonight. I always seem to embarrass myself." I thumb in the direction of the field behind me. "I'm just going to go."

Alex shakes his head, making a move to grab me, but stops. "You don't have to. Honestly, it's kind of refreshing to talk to someone like you."

"Like me?" I give him a puzzled look.

"Someone who doesn't care that I'm a football player. Most people who meet me want to talk about the games."

I bark out a laugh. "I can easily say that I *do* care you're a football player."

Alex crosses his arms over his broad chest in defense. "And why's that?"

"There's not enough time for that tonight."

Alex takes a step closer. If I wanted, I could reach out and squeeze his bicep. His thick, deliciously corded bicep.

God, if only football players weren't so damn sexy.

"Think you could make some time another night?"

"Are you asking me out?" I blurt out. Seriously, where did my filter go? I'm normally not like this with guys. Apparently I am with this one.

Alex glances around, but people aren't paying us any attention. Everyone is wrapped up in their own world. "If you want to call it that, sure, let's go with that."

My gaze lingers on him. He's all hard, rippling muscles, but something about his face is soft. Welcoming.

Don't get me wrong; he has a jaw that could cut glass. But it's his eyes. Something in there tells me I could trust him.

And that makes me wary.

"I don't know. Your schedule isn't very conducive to making time."

More laughter comes from Alex. "You can say that again. Football is brutal on trying to have a life."

"You want to hang out with my brother?" Marley hops over to us from the drink table, her blonde curls bouncing.

"I'm trying to convince him, but don't think I'm doing a very good job."

Marley's eyes light up. She's up to no good. I know it

immediately. "Why don't you go to the comic book convention with him in a few weeks?"

"What? Marley, no." If this guy thought I was cool, any points I had were just lost.

"You're going? I tried getting tickets, but they were sold out by the time I realized I could go."

"You like comic books?" I ask, my voice incredulous.

"I know it's not the coolest thing ever, but it's something my brother and I did together growing up. We spent every last dollar of our allowance on them."

Football player, Carter. Football player.

Maybe if I tell it to myself enough times, it'll sink in.

"That's so perfect!" Marley says. "I was going to go with him, but actually kind of hate it."

"What? Since when?" I ask, turning to face her.

"Sorry, Carter." I notice her holding back her smile. "It's not as fun for me as you think."

"I mean, if you want the company, it'd be fun to go with you." The shy look Alex gives me has me melting.

"Sure."

"Wow, don't sound so excited, Carter."

"Marley, could you please *not* be here?" I whine, pushing her away.

I love my sister—I really do—but somedays I hate her knowing me so well.

"You don't have to if you don't want to. I don't want to impose."

"No, it's fine. My sister can just be a pain sometimes."

Alex nods. "I have an older brother. I totally get it."

"Does he push you to do things you don't want to do?"

"All the time." He laughs, and it's so smooth it feels like hot fudge melting an ice cream sundae.

"Let's never introduce the two of them. They'd be a nightmare together."

"Already meeting the families? Wow, this is moving a lot faster than I thought."

"I'm just going to go bury myself in the mountains. It was nice meeting you, Alex."

"Relax, it's fine." Alex looks as if he's going to reach out to me, but instead shoves his hands into his pockets. What I wouldn't give to feel his hands on me. "Listen, your sister interrupted us, and I know the convention is still a few weeks away, but back to hanging out. Would you want to do it sometime?"

But there Alex goes again with that smile.

Lord help me.

"I'd love to."

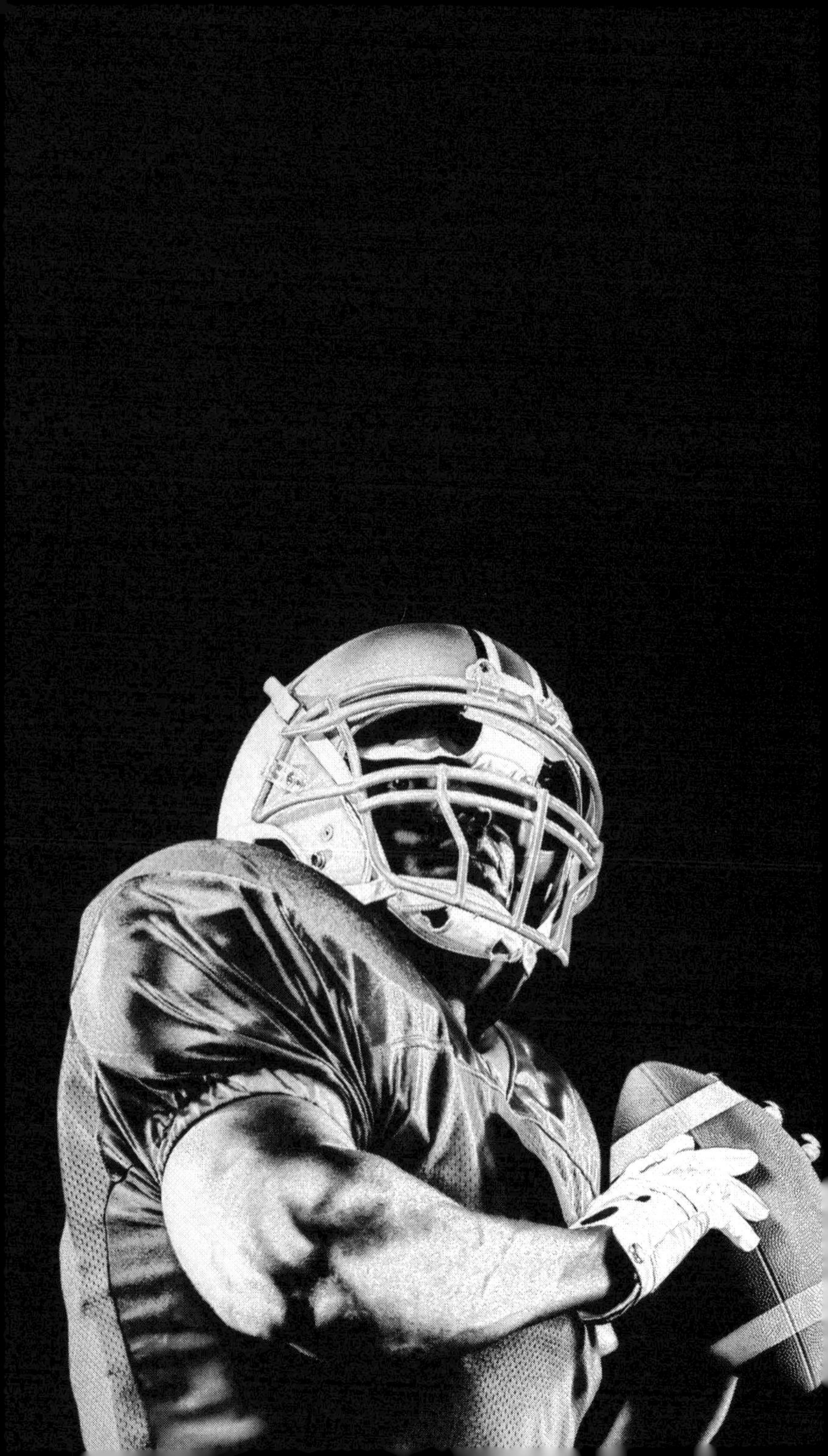

Chapter Five

ALEX

"When you said hang out, this isn't exactly what I had in mind."

I smile at the flustered man on a bike next to me. "Hey, when I asked if you were up for anything, you said you were."

"Is it wrong to admit I said that so you would think I'm cooler than I actually am?" Carter adjusts the strap on his helmet.

"We've already established that we're going to a comic book convention together. I don't think either of us are high on the cool meter."

Carter rolls his eyes at me. "You're a quarterback for an NFL team. Pretty sure that gives you carte blanche to do whatever you want."

I don't know what it is about this man, but I'm ready to break every damn rule I have for him.

Well, almost every rule.

And I only met him last week.

That's why I suggested coming down to the state park

outside of Denver. It doesn't have the big appeal like the national park in the Rockies, but I still love it.

Being outside is peaceful. And there's less of a chance of being recognized because everyone is more focused on the scenery than if the team's quarterback will be biking through the trails.

"You ready to head out?"

"You're not going to make this into a competition, are you?" Carter side-eyes me, unsure if I will.

"If I were with the guys, probably. But I'm not doing this for exercise today."

"Oh, you're not? Already got in your three workouts of the day then?"

"Ouch. You don't mince your words."

He gives me a sheepish look. "Sorry. It's just…past issues. I shouldn't be taking them out on you."

"Care to share those issues with the class?"

Carter shakes his head, his blue eyes wide. With that thick hair of his, he could be a model. The kind that can give a shy look to the camera and sell ice to a penguin.

"Not on the first date."

"So this is a date?" I try to hide my smile, but I can't. "I thought we were just hanging out."

He lets out a long-suffering sigh. "Yes to hanging out. Now, are you ready to go?"

"Lead the way."

Carter takes off down the trail at an easy pace. The path I chose is farther out and a bit more secluded. It's not harder by any means, but because you have to take the winding roads to get here, most people choose the easier trails.

This trail gives me the privacy I like while being out. It's not fair to Carter, but from that first moment we met,

I've felt a pull toward him. And this is the only way to explore that. In the areas I feel safe.

Maybe when things progress—*if* they progress—we can have that conversation about my not being out.

But for right now, I'm enjoying my view. Instead of the mountains and sweeping grasslands spread out around us, I'm observing the man in front of me.

I watch as Carter's arms bend and flex under his white tee in a way that makes me wish we were doing something else.

The trail winds through the park, trees providing shade on either side. A familiar spot is up ahead, one of my favorites. "Want to stop up ahead?" I shout to Carter.

Turning his head, he misses the dip in the trail and his wheel spins out on the rocky path. He slides down the small decline.

"Shit. Are you okay?" I hop off my bike and run over to where Carter crashed.

"Fuck. That really hurt." Carter grabs at his shin, a nasty gash cutting across it.

"How'd you even manage that?" Dumping my backpack on the ground, I feel around for the first aid kit I keep tucked away.

"I'm a math teacher, not a PE teacher. This is not my area of expertise."

"I guess I need to take you places where you are less likely to hurt yourself."

Carter gives me a small smile. "Now that I would not mind. I'm very much an indoors creature."

Handing him an alcohol wipe and a Band-Aid, I let him clean himself up.

"You want to go see the view that I made you crash for?"

Carter reaches up to me, and I help him stand. He's only a few inches from me, his hand still in mine.

I don't miss the way his eyes widen at the contact. Thank God, he is feeling this too, because I might crash my own bike if this was one-sided.

"This view better be worth it."

Dropping his hand, I pick up his bike, giving it a good once-over to make sure it's okay to ride. "Why don't we walk there?"

"You should probably lead the way this time."

We make the short distance down the trail, each of us walking alongside our bikes. Finding the small clearing, I rest my bike against a tree and find the hidden spot.

"You're not bringing me out here to kill me, are you?"

A laugh bursts free. "Trust me, not going to kill you."

"Jury is still out."

Carter brushes by me, his clean scent overwhelming my senses in the best way. All I want to do is grab him and lay one on him. But there's no telling who is around. We only just started this thing, so I do the adult thing and hold myself back.

"Holy shit." Carter makes it through the small clearing to see one of my favorite views. "I can see why you like this."

Behind the tree-lined trail is brushland, leading to the most magnificent view of the mountains. You would never know how close we are to Denver, because the city can't be seen.

"I stumbled upon this when I first moved out here. I always come out here when I need peace."

Carter looks back at me, and I get that same feeling settling in my stomach. I want more with him, but is more fair?

"How'd you stumble upon it?" He hobbles over to a fallen tree and takes a seat.

I follow him, taking a seat next to him. Our thighs touch, and it's hard to keep my focus on the view in front of me. "I may have done something very similar to you."

"Oh I see. You're making fun of me for falling when you did the exact same thing." There's a lightness to his voice that hasn't been there before.

"Aren't people supposed to act cooler than they actually are on dates?"

"I thought we were only hanging out?" A dimple pops out when he smiles. I want to lean over and taste it.

"If you want this to be a date, then a date it is."

Carter nudges me with his shoulder, shifting his attention back to the view. It's one of my favorite spots. The mountains and wide open spaces make me and my problems feel small.

"Glad to know I'm not the only uncool one then."

"Okay, you didn't want me to make this into a competition, but I feel like you're just egging me on now."

Carter shakes his head. "Oh no. I know better than to bet an athlete. I will never be doing that."

"You're still not going to tell me what happened?"

"Not right now."

"You know,"—I rest my elbow on my knee and drop my chin in my hand—"if you were my teacher, I don't think I'd be able to concentrate."

A blush creeps up his neck. "Oh my God. Please stop. You're embarrassing me."

"I'm serious. If you were my teacher, I would've had a serious crush on you."

"Thank God I'm not, because that would be highly inappropriate."

I laugh. "Okay, way to make it weird."

"Hey, you started it."

We're both laughing. It feels like we're a world away, just the two of us here together. I can't remember the last time anything felt this easy.

In my life, nothing is easy. Every move I make is calculated to protect me and my secret. I've been doing it so long, I don't know anything different at this point.

Being here with Carter like this, even though I just met him, gives me a brief window into what life could be like. If I were out.

As great as it sounds, it also sends fear pulsing through my veins. Because as much as I would like to come out, I don't know if I ever will. Not while I'm still playing.

I have so many professional goals I want to hit, and it wouldn't be fair to drag someone into the closet with me.

But I can't resist Carter. When he's looking at me like that, when he's laughing with me, I want more.

And more is going to get me into trouble.

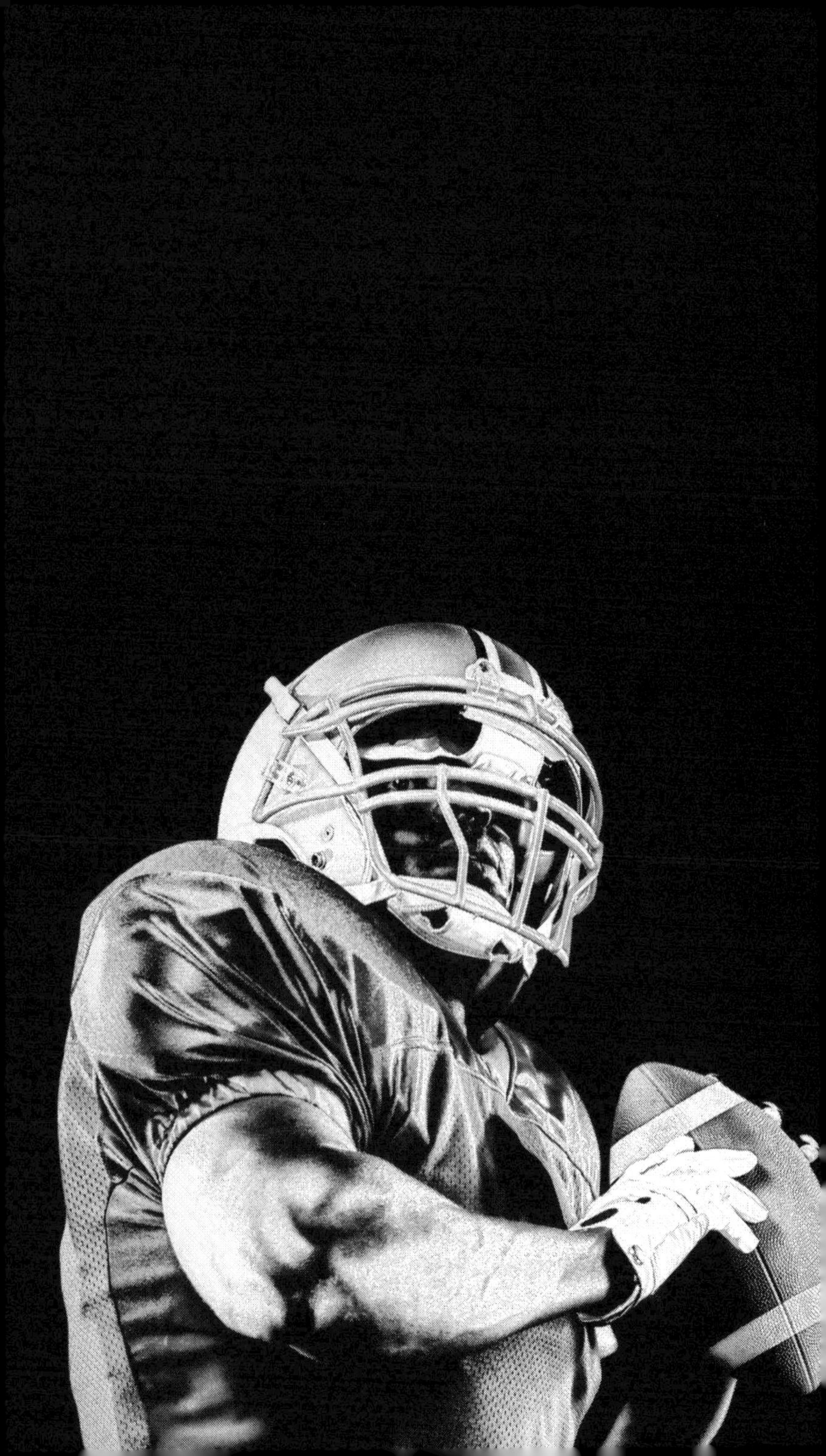

Chapter Six

ALEX

"Why do we have to keep dragging our asses out to the suburbs?" Logan bemoans as I ring Colin's doorbell. "What happened to the cool bar we first went to?"

I laugh. While I enjoy the bar we found, it's also nice kicking back at a place that's within walking distance from my house. "Something about Waffles not wanting to be left alone."

"That's right," Colin says as he opens the door. "Waffles is sad that Peyton isn't here and needs the company."

Looking down at the dog in question, I see his tongue hanging out of his mouth as his tail wags back and forth. "This is Waffles being sad?"

Colin rolls his eyes as we pass him and walk into his living room. Having been here several times, I make my way straight to the kitchen and grab a handful of beers. I love the open feel of his house—that no matter where you are, everyone is together.

"Fine. Waffles isn't sad. I miss Peyton and wanted to

stay at home with Waffles instead of going out to a bar. Happy?"

I can't fight the smirk as it spreads over my face. To think this guy used to be the biggest player on the team. Now he's so far gone for Peyton, I barely recognize the guy.

"Who knew you'd turn out to be such a sap?" Logan smacks him on the shoulder.

"Hey. Watch the arms. They're going to be catching a lot of touchdowns this year."

"Who says you're going to be getting them? According to our math whiz, it's not you."

"Please. I make you look good, Young." Colin shoves me playfully as we make our way out back.

"I dunno. Maybe I'll have to test the prowess of our tight ends."

"Hey, don't forget about the running backs. I still have good numbers," Logan chimes in.

"Nah. We're boosting those receiving numbers this year, aren't we, Young? Gotta prove those stats kids wrong."

Just the merest mention of the stats class that came to the field has my thoughts drifting off to Carter. For the first time in a long time, someone's pulled my attention away from football.

Not that I'm not still focused on the game. But seeing my friends start to settle down, to go home to the people they love, casts a glaring light on what I don't have.

Sipping my beer, I follow the guys outside, trying to stave off the empty thoughts. The Rockies greet me in all their glory. If I didn't have my own house that overlooked the mountains, I'd be jealous. It's one of my favorite things about living in Denver. You can't beat these views.

Lights are strung across the top of the patio as we drop into our seats, no doubt an addition from Peyton.

"Where are the other two slackers?" Logan kicks his feet up on the table.

"Knox had to do more reps. Something about pissing off Frankie."

"Sheesh. Knox gets into more trouble than even you, Colin." Logan sips on his beer.

"Used to. I used to get into trouble. Not anymore."

"Trying to keep any of you guys in line is a full-time job," I say with a laugh as the back door swings open. A tired-looking Jackson comes in, baby carrier in hand.

"Not all of us act like these shitheads," he says, setting Noah down beside him. Waffles scurries over to investigate the newcomers.

"You brought Noah?" Colin jumps out of his chair, grabbing the excited dog.

"Tenley is going out with her sisters, and I wasn't leaving him with a babysitter, so I brought him along."

None of us have met Noah. The few times Jackson was going to bring him around, they couldn't for one reason or another.

"Can we hold him?" Logan peers over Jackson's shoulder at the sleeping bundle. Even with a squished-up face, he's the spitting image of Jackson.

"If you don't drop him." Jackson pushes back the carrier handle and unbuckles him.

"I've got steady hands."

"Is that why you dropped three handoffs in practice this week?" Colin asks.

"I didn't drop them. They were bad handoffs!" Logan yells across the table.

"Keep it down. I don't want you idiots waking him up." Jackson cradles Noah to his chest.

"And from what I recall, they weren't bad handoffs." I eye Logan over my beer.

"I'm not blaming you."

"Then whose fault was it that you dropped the ball?"

Logan and I have been working on new plays. And after the hundreds of times we've run them, we've basically perfected them. Three dropped balls is nothing in the grand scheme of things.

"You guys really suck, you know that?" Logan stalks back into the house.

"It's just too easy to give him crap." Colin laughs. "Now, let me see this little guy."

Setting his drink down, Colin holds his arms out as Jackson hands Noah off to him. "Watch his head."

"Thanks, asshole. I know how to hold a baby."

"That's precious cargo. So I'll remind you again, watch his head." Jackson and Colin glare at each other.

"Relax. He's doing just fine," Logan says, coming back outside, this time, with Knox in tow.

"Look who finally was let out of jail."

Knox cracks his neck as he takes his seat at the table. "I can do nothing right. Never mind the fact that I led the league in sacks last year. Frankie thinks I'm some newbie who has never played a down of football in my life."

"Maybe if you didn't talk back to her so much, it wouldn't be as bad," I point out.

"You're as bad as fucking Hollins," Knox says, taking a swig of his beer.

"What's that douche saying now?" Colin grumbles.

Knox unlocks his phone, taps a few buttons, and flips it to face us.

VgsStarHollins22: There's a storm headed for Denver…new season, new chance to take down those baby Mountain Lions! There's no chance I'm getting kicked out and missing the chance to whoop their pansy asses all the way to the bottom...

"How in the world does the league let this shit fly?" Colin is pissed from the look on his face.

"Because it adds fuel to the rivalry." Shaking my head, I down half my drink. "And Vegas won't do a damn thing about it either. Their fans eat that shit up."

"I only wish I could be out there on the field at the same time as him and lay into him." Knox cracks his knuckles. I would never want to be on the receiving end of a hit from him.

"You? The fucker does nothing but trash talk the entire game. I need earplugs just so I don't have to listen to him," Colin gripes.

"It'd be a great start to the season to see them lose," I tell them.

But Colin has shifted his focus back to the tiny bundle in his arms. He's completely enamored with Noah.

"Did I miss the memo where babies are allowed now?" Knox looks over at Noah, unsure of the tiny bundle.

"It was either that or I missed tonight. And that wasn't an option," Jackson says.

"Besides, we need to break in the future of the Mountain Lions." Logan laughs.

"I'll be happy if he's happy."

"You sound like such a parent," Knox says, shaking his head.

"It's true. You just want your kids to be happy," Colin agrees.

"Your kids? You and Peyton got any hiding that we don't know about?" I quirk a brow in Colin's direction.

"Waffles." Logan goes to interject, but Colin stops him. "And don't say he isn't my kid. Dogs are family too."

"Since when did we turn into a bunch of saps?" Knox looks around at each of us.

"I dare you not to turn into a sap when you find someone, Knox." Jackson tips his beer bottle in his direction.

I don't miss the brief flash in Knox's eyes.

"Maybe that'll make him less cranky," I say.

"I don't see you bringing many women home."

That shuts me up. I take a swig of my beer to cool my suddenly too-warm skin. "I've got football to worry about."

"We all have football," Knox oh-so-kindly points out.

"Maybe Peyton has the right idea and we should get Darlene to set you up." Colin shifts Noah in his arms as he starts to fuss.

"My grandma does not need to be setting anyone up."

"Aww. Are you worried she won't find you anyone?" Colin pokes at Knox.

"She's already all over me to settle down and give her grandbabies." Knox shakes his head.

"Maybe Jackson can come with me to visit her and bring Noah. Get her off your back."

The guys delve into a conversation about Darlene and the safety of baby Noah while playing bingo. Thankful the conversation is off me and my lack of women, I breathe a sigh of relief.

For the last few years, I've been successfully able to navigate any questions regarding my relationship status. Or lack thereof. When you have as much drive as I do, it's easy to deflect the conversation. Football is my focus and no one can fault me for that.

But now that Carter is in the picture, it makes it harder. I wish I could open myself up to these guys. But years spent in locker rooms with *fag* and *that's so gay* thrown around keep me silent. Every time I heard one of those words used as an insult, it added a brick to the wall I keep around myself.

I love what I do. Football is the greatest sport there is. I don't want my sexuality to change that. I want to keep my nose to the grindstone and hopefully win a trophy. Maybe then I can come out. Once I've proven myself in the league.

Each year we keep inching closer, but it's just out of reach. Who knows how much longer it'll be?

Noah's cries bring me out of my thoughts.

"What'd you do to him?" Jackson sighs.

"I didn't do anything. He just started crying!" Colin shouts.

"Shouting isn't going to make him settle down." Jackson takes him back into his arms.

"This is why we don't bring kids to these things," Knox mutters.

"Dude. It's tradition. It's bad luck to break tradition." Colin glares at him. "It's not my fault he was crying."

Jackson rocks the crying baby in his arms and he settles almost instantly. Jackson points to the baby in his arms. "See, Colin? Totally something you did."

"Alright, before you two get into it," I interrupt whatever Colin was about to say, "I think it's time for the traditional toast."

That shuts everyone up. We all hold out our beers.

"I know last year wasn't what we wanted—"

"Fucking Vegas," Colin grumbles. "I hate Hollins."

"But this year we can go far. I know it. We've got the best team we've had in ages. I know we're on the cusp of something great."

The air stills around me, like it's waiting to hear what I say next. Every single one of us is amped-up. After the bitter loss in the first round of the playoffs, we're all ready for this season.

"It won't be easy. But as long as we stick together, we can go far."

I raise my beer and everyone does the same. "To some of the best men I know. There is no one else I would want to play this game with. To the Mountain Lions!"

"To the Mountain Lions!"

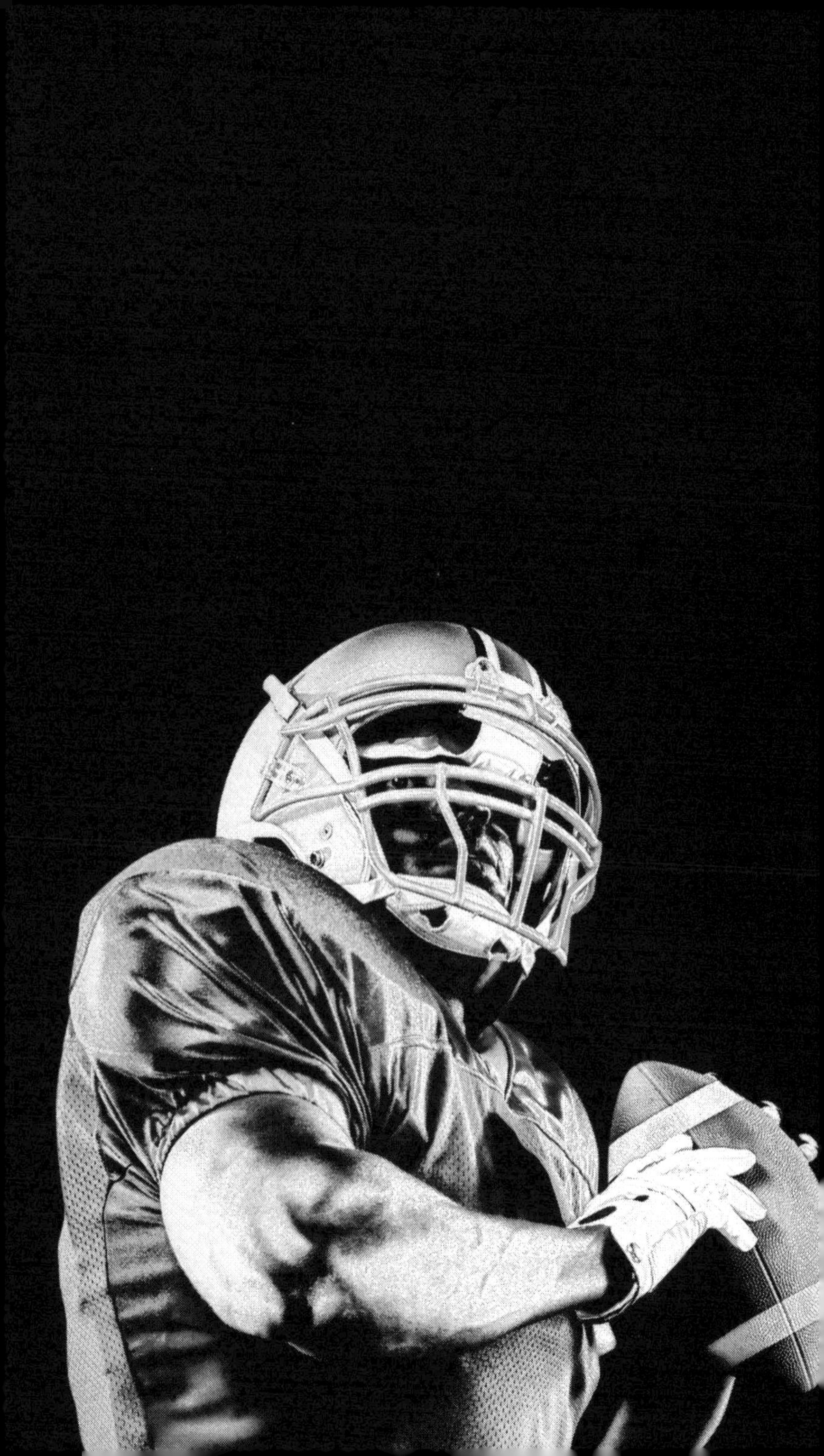

Chapter Seven

ALEX

"First game of the season. You boys ready?" Knox smacks all of our pads as he walks around the locker room. The coaches are gathered in one corner, reviewing strategy. The bare locker room walls are a dull gray, and the metal lockers aren't exactly welcoming.

Being the away team is never easy to start the season. But I know we're ready.

"Fuck yeah!" Colin shouts. "We've got Kansas City's number."

Even better, we're starting with a divisional game. These are the type of games I love.

"Okay, let's not jinx it." I knock on the locker behind me.

"I don't know about you, Young, but the defense has been kicking ass in practice, so we're not jinxing anything. We're ready." As the captain of the defense, Knox has been working with the younger guys on the team to bring them up to snuff. With a few players traded, they needed the work to get them up to speed on our team's plays.

"Hey, offense is ready, so we're not letting anyone down. Fields?" I swing my gaze to Jackson.

"Special teams is ready. Did you see me nail that sixty-yard field goal during warm-ups?" He brushes his hands together. "Game will be a breeze."

"A breeze, huh?" Coach's voice pipes up from the corner.

All of us snap to attention.

"I'm glad you boys are ready, but today will be a tough test. Kansas City has a bright young quarterback that is the talk of the town."

"Nah. No one can beat our guy," Williams shouts.

I smile at the confidence he has in me.

The kid is good.

But I'm better.

"Our team is battle-tested. This is the start of what is sure to be a great season. We've got new guys on offense and defense. We're firing on all cylinders. Go out there and play like we've been practicing and it'll be a good day."

He nods to Knox, who takes the floor for the captain's speech.

"You heard the coach! Let's go out there and show them what we're made of!" The air is electric. Everyone is buzzing to get on the field and start the first game of the season. "Family on three. One, two, three…"

"Family!" we echo.

Cheers and roars bounce around the small locker room, designed to intimidate opposing teams. If anything, it fuels us. Guys are jumping around as we make our way toward the tunnel.

We run out of the tunnel when announced to booing so loud, it could burst your eardrums. Kansas City is one of the worst places to play as an opposing team. Their fans are brutal. Even more so with us because we're a division rival.

It'll make it all that much sweeter when we beat them.

Standing on the sideline, I warm up with my backup quarterback as the pregame rituals start. I drown out the sounds of the opposing team being announced. My focus is laser-sharp on what we have to achieve here today.

No one wants to start the season out with a loss. But to a team in our division who would hold a tie-break in the playoffs? That's the last thing we want.

Jackson, Knox, Colin, and I all walk out to the center of the field for the coin toss, shaking hands with their captains.

"Let's have a good game, gentlemen. Denver, as the visiting team, you'll call the toss." The ref shows us both sides of the coin. "What's your call?"

"Heads," Jackson says.

The coin flips, landing on heads.

We defer the ball to the second half and run back to our side of the field.

"Alright boys, let's fucking go!" Knox is walking up and down the sideline, pumping up the defense. "We've got this boys. Not one yard!"

Adrenaline is flowing as special teams lines up to kick off.

This. This is what I love more than anything in my life. Why I make such big sacrifices in my personal life—because I love this game.

The atmosphere.

My teammates.

The energy of a brand-new season getting ready to kick off.

I fucking love football.

Knox and the entire defensive line are on fire during the game. With two forced fumbles and a pick-six, we take an easy 21-3 halftime lead.

And it only gets better in the second half. My throws have never looked cleaner. A perfect spiral to Colin starts the half with a touchdown.

Games like this, where we take a commanding lead, take the pressure off. It makes the game fun. Guys are joking around on the sidelines as the clock winds down.

Denver wins handily, 34-17.

The happy energy flowing in the locker room is contagious as we celebrate our first road win.

"Great job out there, boys. Offense, defense, special teams—everyone was clicking today. That's what I want to see more of. I'll see everyone on Tuesday to study film for next week, but take tomorrow and be ready for practice this week. Go Mountain Lions!"

Guys are floating in and out of the showers as I redirect my attention to my phone. I hang back, liking to go when it's virtually empty. Less chance for any accusations of wandering eyes. Not that that's ever been an issue, but I don't want to make it one.

Instead, I text the one person I want to share this win with.

> Did you happen to watch the game today?

CARTER
> Oh, was there a baseball game on today? Crap, I think I missed it

> You're actually the worst, you know that?

CARTER
> Would the worst know that you threw three touchdowns today?

That sends a frisson of awareness spreading through my veins. I hoped Carter would watch the game, but with his issues with football players, I didn't want to assume anything.

> Listen to you, talking about football. Careful, you might just start to like it

CARTER
> Don't go getting any ideas

> Too late...all sorts of ideas are running through my head

CARTER
> I guess it was fun while it lasted

I FIGHT the smile at Carter's words. Setting my phone down in my locker, I grab my shower stuff and hurry through cleaning up. I want to get back to Carter.

Drying off quickly, I get dressed and grab my phone.

> Want to hang out tomorrow night?

CARTER
> What exactly does hang out entail?

> I'm going to tie you up in my basement and never let you leave

CARTER
> I knew you wanted to kill me

I snort laugh at Carter's message.

"What's got you so happy?" Colin elbows me as he stands at his locker next to me.

"What? Nothing." I lock my phone and shove it back into my bag. I know there's no way he saw my screen, but it still makes me anxious thinking about it. It's not like I have Carter's number saved under a different name.

"Uh-uh. No way. That's the face of a guy who's met someone."

"Dude, you holdin' out on us?" Knox asks, pulling a shirt over his head.

"Nah. It's nothing special." Even the small lie feels like sand coming off my tongue. I hate lying to these guys—men who have become like brothers to me—but it's easier. Who knows what would happen if they knew the truth.

"I don't believe that for a second," Jackson chimes in. "You have that same cheesy-ass grin I have on my face when I think about Tenley."

"You mean the one you have right now?" Knox ruffles his hair.

"Fuck off, man. I'm ready to get outta here so I can get home to my wife and kid."

"You're such a kept man," Colin jokes.

"Oh, like you're one to talk? You miss Peyton, and we're all coming to your house to keep you entertained." Stepping into my shoes, I grab my bag and follow the guys out of the locker room.

Getting on the bus that will take us to the charter plane, the energy is high as we celebrate our win. I pull my phone out of my bag, hoping to see a message from Carter, and I'm not disappointed.

Sideline Infraction

CARTER
See you tomorrow night

I CAN'T HELP the cheesy-ass grin that spreads across my face.

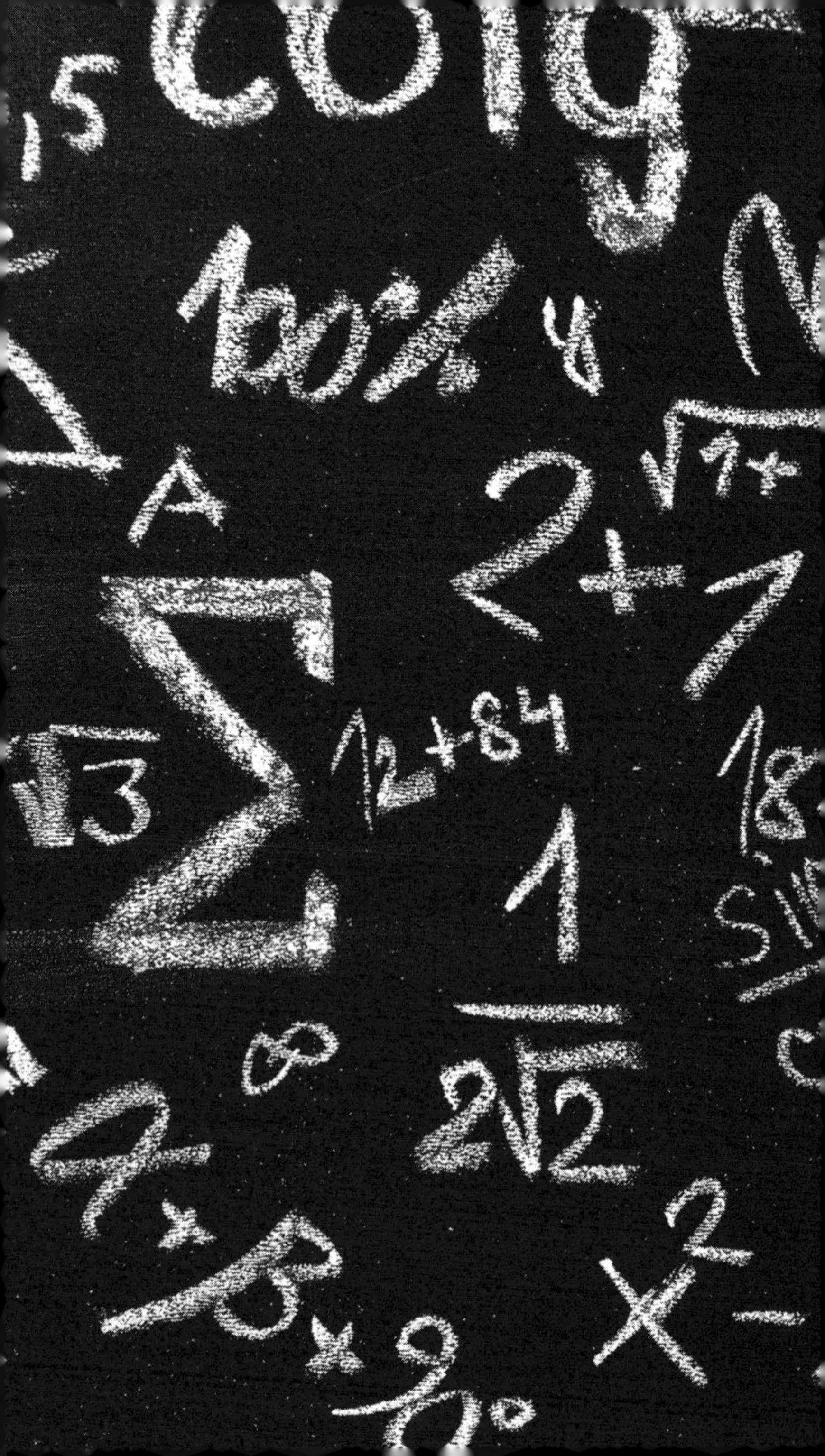

Chapter Eight

CARTER

I told myself I wouldn't come tonight. But I could sense the excitement in Alex's text. It spurred me on against my better judgment.

Ringing the bell, I hear muffled footsteps getting closer. When Alex swings open the door, I have to tell myself not to drool.

Wearing a tight black T-shirt that shows off every ab and the breadth of his shoulders and jeans that cling to his thighs, Alex looks like a walking god. An altar that I would bow down and pray to.

"Hi." My voice is huskier than usual, and I have to shake myself out of my thoughts. "Hi."

"Hi. I'm glad you decided to come." Alex flashes me a pearly-white grin.

"Thanks for inviting me."

Following Alex into his house, I look around the space.

His living room is homey, with oversized couches facing a fireplace with a TV hanging over it. Built-ins flank each side. Instead of displaying football memorabilia, pictures of what I assume are his family line the shelves.

It gives way to a kitchen that any DIY-er would kill for. Granite countertops, shiny appliances, and a kitchen table that looks like it could hold an entire football team.

It's made for entertaining.

"Beer?"

I nod, taking the proffered drink. "This is a great view."

The kitchen opens up to the Rockies in the distance.

"Would you believe I moved in because of Colin?"

"Really?"

Alex nods, sipping his drink. "This neighborhood was still in development when we were drafted. He bought his house, and when I came over to study film one day, I was sold. Bought mine the next day."

"So do all you Mountain Lions live out here?" I circle a finger in the air, referencing the neighborhood. It's a quiet suburb of the city.

"Just Colin and me. Knox doesn't like people going to his house, and Jackson moved in with his wife near Wash Park."

"Damn. You football players and your big bucks." I shake my head.

"It's better than blowing it on things that I don't need." Alex leans back against the granite island, crossing his arms and ankles. "Can you see me with a yacht in the Mediterranean?"

I glance over at him, allowing myself another slow perusal of him. "You are not a yacht kind of guy."

"I wish I could be. Floating in the middle of the ocean away from all the noise of the game? Yeah, that would be nice sometimes."

Seeing him like this—so relaxed in his house—is messing with my head. Like this? He's just Alex. I need to keep remembering that he's a football player.

Sideline Infraction

A player.

One that won't hesitate to screw me over.

"So Mr. Quarterback, are you ready to play?"

He nods, taking a few steps closer to me. "Fair warning, I'm very competitive."

I roll my eyes at his oh-so-obvious admission. "Shocker. The football player is competitive. If you weren't, you'd be playing for participation ribbons."

"I was never very good at losing. I always wanted first place."

Walking over to his table, I set the game Ticket to Ride down. "Well, I hate to break it to you, but I'm pretty amazing at this game. So you might want to get comfortable with second place."

"Want to up the stakes?" Alex sets his beer down and helps me set everything up.

"Please keep in mind I am a teacher. I make pennies to your millions."

Alex shakes his head, a stray piece of brown hair falling in his eyes. God, he is unfairly sexy.

"Which is a travesty. I play a game. You teach kids who probably mouth off any chance they get. You should be making the millions."

"As much as I appreciate that, it's never going to happen." I take another swig of beer to temper the rising heat in my face. Being in Alex's presence is stirring up all sorts of feelings I'd rather not be having. "Back to these stakes…"

"Right." Alex takes a seat and motions for me to do the same. "How about whoever loses has to buy dinner after the convention on Friday?"

I take a minute to think it over. Alex's face gives away nothing. "You're on. But if I win, you're taking me to a steakhouse."

"And if I win?" Alex quirks a brow at me.

"The dollar menu at a drive-thru."

Alex's laugh is deep and sexy and puts a smile on my face. He's making it hard to keep him firmly in the jock box in my brain.

"Why don't you go first then?"

"Fine."

We start the game, each of us taking turns. Each move is polite, neither of us making any big moves. It helps to focus on the game and settle my nerves.

Because being around Alex isn't good for my sanity.

I swore after high school no more athletes. But Alex isn't just any athlete.

Oh no. He's the quarterback on my father's team.

Which would be fine and all, but I can't seem to get him out of my head.

The way he so casually interacted with my students? That never happens.

As I'm getting lost in my thoughts about the man in front of me, he makes an illegal move.

"Sorry. That's the wrong train color for that route." I point to where he played. "You can't play there."

"No, these are the trains that can be played anywhere. It's a legal move."

"You don't have enough to play them. You have to play them all at once!"

"Says who?" Alex leans in closer. There's a fire in his eyes.

"The rules!" I adjust my glasses farther up my nose.

"The rules state if I draw five cards of the same it can be used for that route," Alex states, like he created the rulebook.

"But you still don't have enough! That's not fair!"

"Just because you're losing doesn't mean it's not fair." A

cocky grin spreads across Alex's face, like he knows he's bested me. It's one meant to intimidate opposing defenses. Instead, I feel my dick hardening in my pants.

Planting my hands on the table, I push myself up, getting right into his face.

"You linked your trains incorrectly and that is cheating."

Alex rises to meet me. "Again, not cheating. I used the cards to cash in for the trains that go anywhere."

I shake my head, blowing out a breath. "That's bending the rules and you know it. Rules can't be changed in math."

Dark eyes dip to my lips before meeting my gaze again. "What are you going to do about it?"

"I have half a mind to knock all your trains off the map."

Alex smirks, inching closer. I can see his pupils widen.

"I never thought you'd be a sore loser."

"It's not being a sore loser when you're cheating."

"Not cheat—"

Wrapping my fist in Alex's shirt, I don't think. I ignore every voice in my head shouting at me how wrong this is. I crush my lips to his, shutting him up. I must have shocked him, because it takes him a moment to respond. But when he does?

Wow.

Just wow.

One strong hand cups the back of my neck, taking control of the kiss. Firm lips open mine, his tongue seeking and commanding with each stroke.

Alex tastes like the beer he's been sipping all night. The faint smell of his cologne overwhelms me. Being in his space like this makes me want to crawl across the table and climb him like a tree.

This kiss is that good.

"Fuck." Alex breaks the kiss, his chest heaving. "Fuck."

"I shouldn't have done that." I pull back, sinking into my chair, scrubbing a hand over my face.

"Why shouldn't you have done that?" Alex stalks around the table, standing next to me.

"You're a football player."

"Duly noted. Thank you for pointing that out." There's a hint of laughter in his voice.

"I'm just a math teacher."

"Are you just stating facts here? Because if so, I have one of my own."

"Oh yeah?" I peek a glance up at him.

"I've wanted to kiss you since I first met you."

"Really?"

Alex nods. "And I kind of want to do it again."

"You do?"

Leave it to this man to turn me into a blubbering idiot.

"Can I?"

Licking my lips, I give him the go-ahead. Turning my chair, Alex pushes my knees wide and steps between them. He's confident, just like the way he carries himself on the field.

Tipping my head up with a finger under my chin, he dips down. This kiss is featherlight but sets off a storm of emotions in my belly. He goes back in, his tongue opening my mouth.

I should be embarrassed by the moan that escapes, but I can't bring myself to care. I relinquish all control to Alex as he takes his time.

Tasting.

Exploring.

Learning exactly what I like.

My fingers trail over the muscles his shirt covers, loving

the whimpers that escape. I swallow each one up, as his tongue continues to tangle with mine.

He pulls back, pressing a kiss to the corner of my mouth. I want to reach up and take more. I don't know how much time has passed, but clearly not enough.

Because all I want is his mouth on mine again.

"As much as I'd like to keep doing this," Alex whispers against my lips, "I have an early practice tomorrow."

"And I have school."

"To be continued?" Alex drops another kiss against my lips, but when he goes to pull back, I keep him there, nibbling on his bottom lip.

"I guess so." His eyes are filled with lust, no doubt matching my own.

I stand, matching Alex's height. Cupping the back of his neck, I drop one more kiss on his lips.

Because I just can't help myself tonight. I want to taste and get lost in the feel of him.

"We still on for this weekend?" Alex clears his throat.

We clean up the game, our faces flushed from the heated make-out session. I tuck the game under my arm. "As long as you don't ask for a rematch, yes."

The side of Alex's mouth—still swollen from that kiss—ticks up into a cocky grin. "We'll get that rematch someday. Just you wait."

"It's on, Mr. Quarterback, it's on."

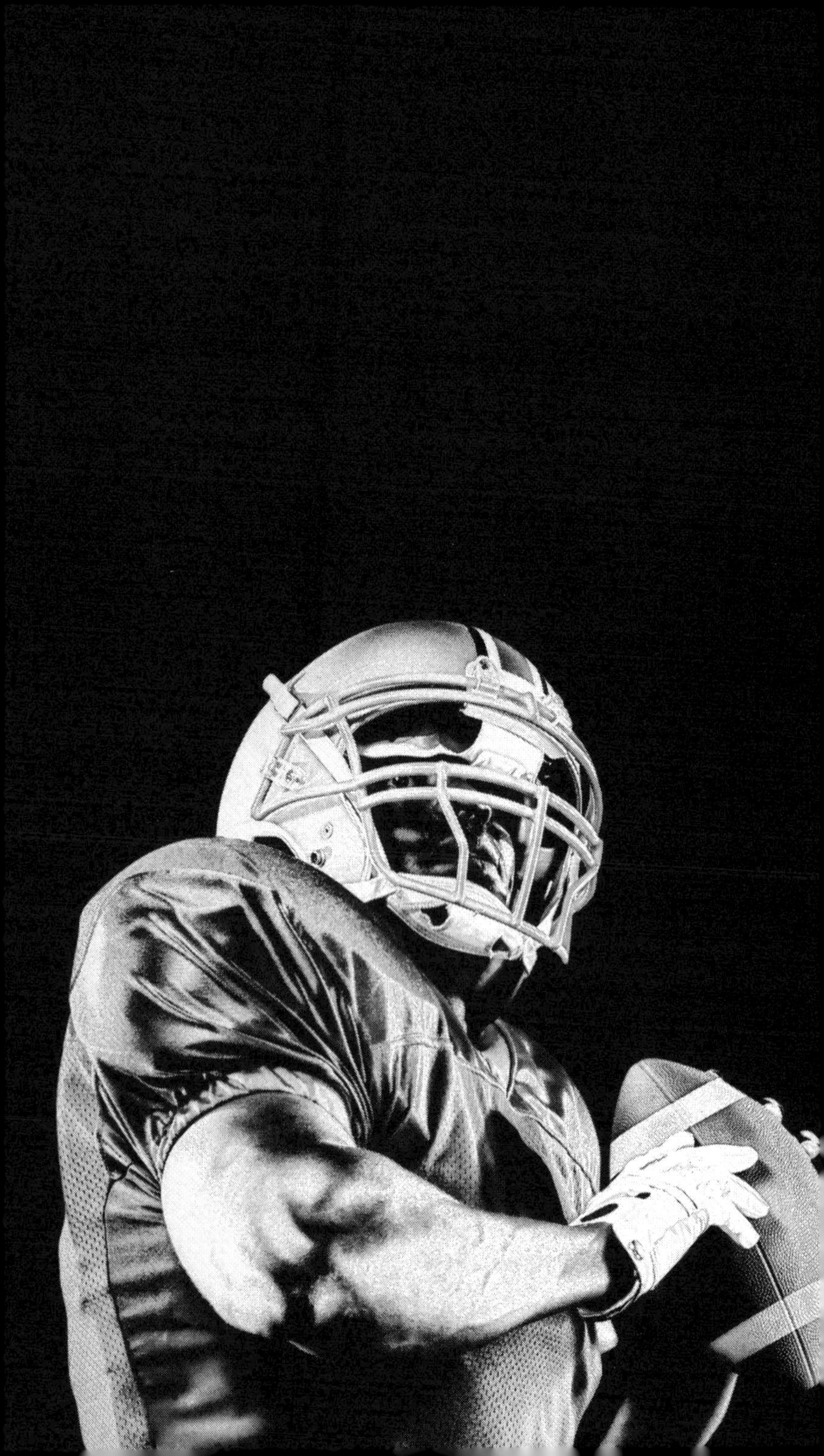

Chapter Nine

ALEX

"What the hell is in these boxes?" I drop the last of the boxes in my brother's new apartment. It's a small studio in the heart of downtown Denver, offering great views of the stadium.

"Hopefully not my dishes, because you just broke them." Tommy shakes his head at me as he comes out of the kitchen. "Beer?"

I take the bottle and gulp it down.

"I needed that."

"I appreciate you helping me move, bro." Tommy claps me on the shoulder as he plops down on the couch.

Leave it to a man to have his couch and TV set up before anything else in his new place.

"You know I could have hired movers to help you."

"I wouldn't want you wasting your money." He waves me off.

"You better hope I'm not sore for the game this week. We're playing in Vegas."

I sit down opposite him as he turns on *SportsCenter*. The analysts are discussing Hollins's latest tweet, aimed at us.

"This Hollins guy never shuts up."

"You try having to deal with him on the field. He's even worse. Yelling stupid shit, complaining about the refs—you name it. He's one of the dirtiest players in the league."

"I hate that we have to play Vegas twice a year. They're the worst of the worst," Tommy says.

I poke him in the shoulder. "You don't have to play them twice a year."

"Eh. Doesn't everyone talk about their team like they're the ones in the game?"

I laugh.

Isn't that the truth.

"You try being chased down by three-hundred-pound linebackers."

"I'll leave that to you."

"Really glad to have you here."

"Hey, I've always wanted to be here. Thankfully, work agreed."

My older brother and I have always been close. He was my idol growing up. When he joined the football team, I wanted to be just like him and play. Whereas he did it for fun in high school, I discovered I had a knack for it.

Ever since, he's been my biggest fan. And closest confidant.

"Earth to Alex. Are you paying attention to me?"

"Sorry, what'd you say?"

"Any guys on the horizon?"

I pick at the label on the beer bottle, suddenly nervous to have this conversation. My brother is one of exactly three people who know I'm gay.

Well, now four.

That'd be an even more awkward conversation with

Carter if I wasn't gay after having kissed the life out of him.

Anyone else and it's a liability.

"You know I can't be with anyone in public."

Tommy fixes his dark-brown eyes on me. When he did that growing up, I'd confess anything to him. Now, it doesn't even faze me.

"That's not what I asked."

I chug down the rest of my beer. I don't want to lie to him, but I don't want to make Carter seem like something more. This thing between us is still so new that I don't want to jinx it.

"I mean, kind of."

"Kind of? Care to share with the class?"

Blowing out a nervous breath, I share my biggest secret with him. "I've met someone."

"Oh shit."

"Yup." Anxious nerves are vibrating now. "Need another beer?"

"Forget the beer. I've never heard you talk about a guy. Like ever."

"Just because I haven't, doesn't mean there hasn't been someone."

Tommy shakes his head. "No. I don't mean hookups. I know you've had those. You had one boyfriend in middle school before we moved. Then you joined the football team and decided you'd be better off if no one knew. There has never been anyone since."

"I want him to be a someone," I confess.

It's my biggest secret.

Well, second-biggest secret.

Because I've never wanted anyone the way I want Carter.

And it's only been a few weeks.

"Does he know?"

"I need a beer." Ignoring my brother, I grab another drink and take a swig.

"Alex."

I can't imagine what my face looks like because my brother's loses its hard edge. "He doesn't know, does he?"

I shake my head. "Do you think he'd be with me if he did?"

"You're not being fair to him."

"Don't you think I know that?" I shout. "But you know the reality of my situation."

"That doesn't mean you should drag people down."

"Oh thanks, asshole."

"That's not what I meant, and you know it." Tommy glares at me. "Clearly you like this guy, but you can't build a relationship on a lie."

Guilt creeps over my skin, eating into me. "I know."

"So why are you doing it?"

"Because I want to see where this goes. What if it doesn't mean anything?"

Tommy scoffs. "It already means something because you're telling me."

"Be straight with me. Am I terrible person?"

Setting his drink down, Tommy grabs my shoulders and turns me to face him. "No."

"But?"

"You're in an impossible situation. I remember what those locker rooms are like. I can't imagine hearing what you hear and not screaming at everyone within a ten-mile radius. No one uses those words in polite conversation, so why they use them as an insult is beyond me."

My head hangs in shame. "You aren't making me feel any better."

"Just promise me something, okay?"

"What's that?"

"If things do get serious, you tell him."

Fears gnaws at my gut. "What if I lose him?"

"It's a decision you'll have to live with."

Fuck.

Life would be so much easier if I liked women. I wouldn't have to hide myself and stay home when my teammates want to go out and pick up women.

All I want is to be with someone I love. It shouldn't matter that I want that person to be a man.

But here I am.

Between a rock and a hard place.

"Why couldn't you have been the NFL star in the family?" I joke, defusing the tension that's grown thick.

"Hell if I know. Good thing I got the good-looking genes of the family."

"Fuck off." I shove my brother over on the sofa.

The moment's gone, but his words churn dread in my gut.

My phone buzzes in my pocket and I pull it out to look at it.

"Oh shit, is that him?"

"How could you possibly know that?"

"Because you have the dopiest grin on your face."

"I do not."

But I know I do. Because Carter's words confirming our plans this weekend make me happy.

Happier than I've been in a long time.

Those happy feelings push down the growing guilt.

What little time I do get during the season, I want to spend with him.

This might be the worst decision I've made in a long time.

But that's for Future Alex to worry about.

Present Alex has a date with a man who is giving him butterflies.

And that's all I want to focus on.

$\sqrt{3}$ $\sum$ $12+84$

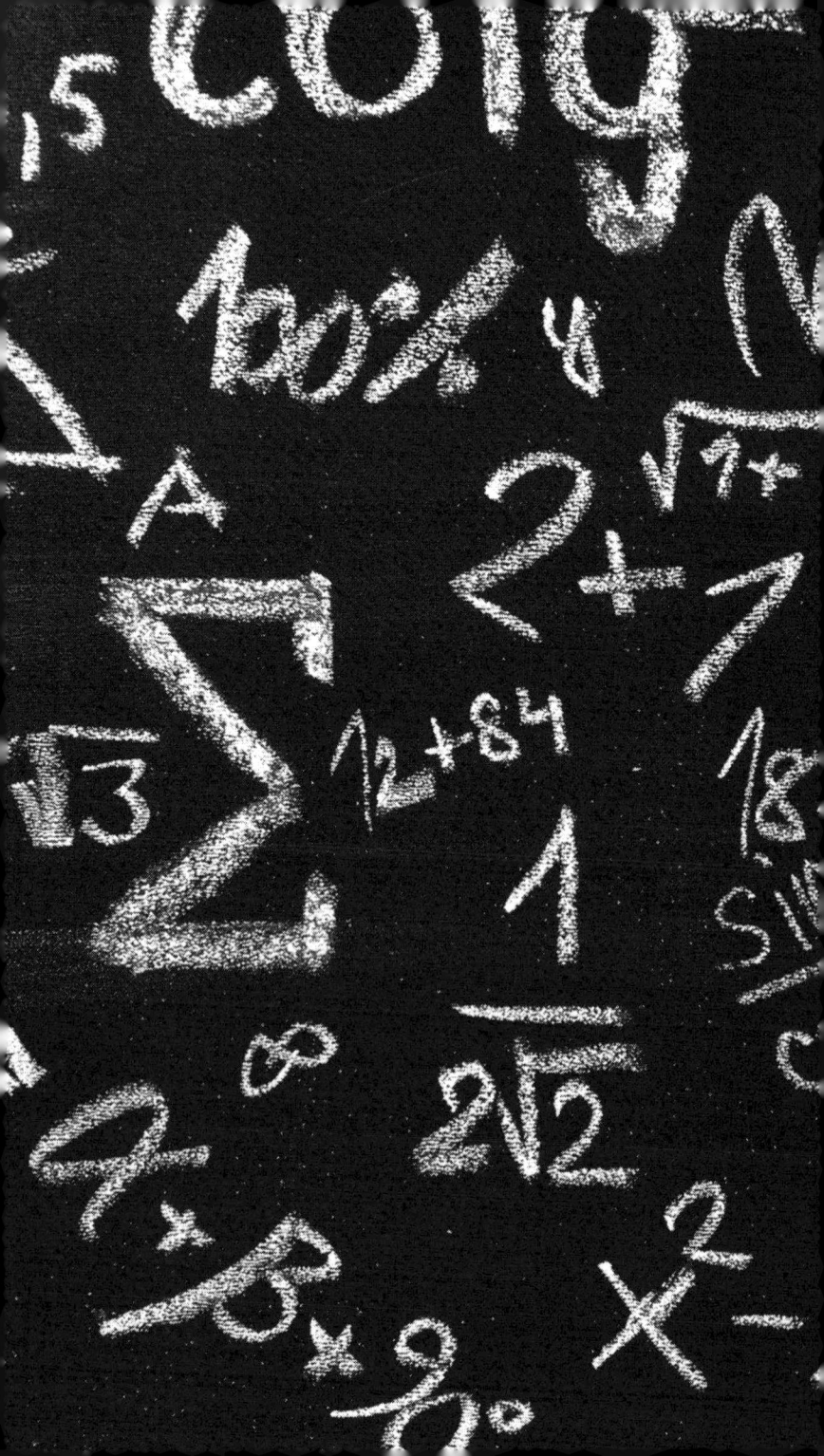

$2\sqrt{2}$

Chapter Ten

CARTER

"I can't believe you got into a fight with someone over Marvel and DC." I laugh as I slide into the booth at the deserted diner. The red plastic seats crack as we sit in them. The smell of fries and stale coffee hangs in the air. It's everything you imagine a diner to be.

With Alex's crazy practice schedule and the game this weekend, we'd had to go to the convention later than I wanted. Being that I was with Alex, I expected to be mobbed. But with the slight change to his appearance—a walking wet dream—no one paid him the slightest bit of attention.

Even when he got into a fight over which characters are better.

"If you had said you like Marvel over DC, we would've had to put an end to this thing right now." He waves a finger between the two of us.

"Don't get me wrong, I still love Superman. But Thor? Yeah, I'd do him."

Alex barks out a laugh across from me as an older

woman drops off two menus. "Evening, boys. Can I get you anything?"

"I'll just take a coffee, black and…"—I glance at the menu and find the first thing that grabs my attention—"cheese fries."

Alex smiles at her. "Same."

"Coming right up."

"Back to this whole Thor thing…" Alex starts.

"You cannot have an issue with Thor!" I bark out, slapping my hand on the table. "You've seen the movies. Even you couldn't turn down those muscles."

"I'm not saying I would, but Captain America gets my vote any day of the week."

I rake my gaze over him, taking in his hoodie and ball cap, and it suddenly dawns on me. "You're dressed up as Cap when he went to the museum."

Alex laughs, deep and long. "Took you long enough to figure out. I figured it was a pretty easy getup."

"I am such an idiot."

"A pretty cute idiot, if it helps." Alex smiles at me as our coffees and fries are dropped off.

"Are you sure this is something you're allowed to eat while training?"

Alex waves me off, shoving three gooey, dripping fries into his mouth. "Doesn't matter."

Even eating fries is sexy. What in the world is this man doing to me?

"If you're puking during the game on Sunday, remember it's not my fault."

"Are you going to watch again?"

I roll my eyes. "Why is it all about you?"

"Hey, I didn't say it was. I just like that you watched the first game. Would you care to know I wanted to play better? Thinking of you watching?"

"I was never good luck to anyone before," I whisper, my voice getting small.

"Okay, I really need to know who I should beat up on your behalf."

"Ryan Cook," I say without thinking.

"And what did this Ryan Cook do to you?" Alex leans back in the booth, crossing his arms. He's getting defensive on my behalf, and I hate that I love it.

I blow out a breath. "It's not a story I like telling. But he's the reason I have an issue with football players."

"What did he do to you?"

"He broke my heart in front of the entire football team."

Alex winces. "As terrible as that sounds, what's the full story?"

"If I didn't know any better, I'd say you're Mantis reading minds."

A soft laugh hits me. "I think it's cute you think you can try and distract me. You can trust me, Carter."

Bricks fall from the wall I built up around my heart. It was easy to not let myself go around the men I've met. No one was worth even trying to let my guard down for. But there's something about Alex that keeps drawing me in.

Underneath all the padding and jerseys, he's just like me.

Loving the most random things.

"We started dating my sophomore year of high school. He was a senior and on the varsity football team. I was out and everyone knew it. One day I was studying at the library and he asked if we could study together."

Alex doesn't say a word. He's letting me process as he sips his coffee.

"We ended up making out more than we studied."

"As would most high schoolers." Alex smiles at me.

"Well, after that, we met a lot after practice. It was a lot of bumbled hand jobs under the bleachers and really sloppy kisses. But I felt something real for him. He said I was his first boyfriend."

"Oh God. This can't be going anywhere good."

I shake my head. "Nope. I was wavering back and forth on asking him to the homecoming dance. I wanted to go. Get a suit, share a limo…the whole nine yards."

"You know, for someone who doesn't like football, you sure know your terminology."

"You're lucky you're cute." I mock a glare across the table at him.

"So I've been told. Continue." He waves a hand, letting me go on.

"I worked up the nerve to ask him to the dance after practice one day. He told me he wasn't gay and shoved me. I ended up tumbling into the water coolers."

Alex's face pales.

"But the best part? He tried to pull me aside after— under the bleachers— and tell me he just couldn't let his friends mock him for liking me."

Scrubbing a hand over his face, Alex faces out the window. The glow from the diner lights reflects off his face, lightly stubbled now.

"Ever since then, I have a very strict no football players rule."

Alex turns back to me, his face having lost some of the earlier edge. "If I were a basketball player, I'd be okay to date?"

"Oh, I would have no issues." I smile, pushing down the roiling feelings that this story always dredges up.

I hate sharing my past humiliations, but I know I'm safe with Alex. He's someone I can trust who wouldn't do the same thing to me.

"Yet, you're still out with me right now."

I roll my eyes. "And I'm still out with you. You're someone I want to break my rule for."

Reaching for his wallet, Alex dumps a hundred-dollar bill on the table. "Care to break any more of your rules tonight?"

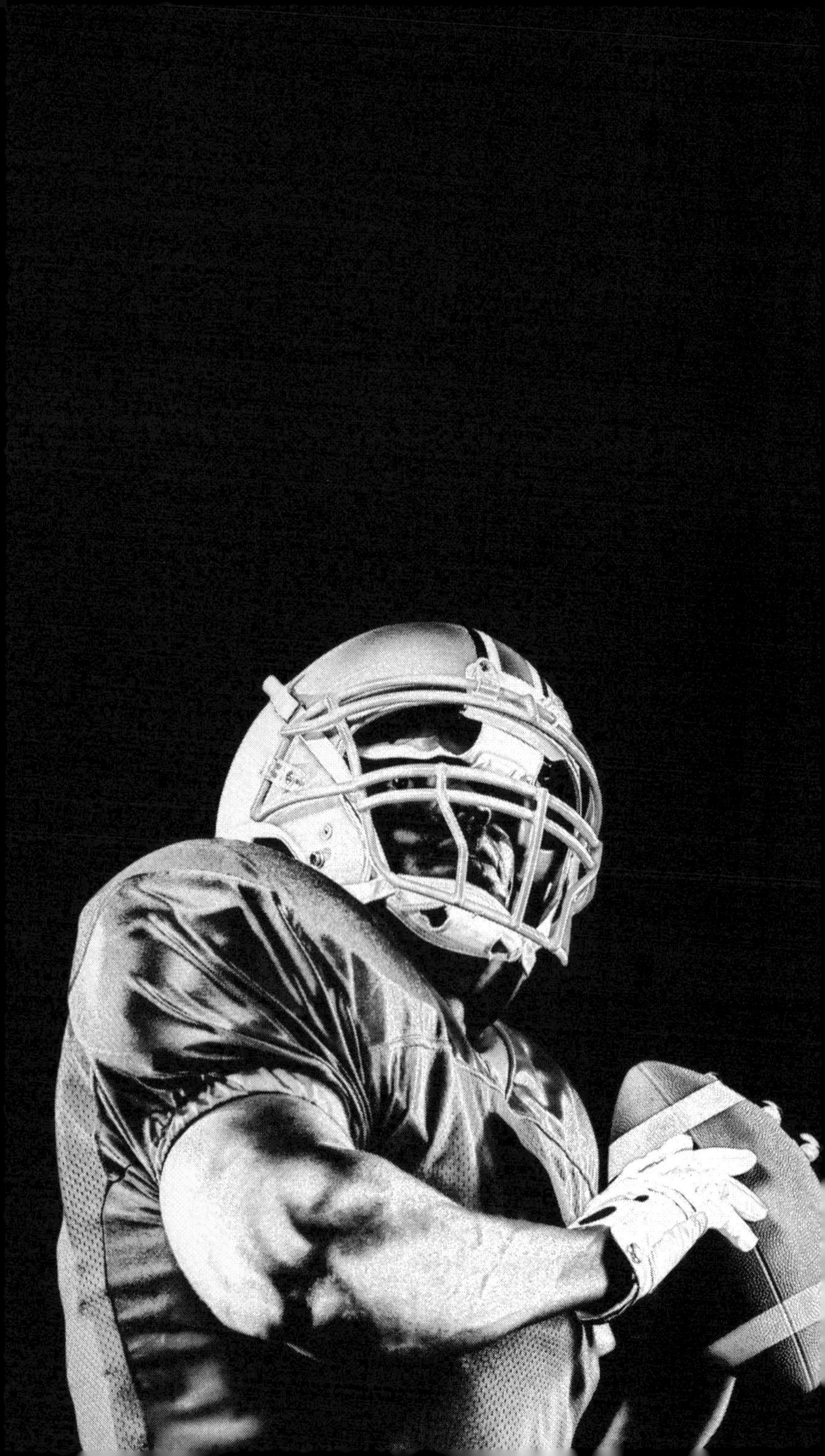

Chapter Eleven

ALEX

Carter is on me before I even have time to close the door. But I don't care. Ever since he picked me up, looking sexy as hell in a simple outfit for the convention, I've wanted to get my hands on him. Dressed up as Clark Kent, he's a walking fantasy.

His lips trail a hot path up and down my neck, sucking and nibbling. I push him off me.

"Is everything—"

I don't let him finish before I take his lips in a punishing kiss. He tastes minty from the peppermint we grabbed on our way out of the diner. I slide my tongue inside his mouth. I want to take my time, to explore and learn everything about this man, but I don't have any patience right now.

I want to feel him pounding into me. To feel his mouth working my cock over. I want it all.

"We should probably move this to somewhere that is a little more conducive to what we want to do." Carter tips his head to the side, my lips now moving down his neck.

"I guess we should."

Pulling my mouth off of him, I take in the disheveled appearance of the man in front of me. His eyes are filled with lust, lips swollen and neck red from my scruff.

I can't wait to see what he looks like once we're both thoroughly fucked.

Taking his hand in mine, I lead him through my house. I don't turn on a single light. My only thought is to get him into my room.

And naked. Definitely naked.

My steps are hurried as I turn the corner into the large master bedroom. Carter is right behind me. The dim light from my bedside table lamp casts the room in a golden glow. Carter's eyes look like they're on fire as he stalks toward me.

Each step he takes has my blood sizzling with need.

I can't remember the last time I've felt like this. I'm never able to fully let myself go. But with Carter? I know—I just *know*—that I'll be able to.

"Thinking some pretty serious thoughts there." Carter grabs my hip, pulling me to him. His own hard dick brushes my own.

"Just thinking about how I want you."

"And how is that?" Carter backs me up against the dresser across from my bed. My very large bed where I can't wait for him to have me. There's a dirty gleam in his eye as his mouth moves closer to mine.

"I want you to take over." My breath ghosts over his lips.

"Wait, what?"

Whatever lust-induced state he was in seems to have been broken.

"I want to feel you inside me."

"I'm so confused right now."

"You do know how this works, right?" I say on a laugh, waving my finger between the two of us.

Carter rolls his eyes at me. "No shit, Sherlock. I have done this before. I figured I'd have to bottom since you're a top."

"What makes you think I'm a top?"

His brows furrow together. "I mean, you're a quarterback. You lead on the field. You have to be in control of everything. I assumed you'd be a top too."

I can't help the smile that spreads across my face. "You would be wrong in that assumption."

"I am?"

I nod, taking his lips in another kiss. "I'm in control on the field. In the locker room. Everywhere. I have to be in order to be the best at my position. The last thing I want is to be in control in the bedroom."

Carter hooks a finger in the waistband of my pants, teasing ever so gently. It sends a flash of heat racing down my spine, tightening my balls. "So you're saying you want me to dominate you?"

The heat in his eyes is back. It has my cock thickening, imagining what this man can do to me. "Dominate me. Control me. Fuck me."

"Fuck, is that ever hot." Carter takes me in a commanding kiss, his lips and tongue moving expertly over mine. His fingers are bruising on my skin as he holds me to him. "PReP?"

I nod and add, "And tested recently."

"Good. Me too. Now, get on the bed."

I don't take my eyes off Carter as I take two steps backward until my knees hit the mattress. Pulling my shirt over my head, I scoot onto the center of the bed, resting against the pillows. Carter moves around the bed. His eyes don't leave mine.

"Hands up by your head. And don't move them."

Who knew my sexy math teacher, whose face lights up with excitement at numbers, likes to dominate in the bedroom?

"God, it's almost unfair how sexy your body is."

"And yet, you're not taking advantage of it yet."

My dick is painfully hard, the leaking tip peeking out from behind my pants. I feel Carter's eyes everywhere. All I want is his mouth to be on me. Somewhere. Anywhere. I don't care where, I just need relief.

Dropping a knee to the bed, Carter's presence takes over the room. It's like a switch has been flipped. Instead of the calm and quiet man I've gotten to know, he's now a man possessed.

"I've imagined this." Carter's hand slides over the bulge in my pants, cupping me ever so lightly. I arch into the contact, wanting more. "Seeing you spread out and being at my mercy."

"Please."

Carter leans over me, his lips a breath away from mine. "Please what?"

"Anything. God, I just want to feel you on top of me." I'm begging. I don't care. Every cell in my body is on fire, reaching out for this man to put me out of my misery and make me feel.

"I should really punish you and make you wait."

Carter's hand drags back up over my stomach, tracing each dip and groove in my abs. I try to close the distance between our lips, but Carter backs up.

I moan in frustration.

"Something wrong?" Carter's fingers brush against my nipple. Just the slightest touch has me ready to come in my pants. He's barely touched me and I'm coming unglued.

"You know there is."

"You know I like solving problems. What's yours?"

A smile pulls at the corner of my lips. "Is this a kink of yours?"

Brushing his nose along my jaw, his lips trace my ear. "Humor me. And maybe I'll help you out with your problem."

Tilting my head toward his, I whisper, "I'm painfully hard and the frustratingly sexy man in bed with me doesn't seem to want to do anything about it."

"That does seem like a problem." Carter swings a leg over my hips, settling over me. His cock lines up perfectly with mine. The tight pants he's wearing do nothing to hide his own straining length. "But you're in luck."

"I am?" I grind up against him, fighting the urge to pull him down to me. I move my hands under my head so I'm not tempted.

His grin is downright sinful right before he kisses me. And holy shit, does he ever kiss me. I'm fighting for air as he unbuckles my belt and slowly slides my zipper down.

When his hand makes contact with my dick, it takes everything I have not to explode at his touch.

"Fuck, that feels good."

"Then you'll like what I do next."

His grin is cocky as he slides down my body. Dark blue eyes stay locked on mine as he pulls my pants down and off my legs. Moving my boxers under my balls, my dick is offered up to him like a feast.

"Your dick is even better than I imagined it would be." His tongue darts out to lap at the precum leaking from the swollen head.

"More. God, please more."

This time, Carter doesn't make me wait. Sucking the crown into his mouth, I get the relief I've been searching for all night. His tongue swirls around the velvet skin. Each pass has my cock thickening in his mouth. He looks even sexier with his lips wrapped around me.

It's a sight to behold.

Carter's mouth slides up before swallowing me to the back of his throat. The heat and wetness is pulling me closer and closer to the edge.

But being the teasing man he is, he pops off, his hand squeezing the base of my cock to prevent me from shooting my load off.

"God, you're the fucking worst!" I groan.

"Worst or the best?"

"Worst. Definitely the worst." I throw an arm over my eyes in dramatic fashion. Maybe if I'm not staring at the sexy, teasing man, it'll help.

"Seems someone doesn't like edging."

I peek open one eye toward him. "You wouldn't like it either if you couldn't come."

Carter drags his tongue along the vein running up my length. "Trust me, you'll end up loving it."

Carter stands, shedding the rest of his clothes.

"I'm loving it more already."

Carter's body is drool-worthy in its own right. Soft hair coats his chest and a trail of light hair leads to a long, thick cock. One that juts out straight toward me.

"Are you going to tease me with that thing all night, or are you going to let me play?"

I reach for him, but he swats my hand away. "Lube? Condoms?" His voice is gravelly as he gives himself a slow stroke.

"Nightstand."

Carter fumbles in the drawer, looking for what he needs. Throwing them on the bed, he climbs over, taking my lips in a searing kiss.

Skin against skin.

Cock against cock.

The feel of this man over me has me rutting against him.

I cry out as he takes both our dicks in his hand, jacking us off.

"Fuck, Alex." His breath is hot on my neck.

I wrap my legs around his waist, pulling him closer. "I can't wait to feel you inside me."

Carter pulls back, a sly smile crossing his kiss-swollen lips. "Then I better get started."

Carter lubes up his fingers as he drags a trail down my eager dick, past my balls and right to my ass. A light tap on the rim has me so close to the edge, I have to bite my fist to stop from coming.

I can't imagine what it's going to feel like when he's inside me.

"Okay there?"

I peer down at him. His fingers haven't moved. "Just get inside me."

Waggling his eyebrows, Carter sinks one digit inside. Slowly. So painfully slow that I can't handle it.

Fisting my hands in the sheets, I rattle off stats to myself to keep from blowing my load.

"You look so good. Taking me in like this." Carter pushes my leg back, further opening me up to him. "It's going to look even better when it's my cock."

Warm breath ghosts over my balls as he sucks one into his mouth and, at the same time, sinks two fingers inside me.

He stretches me open as I push down, wanting more. Needing more. Craving more.

"I'm ready. Fuck, I'm so ready."

This time, Carter doesn't tease. He grabs a condom and rolls it down his hard length. "Turn over. Hands and knees."

I obey immediately as I hear the cap of the lube flick open. He drizzles more onto me before I feel the head of his dick. Strong hands pull my cheeks apart as he pushes inside.

"Yesss," I hiss.

"You look so good taking me in." Carter's voice is full of reverence as he sinks in, past the tight ring of muscle. He goes farther, his balls slapping me in the ass as he pushes all the way in.

"Fuck. Fuck."

It shouldn't feel this good. But God, does it ever.

Covering my body with his, Carter starts to move. Slick skin moves against slick skin. Each time he pounds back inside me—each graze of my prostate—my balls draw up higher and higher.

"Carter. Fuck," I groan. "I'm so damn close. Harder."

Carter pulls back, grasping my hips. "Jack yourself off."

Resting on my forearm, I take my own sensitive length in hand as Carter pounds into me. He's relentless. Every groan, every slap of skin pushes me to the edge.

"I need you to come, babe," Carter whispers.

Carter holds on tight as I take everything he has as the first flashes of my release flare to life.

"You're squeezing the life out of me. Fuck, that feels amazing." With one more pass of my prostate, I explode.

"Fuck, Carter!" I'm yelling. I don't care if people could hear me down the street, because rope after rope of cum is exploding out of me. It's never felt this good.

"Yesss," Carter groans as I feel the pulse of him inside me. "Yes!"

He loses his pace as he settles inside me, losing himself

to his own orgasm. Then Carter collapses on top of me, neither of us moving.

"Damn." I turn my head to see him, and his face is completely glazed over in pleasure.

"If you can still talk, I didn't do a good enough job." Carter's voice is breathless.

I smile at him, dropping a quick peck on his lips.

"Then I guess it's a good thing we have all night."

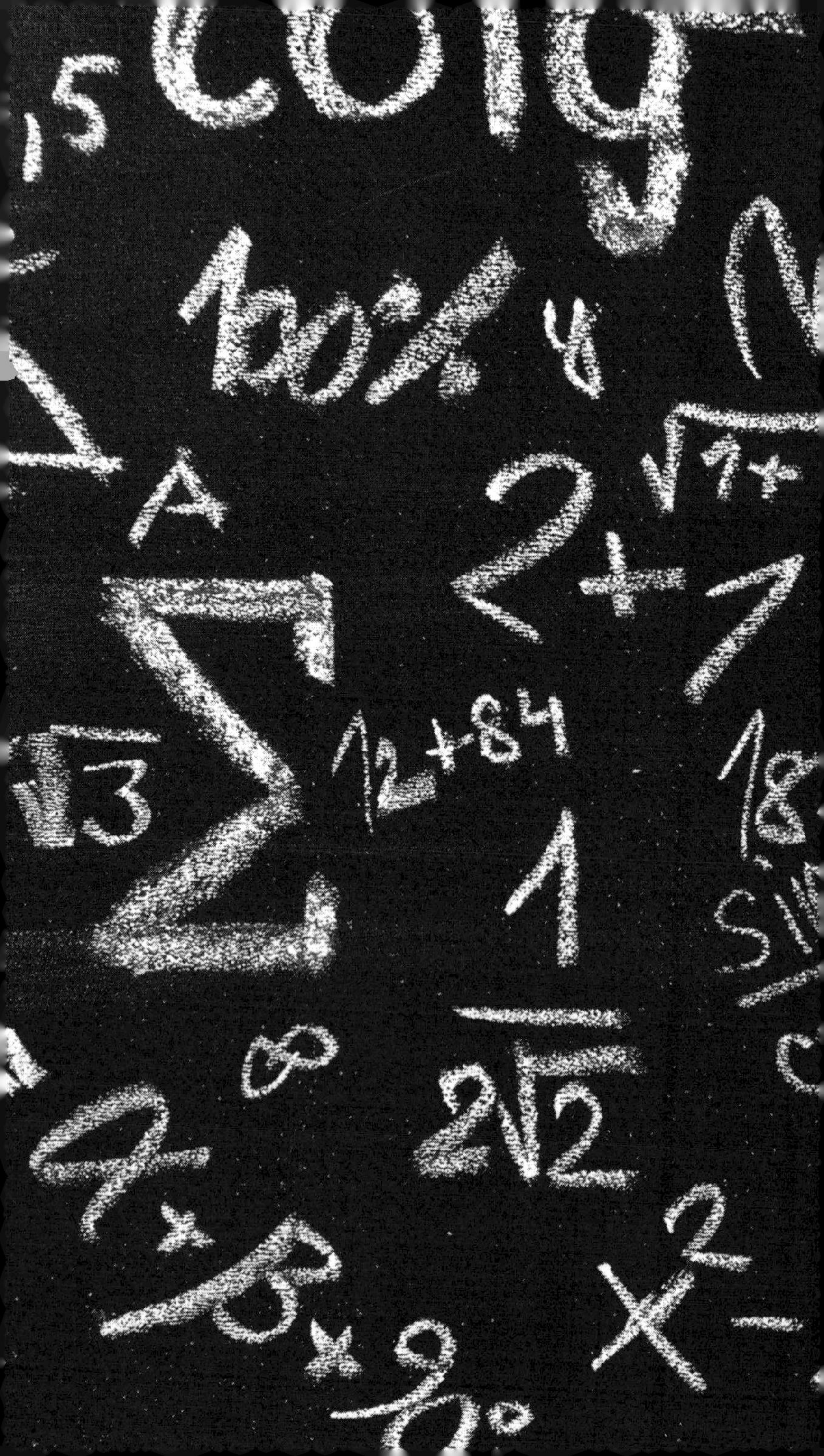

Chapter Twelve

CARTER

Rolling over, I feel the bed beside me is cold. The sunlight streaming in through Alex's windows is nearly blinding. But it doesn't hide the fact that there isn't a certain stud of a quarterback lying next to me.

Faint sounds of music drift upstairs. A groan escapes as I stretch. My body is tired after last night. I got to know Alex's body very well—every spot that makes him light up.

It makes my own dick get hard. Pushing down the thoughts from last night, I grab my boxers from the mess of clothes on the floor and follow the sounds downstairs.

I was too focused on Alex last night to really look at the upstairs of his house. It's homey, with pictures of friends, family, and him playing lining the walls. I love the homey feel. I expected something way more modern, but Alex continues to surprise me.

Especially when he's standing in front of the stove.

In nothing but a pair of black boxer briefs.

Fuck, if he isn't the sexiest man I've ever seen.

It's unfair for anyone to have that sexy of a back.

But Alex does.

The way his muscles ripple with each movement has me envisioning other ways I want to see him respond.

Christ, one night with Alex and he's turned me into a sex machine.

"You going to keep staring, or do you want some breakfast?"

Busted.

He didn't even turn around to know I was behind him.

"Sorry, just enjoying the show." I step closer to him, resting my chin on his shoulder.

"I can tell." His gaze shifts to mine, and I can't help myself. I take his mouth in a long, slow kiss.

After those drugging kisses last night, I can't get enough.

"Morning." His voice is scratchy.

"Good morning." I wrap my arms around him, peering down at what he's making. "What did I do to deserve such service?"

"I think you know." Alex leans farther into my hold as he whisks the eggs and veggies around in the pan. Coffee is gurgling in the pot next to the stove.

"A guy could get used to this." Dropping a kiss on his neck, I pull away. I grab a *Nerds are cool* coffee mug, pour myself a cup, and hop up to sit on the counter.

"And a guy could get used to seeing you in their kitchen every morning." Alex gives me a sly grin as he plates our breakfast.

When he spins in my direction, I notice the purple mark marring his pec. "Oh shit. Did I really do that?" I finger the hickey on his chest.

Alex steps in between my legs, resting his hands on either side of me. "You did."

"Hopefully the guys won't give you shit in the locker room."

Sideline Infraction

Alex gives me a lazy smile. "I'm not worried about them." He drags a finger around my own pec muscle. "I'm more worried about you not having a matching one."

His eyes are dark with need. But the rumble of my stomach interrupts whatever was about to happen.

"Looks like someone worked up an appetite."

Pulling the pan off the stove, Alex splits the eggs between two plates and hands one to me. Alex stands right beside where I'm sitting on the counter, shoveling a mouthful in.

I groan in delight. "This is delicious."

"I'm glad you're so easy to please."

"I would call this a symbiotic relationship." I drop a peck on Alex's lips before taking another bite.

"I thought you were a statistics teacher." Alex quirks a brow in my direction.

"Yes, but it doesn't mean I don't know what all my students are studying."

Alex sets his empty plate down, having inhaled his breakfast. "You're a good teacher, you know that?"

I shrug my shoulders. "Somedays it's hard to get anyone to listen, but I'm glad you think so."

"Hey, if it wasn't for you teaching, we wouldn't have met."

My gazes rakes over the man standing in front of me. That would be a damn shame.

Not just because of his amazing body. But because he might be the biggest surprise ever.

Who continues to surprise me with his choice of music playing right now.

"Any particular reason you have boy bands playing right now?" I try to hide my amusement at his choice in music, but I can't.

"What, you don't like the Backstreet Boys?"

I shake my head. "That's not it at all. I just didn't peg you to be a BSB fan."

"What, just because I'm a football player I can't appreciate their music?"

"You can. I just thought I was the only man near the age of thirty to listen to them."

Alex arches a brow in my direction. "So you're a fan?"

"I guess you could say that." I try to play it cool.

Alex grabs my plate and sets it on the counter next to his empty one. "Let me guess, you had posters of them in your room when you were growing up."

"Not quite. My sister did."

"And you'd go into her room when she wasn't home, and what, stare at them?"

"It might've been the reason I realized I was gay in the first place."

Alex is beaming at me. I can feel how excited he is when he rests his arms on my shoulders. "Let me guess…Nick?"

I roll my eyes. "Am I that predictable?"

Alex laughs. "Oh my God. If you married him, you would've been Carter Carter!"

I swat at his chest. "He would've taken my name, thank you very much. Nicky Brooks has a nice ring to it, don't you think?"

Alex shrugs his shoulder. "I guess if you like blonds."

I sink a hand into his hair, tugging on it. "I'm an equal opportunist in the looks department. You were probably into Kevin since you like older men."

"Oh please, you're three years older than me."

I lean in for a kiss. "You're not disproving my theory."

"Backstreet Boys was only one of the ones I liked. My brother's girlfriend used to play them all the time. He hated it, I loved it. She taught me everything she knew. They aren't the only ones I like."

"I'm afraid to ask. Was it some obscure British boy band no one has heard of?"

Alex shakes his head. "O-Town."

Thank God I'm not drinking my coffee, or I'd spit it out all over him. "O-Town? Are you serious?"

"I'm sorry," Alex looks affronted, "but did you see Ashley Parker Angel?"

He's got me there. "Okay, I'll agree with you on that. I bet you had all the 'Liquid Dreams' about him."

Alex smacks a hand over my mouth. "Please don't ever say that again."

I smile against his palm before clasping my hand around his wrist and pulling it down. "What? You don't like me using *liquid dreams* against you?"

"If you ever want to sleep with me again, you'll stop."

That shuts me up. I mime zipping my lips.

"Good." A cocky grin spreads across Alex's face as he closes the distance between us. "I'd hate to have to get rid of the first guy who actually has the same taste in music as me."

My hands travel up and over his pecs, linking around the back of his neck. "Then I guess I should thank my sister for it."

Alex smiles before kissing his way down my jaw. "We should also thank your sister for suggesting I take her place for the comic book convention."

The groan he elicits from nibbling on my ear is downright dirty. "I don't really want to think of her right now."

"Oh yeah? What'd you have in mind?"

Alex's lips continue their descent, licking and sucking down my neck. It's hard to focus on anything when his lips are on me.

"When do you have to be at the practice field?" I'm surprised that I can string a sentence together. Alex makes me *that* crazy.

"Not for another few hours." When Alex pulls back, his eyes are heavy with lust.

"Then why don't we make the most of them?" I trace my finger around his nipple, loving the way goose bumps break out over his skin.

"Let's get that workout in before you go then."

I hop off the counter and grab Alex's hand in mine, leading us toward the stairs, ready to spend the morning buried in the man who is quickly becoming one of my favorite people.

$\cot g$

100%

$\sqrt{1+}$

$2+1$

$\sqrt{A}$

$\sqrt{3}$

$\sqrt{12+84}$

1

18

$\sin$

$\dfrac{}{2\sqrt{2}}$

x^2

Chapter Thirteen

CARTER

"Alex, what are you doing here?"

"Gabe. Show our guest some respect." I peer over at Alex, who's grinning like an idiot. "It's Mr. Young."

"Sorry. Mr. Young, what are you doing here?" he repeats.

"Carter—sorry, Mr. Brooks—invited me to come and see how you guys are doing on your project."

I aim a sly smile his way. Alex and I have been seeing each other for a few weeks now. With the insanity of football season in full swing, it's a lot of stolen nights at Alex's house.

Normally, I'd begrudge him for having to hole up there, but I don't mind it. Not when we can get lost in one another.

"So, talk stats to me. Are the Mountain Lions going to win the Super Bowl this year?" Alex claps his hands as eager hands shoot into the air.

"Austin, why don't you start us off?" I point to him, not wanting everyone to start shouting over each other.

"Your passing statistics are sound this year," Austin

states without pretense. He's probably the brightest student in my class. "Mr. James is also having a good season as well."

Good was putting it mildly. He was having the best season of his career, according to Alex.

"He is. How's the defense looking?"

"Limiting opposing offenses' run game to less than one hundred yards per game leads the league."

"Knox Fisher is also having a career season." Alex is beaming with pride. You can't miss how much he loves his teammates.

"Based on all the calculations, and the rest of the teams, my estimation is that the Mountain Lions will win two Super Bowls in the next six years."

"Only two?" Alex looks slightly taken aback.

"My number is closer to three,"—Austin fiddles with his pencil—"but I don't want to overestimate."

"How about we say three, and if it doesn't happen, I won't hold it against you if we only win two?"

The students all cheer for Alex. He wins everyone over wherever he goes.

"Hey, why don't you come chaperone the dance with Mr. Brooks? Mrs. Phillips is out and we need an extra!" Ben calls out from the back.

"How in the world do you know that, Ben?"

"My mom told me. She got a call for more parent chaperones. Apparently no other teachers can do it."

I snort. I highly doubt that. No one wants to spend the night before fall break chaperoning the school dance with these hormone-filled kids. "He does not want to chaperone our school dance."

"Who says I don't?" He crosses his arms and leans against the wall. My students are busy glancing between the two of us.

"You know it's a high school dance, right?"

Alex fights the smile. "I gathered as much. Why not? It's the bye week. I don't have anything going on."

I know Alex doesn't have anything going on, because it's also our fall break. How they managed to align perfectly, I don't know. But we planned on spending the whole weekend together.

"Don't talk him out of it, Mr. Brooks! How cool would it be to have a Mountain Lion at our fall dance?" Ben shouts.

I quirk a brow in Alex's direction. "Are you sure you know what you're getting yourself into?"

"Sign me up, Mr. Brooks."

"ARE you sure you're ready for this?"

Alex is standing in front of me, in my classroom, before the dance starts. "You trying to talk me out it?" He gives me a sly grin.

"These are high schoolers. If they sense any fear, they are going to eat you alive."

"A bit dramatic, don't you think?" Tucking his hands in his pockets, Alex leans back against my desk. "They were just fine this week. I'm used to them."

"My kids already like you. The rest will want to act all cool to impress you."

"Kind of like you tried acting cool when you first met me?"

I straighten his tie, not looking at him. "I have no idea what you're talking about."

Alex grabs my hand, dropping a kiss to my palm. "Sure you don't, stud."

"Fine. But it doesn't change the fact that these kids will try to impress you. They are like the worst opposing defenses, reading your weaknesses, plowing through your offensive line, and sacking you on every play."

Alex's shoulders go rigid.

"Now you get it. Teens are the exact same way. Especially ones with a lot of hormones."

"Okay, yes, that does sound terrible. But can we also talk about how hot it is when you talk football?"

"You are not focusing on the right things." I go to leave, but Alex pulls me back.

"Oh, I believe I am, Mr. Brooks."

"Fine, but don't say I didn't warn you."

"Relax. I knew what I was getting into when I signed up. Besides,"—Alex shrugs a perfectly muscled shoulder—"I have you. They'll go easy on me."

Grabbing his hand, I pull him closer to me. "Okay, babe. Whatever you say."

I drop a kiss on his lips. Quick and easy. But Alex pulls me back, lingering just a moment longer.

"You know this is frowned upon at school dances?"

He laughs, his breath hot against my cheek. "I know. That's why I figured I should get it in now while I can."

"As long as it's not the last one you'll ever give me." There's a slight edge to my voice. Alex and I have only been seeing each other for a few weeks. Yet, it feels different from anything else I've ever had.

"I volunteered for this. I know what I'm getting myself into."

Alex

Holy shit. I did not know what I was getting myself into.

Already, I've confiscated two flasks, stopped two teenagers from dry humping in the hallway, and broken up a fight.

And that was the first thirty minutes.

With the lights in the school gym lowered and a disco ball reflecting everywhere, it's made it easy for the kids to sneak around.

"Are you regretting this yet?" Carter comes up beside me. His presence is soothing, but I'm still on edge.

"You didn't tell me it would be this bad."

"You didn't believe. Did you think they'd all be angels?"

"I figured they'd all be like your students. They were respectful when they came to the practice field."

"My students are in AP Statistics. Not everyone is like them," Carter laughs.

"Is this what you imagined your own high school dance to be like?"

"I guess I figured it'd be more dancing and less grinding."

"Are you sad you never got to experience it?"

Carter shrugs a shoulder. "Yes and no. I wish I could've had a hot date on my arm to impress people, make me stand out less as one of the only out kids, but it doesn't matter. I don't need it if it's like this."

An idea comes to mind. One that Carter would hopefully like.

As my gaze shifts back to the dance floor, two students are grinding on each other. It's an assault on the eyes.

"Can you deal with that? I just can't." I pout, hoping he'll take pity on me.

"It's taken care of." Another adult has already pulled the two apart.

"God, if I ever have kids and they act like this..."

"What will you do?" Carter crosses his arms, his brows quirking up at me.

"Fuck if I know. But they will not behave like this when I'm not around."

This time, Carter bursts out laughing and doesn't stop. I pin him with a no-nonsense stare.

"Oh, you're serious?" Carter wipes a fake tear away. "That's even better."

"Stop laughing at me!" I shove at his shoulder and it diminishes his laughter.

But only slightly.

"I'm sorry. But do you really think you'll be able to control kids when you're not there?"

"Now I don't." I cross my arms, turning away from him. "So much for my angel of a daughter who won't even look at another boy until she's forty."

"Yes, that is going to be your children to a tee. Never doing anything to upset you. They'll be perfect."

"Now you're just patronizing me."

Carter stuffs his hands in his pockets and turns his focus back to the kids. "I deal with these balls of hormones on a daily basis. Sorry to burst your bubble."

"How much longer do we have?"

"About two more hours. Think you'll be okay?"

"If I ever agree to this again, please slap me upside the head."

Carter gives me a grin before walking away to a group of students that are yelling at each other.

"You got it, Mr. Quarterback. You got it."

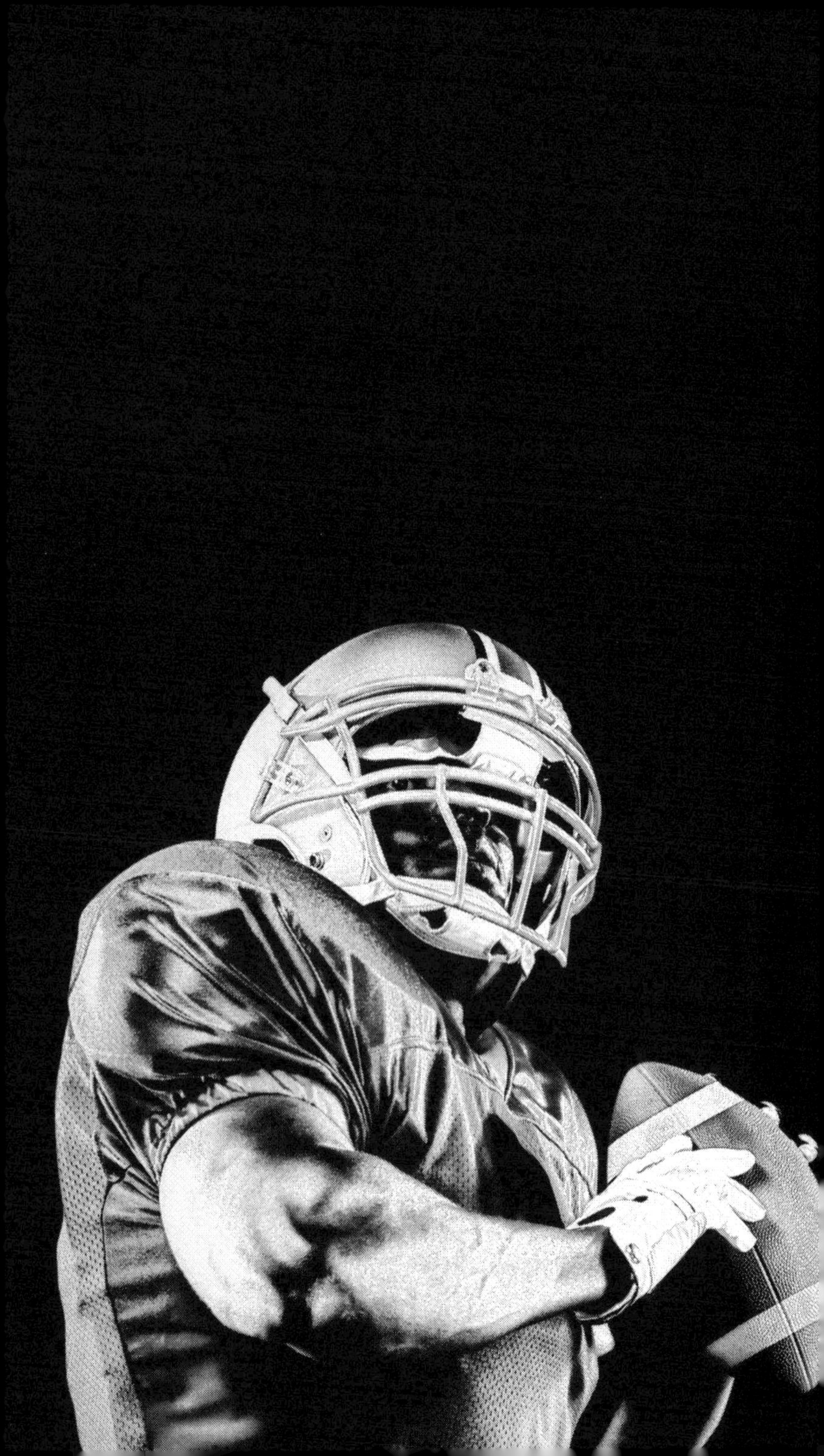

Chapter Fourteen

ALEX

"I appreciate you coming by to help me on such short notice."

I wrap another strand of lights around the back patio column.

"Are you still not going to tell me what this is all about?" Peyton asks, jumping down from the chair on the other side.

I shake my head. "Nope. I want it to be a surprise for everyone involved."

"Well, whatever it is, I think it's cute you're pulling out all the stops. She's a lucky girl."

I focus my attention on detangling the last set of lights, keeping the smile locked on my face.

"Damn. I was hoping that would get it out of you," Peyton says, elbowing me in the side.

"Has anyone told you Colin is rubbing off on you?" I laugh, dropping down into one of the chairs.

Peyton grabs a water bottle from the table. "Wouldn't be the first time."

I eye the woman I've gotten to know over the last few

months. "You know you've changed Colin for the better, right?"

"He's pretty easy to love."

I know it wasn't an easy road for them, and I like seeing both of them happy. Seeing these two together, and Jackson and Tenley together, gives me a sliver of hope.

That maybe someday I could find someone like that.

Except I already have.

Because there is no one else I would do this for.

Except Carter.

"And there's no one special for you?"

Peyton's eyes are studying. It's hard not to squirm under her fierce stare. She's a force to be reckoned with.

"Not really, no."

The lie is getting harder and harder to keep. Yet, it's the reality I'm living on a daily basis.

I want to be able to trust these people with my secret. I trust them with everything else, so why not this?

Because it could accidentally slip out and then I'd be fucked.

I shake the guilty thoughts from my head and focus on what I'm doing right now for Carter. Whether I'm out or not, I know he'll love this.

"I believe what you're doing begs to differ."

I give her a cunning smile. "You don't know what I'm doing."

Peyton looks around at the lights that she helped me string up through the yard. "Whatever it is, they'll love it. Even if you won't tell me."

"I'm just glad the guys were busy and you were free, because they'd give me so much shit over this."

Laughter bursts out of Peyton. "Oh my God, they would give you so much shit. This is definitely better left to a woman for help."

I hold my water bottle up to her in a toast. "Then I'm glad you were around to help."

"I'm always here for you, Alex. I hope you know that. You've done so much for me since I started, and I don't know if I could ever thank you enough."

"Hey, you're part of the family now. We've got each other's backs."

"Well, let me know how it goes." She stands, heading back into the house.

I glance around at the work we did. I have more left to set up, but that'll be later before Carter comes. "I hope they love it," I say as I follow her to the front door.

Peyton hugs me before heading out. "They will. Trust me."

CARTER

FOR SPENDING the long weekend together, Alex had no problem kicking me out of his house today. But when he said to come back tonight, it took everything I had not to get here early.

Walking into the house, I head out back, as instructed. Nerves are racing through me at his mysterious words from earlier today.

Cold air hits me as I step outside. But it's not what takes my breath away.

It's the man standing in front of me.

Alex is glowing under string lights, looking sexy as hell in a well-fitted black suit. His usually messy hair is slicked back to the side. A few bottles of beer chill on the table that is covered with flower petals. Music plays softly in the background.

"All I Have To Give" by the Backstreet Boys, if I'm not mistaken.

"What in the hell is all of this?"

Alex closes the distance between us.

"Carter Brooks. Will you go to the homecoming dance with me?"

I open and close my mouth, words not coming. It feels like butterflies could burst from my stomach.

Alex Young, the quarterback for the Denver Mountain Lions, is asking me to the dance.

This single moment here with Alex is wiping out every bad memory left from high school. Instead of the jock who shoved me and lied to me, Alex is here. And he's asking me to the dance in the most romantic way ever.

Tears gather in my eyes at what this means. And based on the look Alex is giving me, he knows what it means to me.

"You're not answering me. I hope I've stunned you into a good silence."

"Alex…"

He really has stunned me.

Alex wraps an arm around my shoulders and pulls me closer to him.

"I know you never got to go to the dance with the guy you liked, but I'm hoping maybe this might make up for it."

I blink, chasing away the wetness that has gathered.

"This is without a doubt the most thoughtful thing anyone has ever done for me."

Alex's warm breath ghosts my cheek. "Thank God. You were starting to worry me there for a second."

"I'm speechless."

"You deserve to have your own dance."

I shake my head, pulling back to gaze into Alex's eyes. I have all sorts of emotions careening through me. "This is better than any high school dance I would've gone to."

"It will be because we also control the music."

"Backstreet Boys was an excellent choice, Mr. Young."

He winks at me as he leans back to grab a plastic container on the table.

A white rose boutonniere.

"Wow, you really thought of everything."

Alex laughs. "This is our first dance together. Of course I had to."

Shaking hands pin the boutonniere to my sweater. "This really is the full experience, right down to the nervous date."

"It might not be like a regular dance,"—Alex waves a finger between the two of us—"because it's just us and there's alcohol."

I wrap my arms around Alex's shoulders. "You were at the dance. You saw how many kids tried to sneak in alcohol."

Alex kisses me, warm and sweet. "Difference is I didn't have to sneak it from my parents' liquor cabinet. I was able to buy it myself."

"So if this really is like a high school dance, did you book us a hotel room?" I waggle my eyebrows at him.

Alex laughs, starting to sway with me in his arms. "I'd much prefer to have you take me in my own room."

I gaze around the backyard with the lights and the soft music, Alex in my arms as he spins us in a circle. I trail a path of kisses up his jaw, whispering into his ear, "Thank you, Alex."

"Hopefully this is changing your mind about football players."

"It is. It definitely is."

"Now, do you want the full high school dance experience?"

"If you're talking about sex, yes. Bumbling, awkward sex? I'll pass."

Alex barks out a deep laugh, washing over me and filling every cell of mine. He spins and dips me, lips hovering over my mouth.

"I promise you, it will be anything but bumbling."

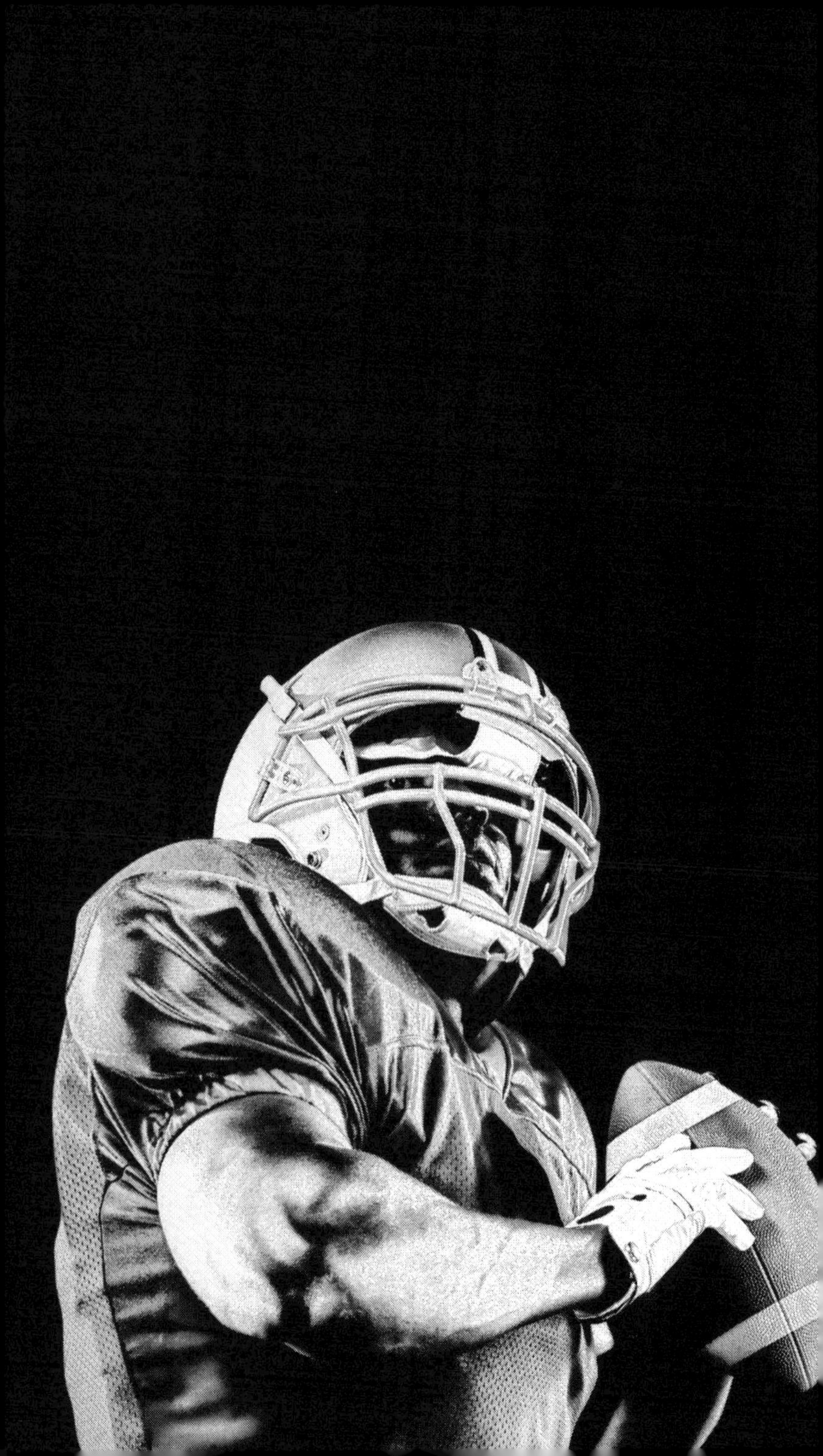

Chapter Fifteen

ALEX

The entire night went off without a hitch. Carter's reaction was everything I hoped it'd be and more.

Dancing with him was even better.

Spending the evening with him like that had me falling that much further for him. Because of the big heart he has hidden away.

I love that he's opening it up to me.

After sipping on beer and dancing to every horrible dance song I could find—all in the name of the true homecoming experience—Carter takes my hand and guides me to my room.

Shutting the door, Carter is on me, his lips kissing my entire face, neck, jaw—you name it.

"If this is how you are when I invite you to a dance, I'm going to do it more often."

Carter steps back, a hazy, happy look ghosting over his eyes. "I can't believe you did all of that for me."

I step into his space, my hand cupping his cheek and bringing him closer. "I would do it again a hundred times over." I kiss his warm, beer-tinged lips. "You make a pretty good dance partner."

"Mmm, yes," Carter chuckles against my lips. "My swaying skills were top notch."

Carter grabs me, shedding my jacket and shirt on the way to the bed. "Maybe next time we can take some dance lessons."

The thought of dancing like that with Carter has guilt rising inside of me. I want to do that. I want to be out with him. But I can't.

"Maybe you can give me some lessons of your own right now." Unbuckling my belt, I make quick work of my pants as Carter stands fully clothed in front of me.

"What lesson would you like first?" Carter pulls his sweater off.

"Fuck, you're sexy."

"Not a lesson." Carter's mouth is pulled into a smug grin as he moves to lie on the bed. "How about since you were so wonderful tonight, you take what you want?"

The thought of riding Carter has me pouncing on him.

"Someone's excited."

"What can I say? Getting to be with you makes me excited."

Carter pulls me down on top of him, giving me a mind-melting kiss. Warm hands skate up and down my back, sending pleasure coursing through me.

Every time this man touches me, it makes me crazy with desire. I'm so far gone for him, it should scare me.

When he's kissing me like this? Like he has all the time in the world with me, it makes me feel settled for the first time in my life.

I'm rutting against him, needing more.

"You still have too many clothes on."

I kiss my way down his chest, sucking on his hard

nipples. Playing and flicking them with my tongue. Each groan of his has my own dick taking notice. It wants to get in on the action too.

"I love that mouth of yours," Carter groans.

"You'll like it even more in a minute."

I kiss and suck my way down his stomach, undoing his pants and pulling them off with his boxers.

His dick springs back, thick and throbbing, against his stomach. I kiss my way up his legs.

"I thought you were supposed to be the one getting what you wanted tonight?" Carter's voice is breathless as I suck a heavy ball into my mouth.

"What makes you think this isn't exactly what I want?" I reply as I pull back and look him in the eye.

"You've already given me so much tonight."

I give him a wicked smile, taking his cock in hand. "Then let's just say it's all part of the experience. I'm making this night all about you."

I suck his dick to the back of my throat and he bucks off the bed. "Oh shit!"

Smiling, my hand and mouth work him over. His cock thickens in my mouth as I pull him close to the edge.

"I'm not going to last much longer," Carter whines. "I want to be inside you when I come."

I pop up off of him and reach across to grab the condoms and lube. Pushing my boxer briefs down, I lube my own fingers and start stretching myself.

"You're not going to let me do that?" Carter asks, as I pick up where I left off.

I moan around his dick, prepping myself with no finesse. "No."

"You're being a very bossy bottom tonight."

"No, I just don't want to drag this out any longer."

Pulling my fingers out of my ass, I open the condom and roll it down Carter's cock.

"Fine by me." Carter pulls me forward and I line his dick up with my hole. I sink down, slowly, adjusting to his size.

There's a slight sting, but I don't care. The feel of him inside me is fucking amazing.

"Fuck, you're tight," Carter hisses.

"It feels incredible." I still as I'm filled to the brim. Sitting up, Carter wraps an arm around me as he attacks my chest with kisses and bites.

I hold him to me as I start to move. Each thrust sends blazing heat through me as he pegs my prostate. I'm making a mess all over his chest, but I don't care. All I want is to feel him explode inside of me.

Words are tumbling out of my mouth. None of it makes sense as the edges of my vision start to blur.

"Go harder. I'm right there with you." Carter brings my face down to his in a bruising kiss. My tongue matches my thrusts as I drink him in. Each pass of his cock inside of me, of his tongue, is like gasoline on the fire.

I'm out of my mind with lust as my orgasm slams into me.

"Fuck!" I rip my lips from his, shouting as my movements falter. Grabbing my dick, Carter strokes me through my release as I feel him come apart in my arms.

My limbs are boneless as I collapse on top of Carter. Strong arms wrap around me. Neither of us moves, happy in our embrace.

"Best night of your life?" I ask, kissing the fluttering of his pulse in his neck.

"Best night ever."

$\cos g$

15

100% y

$\sqrt{1+}$

A

$2 + 7$

$\sum$

$\sqrt{13}$ 12+84

18

1 sin

8 $2\sqrt{2}$

$9 \cdot 3$ x^2

%

Chapter Sixteen

CARTER

"You know, I'm starting to think my dad isn't working you hard enough," I huff out a breath as we hit the next mile marker.

"Football is an entirely different kind of exercise. You have to focus on about a dozen different things at once. I like this—"

"Because you don't have to focus," I interrupt, smiling to myself. "I guess I shouldn't be complaining."

Alex pulls to a stop in the middle of the trail. The sun is heading toward the horizon. Long shadows from the trees stretch across the path ahead.

"You're making it very hard to want to continue this hike and not take you home."

Alex's heated gaze cuts through whatever cold I'm feeling from the wind.

"Then you better get your ass in gear and show me what you want to show me."

Alex smirks before turning back on the trail. With the wet weather we've been having, the trail is virtually deserted. It's like the two of us are out here in our own little world.

"We're only about five minutes away."

"Take your time. I'm enjoying the view."

Alex turns, walking backward. "You are?"

"I was." I twirl a finger in his direction. "Pay attention. I don't want to be the most hated man in the city because you injured yourself on a hike that my grandma could do."

Alex's booming laugh fills the quiet space. "I won't hurt myself." Alex peeks over his shoulder. "Besides, we're here."

The trail ends at a picnic table with a view overlooking the mountains. The sunset is exploding across the sky, clouds disappearing into nothing.

"How do you know about all of these places?" Alex spreads out a black-and-yellow striped blanket. I drop the small cooler on top. Reaching inside, I grab a water bottle and pass him one.

"I like being outside. I spent every free weekend I could during the off-season exploring."

I drop down next to Alex. "Must be nice having all that free time."

"You're a teacher. You have summers off."

This time, I'm the one laughing. "I have to teach summer school for my delinquents who won't get off their phones. I get maybe two weeks off."

"So you're saying if this thing continues, I won't be seeing much of you?"

"Probably about as much as I'm seeing you right now." I quirk a brow in his direction.

"One of the downsides of playing football."

"Did you ever think you'd do something else?" I kick my legs out on the striped blanket.

"Other than football?" Alex sips from his water bottle.

"Yes."

Alex shakes his head. "Once I realized I was good at it, I threw all my energy into it."

"And you never wanted to do something else?"

Alex laughs at me. "You know I'll have to do something else eventually."

"Because you'll retire?"

"Hopefully not too soon. I still have a lot of football left to play."

"What would you do after?"

"I haven't thought about it."

"Really?" I don't try to hide the shock in my voice. "Someone as cerebral as you? I figured you'd have a thirty-year plan."

Alex leans back on his elbows. His long body is stretched out, easy for me to drink him in. It's about the only thing to distract me from the sunset.

"Are you trying to make me consider my entire future in one night?"

"Wasn't my plan." I take a swig of my water, staring out at the views in front of me.

"It's hard to think about because it's always been so up in the air."

I turn to face him, the dying light of the sky reflecting in his eyes. "Are you always worried about being cut?"

"Not necessarily that. Sure, it's something every athlete could face in their career, but more so the fact that I couldn't even get married if I wanted to up until a few years ago."

"Ah."

"Sorry. Don't mean to bring down the evening."

I lean over, moving a bit closer to Alex. The only noise is the rustling of leaves in the trees. "I like getting to know all these sides of you."

His lips turn up in a small smile. "You're about the only one who does."

"I find it very hard to believe I'm the only one."

Alex shifts to his side. I mirror his position. "Fine. You're the only one who I've let get close enough."

"And yet you're the one who pursued me."

Alex links his free hand with mine. Sparks instantly pulse through me.

"Can you blame me?"

I look around me, taking in everything. The trees. The mountains. The last fading rays of the sun.

Everything about this is the perfect evening.

"I'm glad you did, because otherwise we wouldn't be here together."

And I'm happier that I put aside my rule to ignore football. As someone who grew up around football, after high school I paid little to no attention to the game. I knew that Alex was the quarterback for the team, but nothing else about him. People would give me shit about it, but I didn't care.

The less I knew about football, the better. My dad never pushed. Maybe if he had, I would've known about Alex sooner.

I'm glad I came to my senses because I wouldn't want to be missing out on this—being here with Alex.

"I mean, I might still have some sanity after the dance…"

I bark out a laugh as I shove Alex back. "How ever will I make it up to you?"

"I've got a few things in mind."

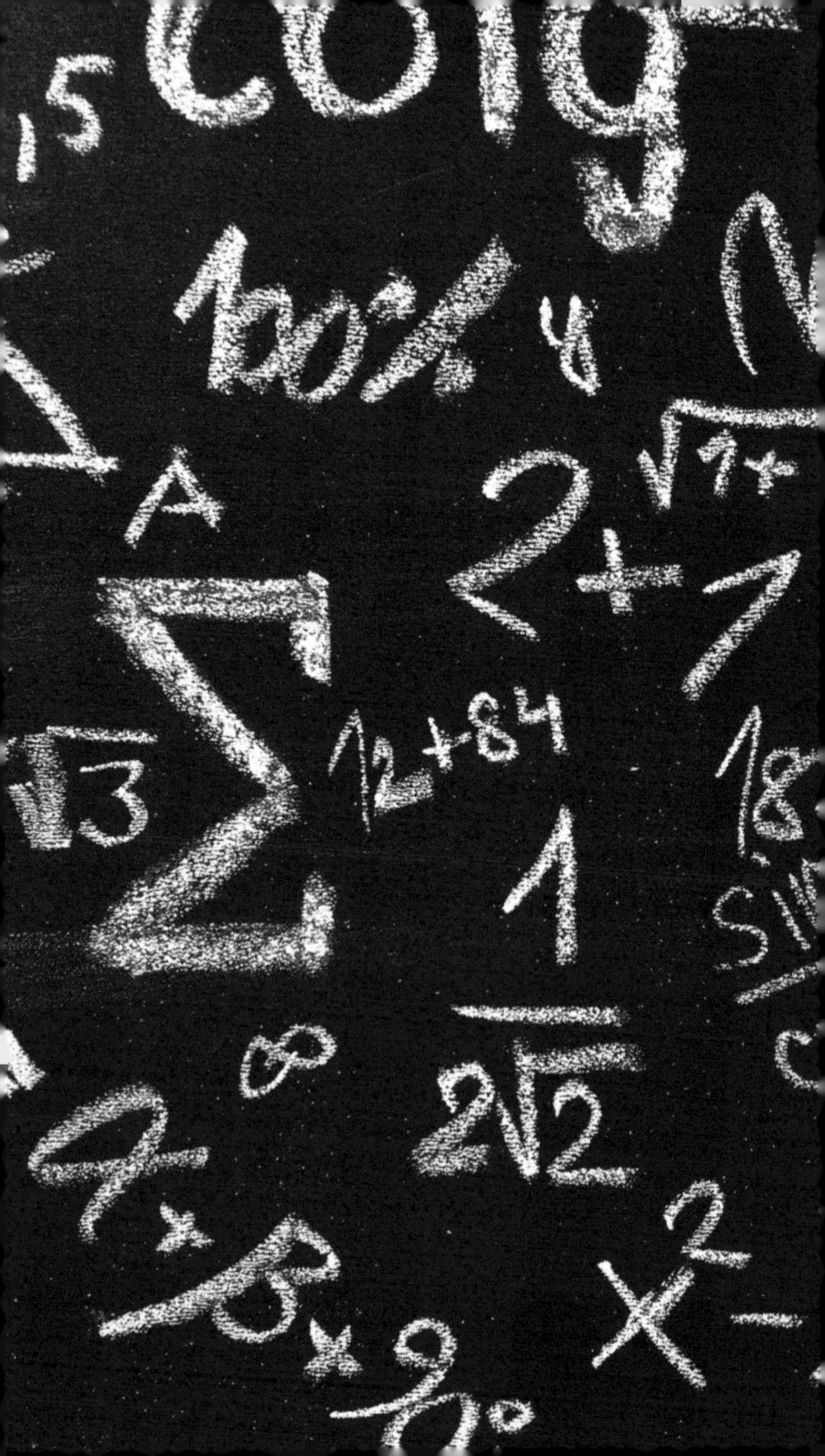
cotg
100%
A

Chapter Seventeen

CARTER

"I kind of like you having fall break." Alex kisses the back of my neck.

"Why? Because I'm here all the time?" I ask as I stir the risotto in the pan.

"Yes." Alex wraps an arm around my waist. "I like this way of you making it up to me."

"Okay. You need to back up, or I'm going to burn this dinner." I shove Alex back a step or two.

We've spent the last few days together. Aside from our hike this afternoon, we haven't left Alex's house. If it were any other week, we wouldn't get to be here together. But because of the bye week, we've locked ourselves away.

I suggested we go out, but Alex wanted to stay in. Normally I would have pushed, but he says he doesn't like being in the spotlight and just wants to be with me without interruptions.

It's hard to argue with that.

"I can't help it if you look good cooking. Are you sure I can't help?"

"No. You've spoiled me enough. Now go sit."

Alex grabs a beer and stalks around the counter, sitting at a bar stool. "You know, a man could get used to this."

I point the spatula at him, mushrooms dripping off. "Don't get any ideas. I like you cooking for me just as much."

"That would mean you'd have to spend more nights here. You know, breakfast is my specialty." Alex waggles his eyebrows in my direction. Finding the bread I laid out for us, he drags a piece through the oil and spices and takes a hearty bite.

"What a hardship. Having to spend the night next to you." I take my own sip of beer and turn down the burner. "Waking up next to those hard muscles. Yes, it would be the ultimate sacrifice on my end."

Alex tears off a piece of bread and chucks it at me. "Then maybe I won't cook you breakfast."

"Then no more dinners for you." It's hard to fight the smile as I turn back to the stove.

"Maybe I'll just handcuff you to my bed then and never let you leave."

Laughter bursts out of me. "I don't think that's quite the punishment you think it is."

"Then I wouldn't be doing my job correctly."

My gaze flits back to Alex. He's sipping his beer, an air of indifference around him. I know him better than that. I can see the flush crawling up his neck. The throb of his pulse in his neck gets a little faster. "Maybe I should come willingly then."

"Ugh. You're killing me, Carter."

I smile to myself as I drop in the scallops. Something about making this man lose his mind makes me inordinately happy.

Because the last player I was with? He didn't give me the time of day.

The one whose house I'm currently at, where he gave me the dance I never had? I'm scared at how fast I'm falling for him.

It feels like things are moving fast, lightning fast, but it's been a couple of months. With Alex and his crazy schedule with the team, the time we get is limited.

Time that I want to hold on to with both hands and drag out for as long as possible.

"Earth to Carter. Where'd you go?"

Alex is resting his chin in his hand. With the sweater clinging to his muscles and his hair still wet from his earlier shower, he's the picture of relaxed.

"Just thinking about you."

Alex stands, walking around the counter and coming to a stop next to me. "Hopefully good things."

There's a nervous note to his voice. It tells me he's just as invested in this relationship as I am.

"Why wouldn't they be good things?"

"I know it's been hard with how crazy my schedule is and all the traveling. I just don't want you to think I'm not making time for you."

I place the lid on the pan, turning the heat down so dinner can simmer. Stepping between Alex's legs, I pull him close. "I don't feel that way at all. I'm happy with the time we do get. Is it bad that I'm already looking forward to the off-season?"

Alex smacks my shoulder. "No off-season talk. You don't want to jinx us."

"I take back what I said. You football players and your superstitions."

I go to move away, but Alex wraps an arm around me, locking me tight in his embrace. "Nope. You already said it. You like me. No take backs."

"I'm pretty sure I said I'm happy with the time we do get. Not that I like you."

Alex quirks a brow. His brown eyes are playful. I wish everyone could see Alex the way I see him.

He's more than just the intense football player he projects to the world. This fun and light side is something very few people get to see. And I'm thankful I'm one of those people.

"You wouldn't be spending time with me if you didn't like me. I'm pretty sure that means something in statistics."

Alex looks so proud of himself; I can't help but laugh. "I will give you an A+ for effort. God, you're such a nerd."

I nuzzle his neck, dropping a warm kiss over his pulse.

"Okay, you are giving me some very dirty fantasies, Mr. Brooks."

The timer dings, breaking the moment. Alex's eyes are hazy with lust. "Save those thoughts for later."

I try for a quick kiss, but Alex pulls me back in, lingering just a moment longer.

"Dinner will burn," I whisper against his lips.

"Fine."

Shutting off the stove, I grab the two plates and scoop out a hearty portion for each of us. Alex grabs two beers and I follow him into the living room.

"I figure dinner can be in front of the fire tonight."

The temps took an unexpected drop this morning. Instead of a nice fall day, they're calling for snow. And nothing sounds better than curling up in front of the fire with Alex.

"This smells delicious." Alex settles on an oversized cushion that we moved onto the floor. The lights are dim as the sun has already set.

"I only do my best work for you." I take the seat next to

him, resting my back against the coffee table. Stretching my legs out, our feet tangle.

Alex scoops a hearty bite, his lips closing around the tongs of the fork. "Holy shit, Carter. This is amazing."

I smile, taking my own bite. I give him a satisfied smile as I chew.

"Seriously. Why haven't you made anything like this before for me?"

"Do you need me to make an honest man out of you?"

Alex sets his plate next to him and throws a leg over my lap. I set my own plate down and wrap my arms around him.

It's like we can't be together and not touch. It's a constant need. I've never been like this before. But then again, I've never felt what I feel for Alex.

"You keep talking like this, and I might just have to." Alex kisses his way along my jaw to my ear. "Because the thought of anyone else touching you? It makes me want to punch someone."

A shiver racks my body. "I know violence shouldn't be sexy, but when you talk like that, it really does something to me."

"You make me crazy." Alex drops a kiss on my neck. "You drive me absolutely wild, Carter Brooks." Another kiss. "And I can't fucking get enough of you." Alex pulls back, his face mere centimeters from mine.

"How in the world did you manage to get around every single wall I have?"

"I have good biceps. Great for climbing."

I squeeze said bicep. "I can confirm. You do have great biceps."

"In all seriousness, Carter…I don't know how or why you came into my life when you did, but I'm thankful you did."

The burning need in Alex's eyes lights a fire inside me. I've never seen this kind of passion or desire from anyone. It should scare me.

Instead, it makes me feel needed. Craved. Desired.

Everything I want to mark on Alex, he makes me feel.

And I give in to it. Letting him take what he needs from this kiss as he sweeps his tongue into my mouth. Letting him taste and explore.

It feels like we have all the time in the world together.

Time I have no intention on wasting.

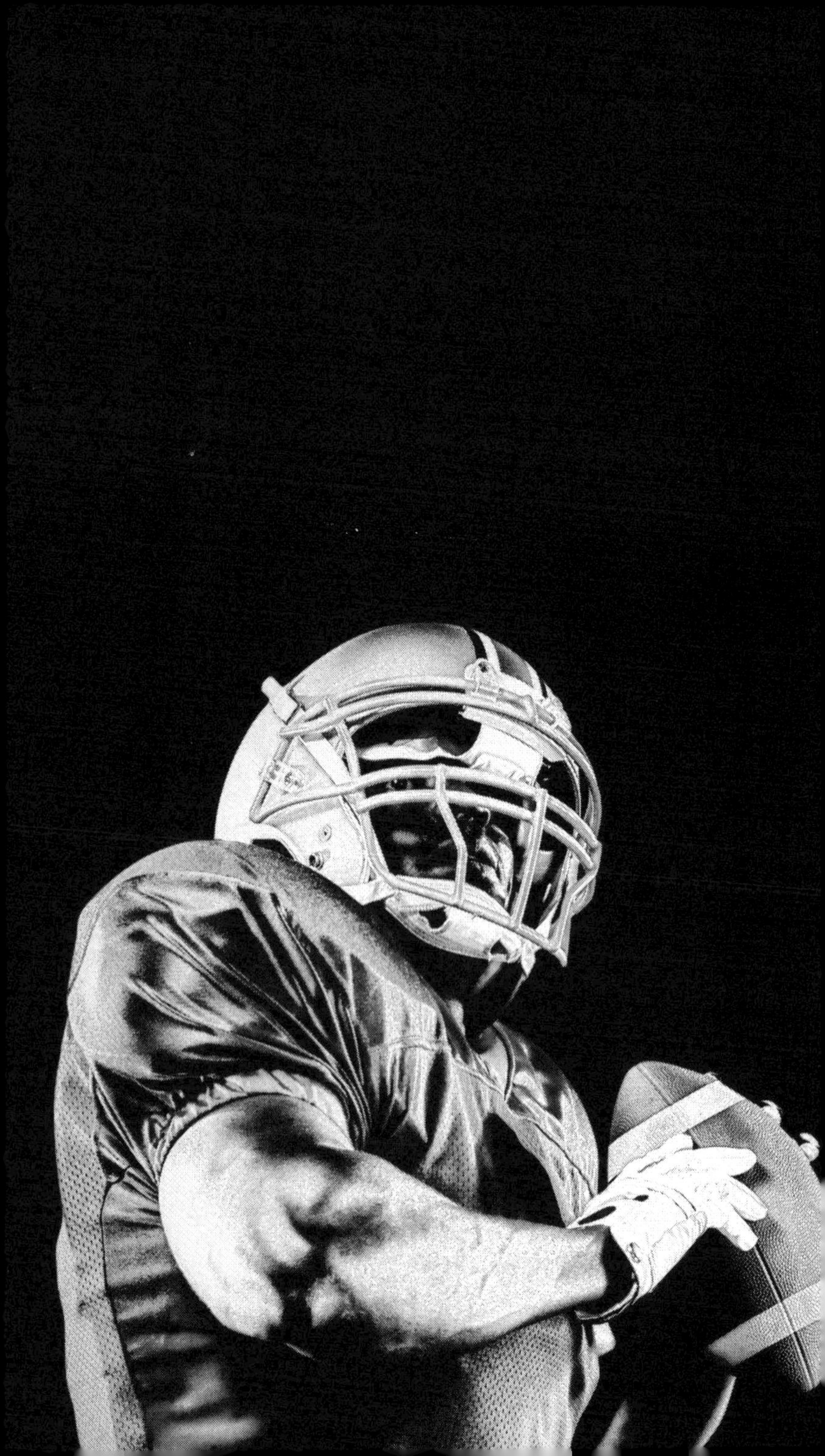

Chapter Eighteen

ALEX

"Are you sure you want to watch the game? We don't have to."

Carter rolls his eyes at me. "It's fine. I figured I'd have to watch a game or two when I started dating an athlete."

A satisfied smile I have no right to feel stretches across my face.

"Ugh. You look way too cocky right now."

I flop down on the couch next to Carter, leaving no space between the two of us. I love how at home I feel here with him. "I've just never had someone to watch the games with on bye week."

"Are you going to be really obnoxious and pick apart every play while we watch them?"

I shift, pinning him with a duh face. "I mean, that's why I watch them. I need to know my opponent. We play Indy in a few weeks."

"God, it's like watching the games with my dad."

"I hope it's not quite like that."

Carter quirks a brow in my direction. "Why do you say that?"

This time, I lean in even closer, dropping a kiss on the spot on his neck that I know gets him riled up. "There will be a very nice reward for you at the end of the game if you watch it with me."

"At the end of the game?" His voice is husky. "Are you really going to make me sit here with a hard-on the entire game?"

"Consider it incentive for you to keep wanting to watch games with me."

"You're a sadist," Carter grumbles.

I nip at his ear. "Not a fan of turnabout?"

"How is this turnabout?"

My gaze drifts down to his hard cock, tenting his pants. "I seem to recall you enjoying edging me."

Carter groans, low and deep, and it sends sparks of pleasure straight to my own cock. "I really hate you right now."

"Just remember that when you're pounding into me later."

"Okay, seriously. How am I supposed to watch the game with you doing this to me?"

"Stats. Think you can use that big brain of yours to help me find an edge against them?"

Carter huffs out a breath. "I mean, if you really want to know, I could give you some tips."

"Wait, really?"

"Oh, what, now you don't want my help?"

I pull back from him, all teasing gone. "Do I really need it?"

"I've been watching your games," he says quietly.

"You like watching me play?"

"Don't get a big head about it. But you're losing some power in your legs because you rotate too far when throwing."

Sideline Infraction

I look down at said legs, as if they've done me a world of hurt. "So how do I correct it?"

"I thought we were supposed to be watching the game?"

Grabbing the remote, I flick the TV off. "Get your shoes on. You're helping me now."

This time, when Carter groans, it's not in pleasure. "I'm a math teacher. How am I supposed to help you?"

Stepping into my shoes, I rest my hands on my hips. "You can't tell me I'm losing power when I'm throwing and expect me to just take it lying down."

"I'd rather have you lying down," he mutters to himself.

"You'll get that." His ears perk up as he ties his laces. "But only after you help."

"Fine. But I'm doing it under protest."

I fight the laugh that threatens to burst free. "Duly noted."

It's moments like these that make me think being out in the open with Carter would be easy. He's not one to draw attention to himself. Couple that with my need for privacy from being in the spotlight, it's easy to see how this could work.

But that gnawing sense of dread still weighs heavy as we step out into the cool fall day. I try to push it down as I go to the shed to grab a football. The lights are still strung up on the patio, as we head out into the backyard.

"Okay, smarty-pants. Please tell me what it is that I need to do in order to work on my throw."

"Okay, Mr. Quarterback." The hint of teasing in his words goes straight to my groin. Fuck, this is going to be harder than I thought. "I've been studying you."

"I like the sound of that."

"Purely educational reasons."

"Mm-hmm." I lick my lips as I take a step closer to him.

"Now,"—he throws a hand out to stop my approach—"get in your throwing stance and mimic what you would do."

I do exactly as he says. Twisting my hips, I throw the ball across the yard.

"That right there!" He points.

"That right there what?" I widen my stance, trying to figure out what he means.

"Can I?" He motions to my hips.

"I think we've established you have free rein here."

Carter drops his arms, his gaze going straight to my groin. "Please don't make this any harder—oh, please don't."

I can't help but laugh as I wrap him in my arms. "You make it so easy, babe."

"Do you want me to show you or not? I have half a mind to tackle you right now and call it a day."

"Again, not saying anything that I wouldn't want to happen."

"Just remember, payback is a bitch."

Carter steps just out of reach and indicates for me to get into position again.

"This time, stop your rotation a fraction of a degree before you throw the ball."

"Do you know how hard that is when you have linebackers charging at you?"

Carter smiles at me. "Humor me."

I roll my eyes. "Fine."

This time, as I get into position, I concentrate on throwing. On where my hips and legs are as I twist to throw the ball. I know the moment I let go of the ball.

"You felt it, right?"

Sideline Infraction

"Holy shit. How did you know?"

"It's that fraction of a second. You turn just a degree too much, but if you're aware of it, it'll help your passing game. I think it happened when you took a pretty big hit last season. You fell awkwardly, and to compensate for it, you don't put as much onto that leg," he points out.

"You know, for someone who says he doesn't like football, you sure know a lot about the game."

"I guess it's through osmosis."

"It's okay to admit you like the game."

"I'll do no such thing." Carter crosses his arms, trying to throw me off.

But in the few weeks we've been together, he's easy to read. "It'd be hard *not* to like football when you're dating the quarterback."

"Maybe we could say I'm bad luck for you and don't need to go to any of the games to throw you off."

"No way." I shake my head at him. "There's no way you could be bad luck when you're helping my game."

"What can I say? I understand high school science classes too."

Carter's cheeks are cold as I pull him to me. "It's very sexy what a good teacher you are."

"Does it mean we can go inside?" Cold hands slip under the T-shirt I'm wearing.

"Is it a reward for me or you if I let you do dirty things to me?"

"Both." Carter drops an innocent kiss on my lips. "Definitely both."

"Good. Then get your ass inside."

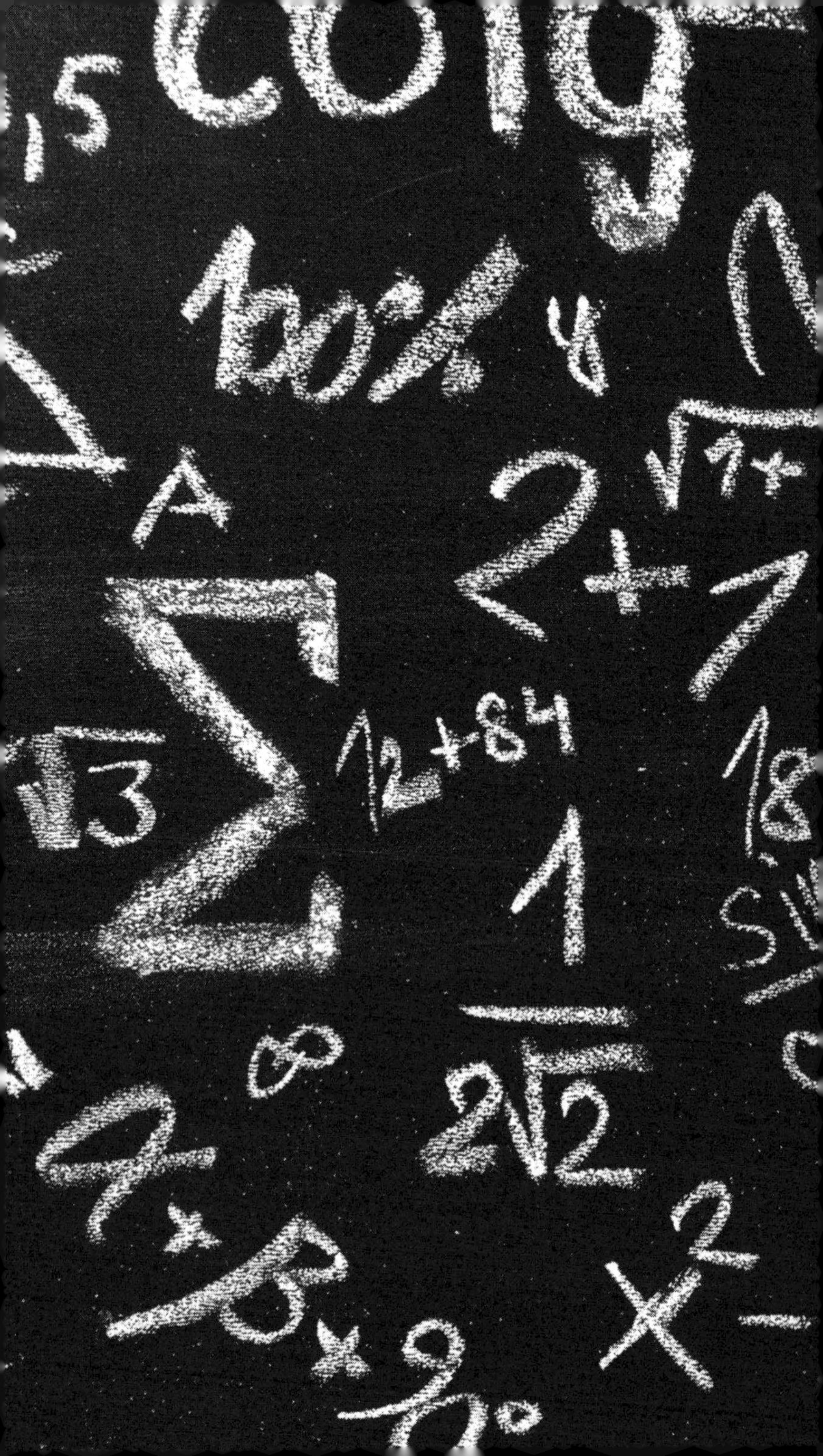

Chapter Nineteen

CARTER

It doesn't take much for me to appreciate Alex's athletic abilities. Not when he's chasing me through his house to his room.

So much for watching the game this afternoon.

His lips warm my cool skin from being outside as we crash into his bedroom.

"I feel like it's been forever since I've been with you."

"You mean since last night?" Alex tilts his head to the side as I kiss and lick over his Adam's apple.

"What can I say? I'm addicted to you."

I smile against his skin before shoving him down on his bed. "Then I guess it's a good thing I have the cure."

Alex tries to stifle a laugh, but is unsuccessful. "I'm sorry, that was just super cheesy."

I straddle his hips, his hard length already pressing against mine. "I think we've already established we do cheesy just fine. But if you don't want cheesy, I guess I can just take care of myself."

I don't miss the way his eyes widen.

"You like that idea, don't you?" Reaching into my

sweats, I take my dick in hand, shoving my pants and boxers down.

Alex licks his lips. "I very much like that idea."

I give myself a slow stroke. "Would you like it even more if it were your mouth?"

I love that Alex brings out this side of me. Sure, I love topping, but I've never been like this before. Something about this man makes me want to command him. Possess him in a way that no other man has.

I growl at the thought of anyone who came before me touching him.

Because he's mine.

"You okay up there?" Alex's eyes are playful.

"Thinking about how much I want to mark you with my cum."

"Then do it."

Alex grabs my ass and tugs me farther up his body. I waste no time, straddling his broad chest and teasing his lips with my dick. Precum spreads across them as he opens, sucking the head in.

"Fuck."

Alex's eyes lock on mine as he hollows his cheeks and sucks me in even farther.

"Damn, you look good taking my cock like this."

Pitching forward, I rock my hips, hitting the back of his throat. I try to pull back, but Alex keeps me there a moment longer.

"Use me," he says after I pull out. "I want a sore throat tomorrow from you fucking my mouth."

"You sure?" I run a slow hand through his hair, wanting to make sure he wants this.

"Yes. I want it all with you, Carter."

The fierceness in his eyes has me dipping down to take

his lips in a kiss. The saltiness of my precum pulls a moan deep from within me.

"Do it," Alex whispers against my lips.

This time, when I thread my fingers through his hair, I hold on tight as I shove my dick into his mouth.

I keep my eyes locked on him as I do exactly what he says. I fuck his mouth. It's pure bliss, the ecstasy of having his lips wrapped around my dick. Each time I push back into his mouth has my balls drawing up tighter.

I'm not ready to come. I want to draw this out. To make this last as long as possible. Commit everything about this to memory because it's hot as sin.

I pull out, tracing my wet dick around Alex's lips. He smiles as he tongues my slit. Strong hands move up my thighs before pulling me back in.

"Someone's eager."

He does his best to smile, but waggles his brows at me instead. Thick fingers start playing with my balls.

"I love it when you do that."

Alex keeps sucking me down as heat and fire race down my spine. I throw my head back, trying to stave off my impending orgasm, but I don't know how much longer I can hold on.

"I'm so close," I moan.

Goose bumps break out over my skin as I look down at the man whose mouth is full of my cock. One more squeeze from his hand on my balls has me exploding down his throat.

It feels endless as my entire body is filled with a pleasure I've never felt, unleashing my cum down Alex's throat. His hand is bruising on my hip, keeping me grounded as he takes every last drop. I don't know how much time has passed before I'm collapsing next to him.

"I'm calling it. World's best blow job." I'm breathless.

Alex shifts, lying on his side next to me. "That's a pretty big compliment there."

"I think you sucked every last brain cell out of me. Fuck, Alex."

Alex doesn't say anything, but leans in for a kiss. It's a heady sensation, tasting my release on him. I lie back, pulling Alex on top of me. It's then I feel his very noticeable hard-on.

"You want some help with this?" I drag a hand over the bulge.

"I wouldn't say no." Alex buries his face in my neck, licking and sucking as I reach into his pants.

Shoving his pants down enough for his dick to spring free, I twist and turn my hand in the way I know he likes, smearing precum as I go.

"Why does this feel so good?" Alex drops his forehead to mine, pleasure etched into every crevice on his face.

"Because it's you and me," I breathe against wet lips.

My strokes are lazy, unhurried, as I jack him off.

"Are you trying to drive me out of my mind?"

"Only returning the favor." I lean up to capture his mouth again. Alex tries to take control, to hurry the kiss.

With my free hand, I hold his head to me, slowing him down. I don't know what it is about this moment with Alex, but I want to remember it.

The way he tastes.

His calloused hands as he holds my face.

The soft strands of his hair as I hold him close.

Without warning, hot ropes of cum hit my hand.

"Fuck." Alex pulls back, the muscles in his neck strained as I work him through his orgasm. I lean up, licking the throbbing pulse of his neck.

It causes one last rope of cum to release as he collapses on top of me.

Sideline Infraction

Both of us are still mostly clothed, our need too great to even get fully naked.

Wiping my hand on my boxers, I hug Alex to me.

He smells of sex and the outdoors.

"If we're giving out awards today, I think you win best hand job."

I laugh, shifting us up so we're lying on fluffy pillows. "Not world's best hand job?" I poke at his side.

A lazy smile drifts across his face. "Definitely world's best hand job. Happy?"

"Very."

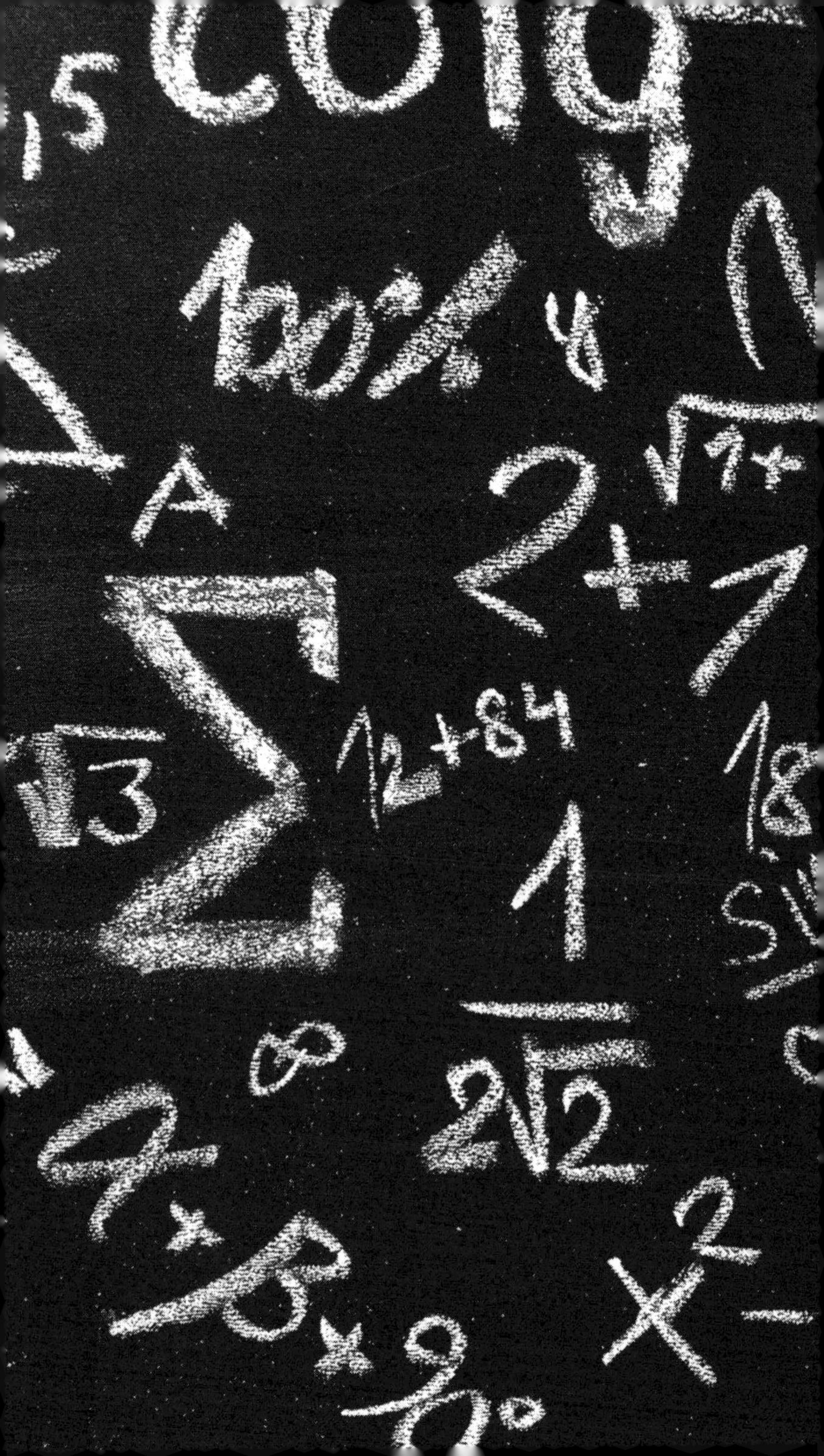

Chapter Twenty

CARTER

"Since when do you want to watch the football game?" Marley jabs me in the leg with her toe as we settle in to watch the game today. We're in my parents' living room. With the cold weather Denver is having and the roaring fire in the living room, it's the perfect place to cozy up and watch the game. It's the first trip after the bye week, and Denver is playing in New England.

"I'm supporting Dad." Except I don't look at her when I say it, because Marley can read me like an open book. And she'll know I'm lying.

"And you haven't supported him the rest of the season?"

"Is it so hard to believe that I want to spend time with my stupid older sister?" I grab a handful of popcorn and shove it in my mouth.

"Yes. You've never gone to a football game once in your life."

"Do we really need to rehash this again?"

"Marley, give your brother a break," Mom says, dropping onto the love seat opposite us. "We want to watch the game in peace." The large TV dominates the space.

Marley throws a piece of popcorn at me as the players run onto the field. My eyes land on Alex. It's criminal how good he looks in a football uniform. The way those pants cling to him and his arms flex as he runs?

He's a walking wet dream.

One that woke me up this morning with a very inconvenient hard-on. I really do hate his schedule.

"After years of hating football—" Marley starts.

"Football players," I correct.

"Fine. Football players. You're all of a sudden Denver's biggest fan?"

"If you must know, the students did a project with the team and I feel more invested with the Mountain Lions now."

"Your dad said that has been going well," Mom comments. Her blonde hair hardly shows her age, but the wrinkles around her eyes give her away.

"He's mentioned it?" I ask, popping another piece of popcorn in my mouth.

Mom nods. "Only that it was nice to see you at training camp. And again at the family cookout."

"See," Marley jabs, "you really need to do more."

"Marley," Mom says, her tone laced with a warning.

"Would you drop it?" I sigh as the game kicks off.

"Which one are you in love with?" Marley says on a sigh.

"I'm not in love with any of them."

Love? Alex and I haven't said the words yet. But how could I not after that surprise dance? Whatever this thing between us, it still feels too new. The last guy I introduced to my family was gone within a week. It feels like I'll jinx us by telling my sister.

And the last thing I want to do is send Alex running for the hills, so I keep it to myself.

Alex and his superstitions are really rubbing off on me.

"It's fine if you are. Not all of them are going to be like that douche in high school."

"Marley. Honestly,"—Mom shakes her head—"you'd think I raised you two in a barn with how you talk."

We both laugh at the exasperated look on her face.

"It's true though, Mom. That guy was a douche."

Mom can't hide the smile on her face as she turns back to the game.

"Trust me, I know," I tell Marley. I settle back into the worn-in couch to focus on the game.

Marley leans across the couch and grabs my hand. "Carter. It's not the end of the world—Wait, did you just agree with me?"

I roll my eyes. "Try not to let it go to your head."

She shakes her head. "I didn't think this day would ever come. You liking a football player."

"What can I say? The Mountain Lions are really good guys." I laugh. "Not at all like a player. Even though they technically all are players."

"God, whoever this guy is, I hope he has the patience to put up with you."

My focus shifts back to the game. Alex easily takes the team down the field to score on the first drive.

"That was a great first drive," I say casually. "Maybe Dad will finally get that Super Bowl ring."

"Seriously, who are you and what have you done with my brother?"

"Whatever's gotten into you, I like it." Mom winks at me.

I smile to myself, thinking about the man on TV.

Before I was worried he'd easily ditch me to find someone more interesting.

But underneath all that padding and that football player mentality is someone who is just as nerdy as I am.

These last couple of months together, it's been harder and harder to hold myself back with Alex. I want to give him everything. I thought it would be scary falling for another player.

Turns out, losing my heart to him might be the scariest thing of all.

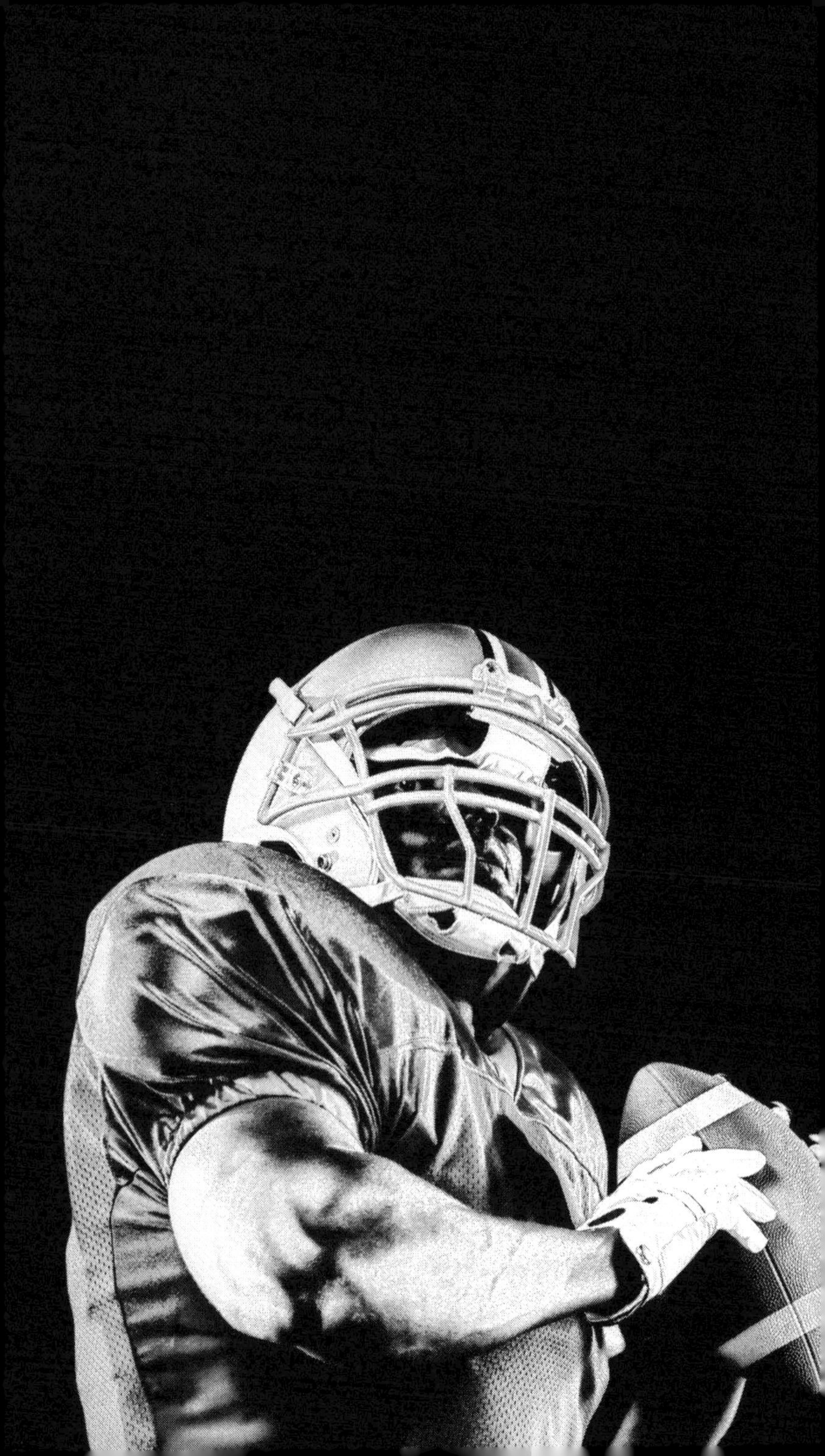

Chapter Twenty-One

ALEX

"Someone's looking nice tonight." I ignore Carter's words as he gets in the car. His clean scent fills the small space, something I find I'm quickly becoming addicted to.

"When you don't get many nights out, you want to do it up right."

Carter leans across the console, his eyes drinking me in. "Yes, when you look like that, I'm sure you want to show it off as much as possible."

Grabbing his chin, I pull him in for a quick kiss. "Someone's feisty tonight."

"When someone is keeping me out late on a school night, maybe I am."

"You could've said no."

Pulling out onto the street, I head toward the restaurant in question. "And miss a rare night out with Mr. Quarterback after that win today? I don't think so."

I fight the ever-present twinge of guilt at Carter's comment. El Five is one of the few places I go and will be left alone. Anonymity is key—only one person there knows me, and that's how I like to keep it. And because he doesn't work on Sundays, it's easier to be out like this.

"Mind you, the manager is keeping the place open a tad later for us than usual."

"Is it cheesy to say that I'm happy you can make the time?"

Stopping at a red light, I glance over at him. The streetlights cast him in a low glow. In a simple button-down shirt with the sleeves rolled up, he's still one of the sexiest men I've ever seen.

"We've established we like cheesy. I'm glad we got back earlier than expected. I was afraid we'd be snowed-in in New England."

"I think I can safely say that I never want to get stuck in New England. Even I know they have terrible fans."

I smile, adjusting myself as I drive to the restaurant. "You really do have no idea how hot it is when you talk football."

"About as hot as when you talk comic books to me."

Reaching across the console, I squeeze his thigh. "This really isn't a conversation we should be having when we can't do anything about it."

Bypassing the valet, I drive to the underground parking garage and find a spot. This late at night, it's empty.

Another added perk of coming so late.

"I feel like you might try to kill me."

I laugh as I lock the car and pull him toward the elevator. "I think we've established that I won't try and kill you."

"Maybe you're just buttering me up."

Stepping into the waiting elevator, I let my gaze trail over Carter.

I never thought I'd go for someone like him. The men of my past? Big and dominating. People who had no idea who I am. It let me escape my reality, even for a short while.

Maybe that's why I was drawn to them. Because they would never be the type of person I would settle down with.

Whereas they all had hard edges, Carter is soft.

They were one-and-dones. Carter? Carter is the worst kind of trouble because even just a few months with him has me wanting more.

Imagining more. Hoping for more.

But more is dangerous.

It could take everything from me in the blink of an eye.

"Thinking some pretty heavy thoughts over there." Carter's voice is quiet as the elevator takes us to the top floor. A small smile plays at the corner of his mouth.

It shoves down the guilt I'm feeling at lying to this man.

My grip on the handrail tightens. I want to reach out to him. To pull him closer. But that thought is always there—someone could get on this elevator at any floor and see us.

At least with the restaurant, I know it'll be empty.

Because I paid for it to be that way.

"Taking in the sights."

There's that blush again. "I feel like I have more to be looking at than you."

"I wouldn't say that."

The air tightens in the small space. The way Carter's eyes widen no doubt mirrors my own.

Before I can take a step toward him, the elevator opens to the restaurant. A blissfully empty restaurant just for the two of us.

"Good evening, gentlemen," an older man with graying hair greets us. "Welcome to El Five. Your table is this way."

Colorful paintings decorate each wall. The mirrored ceilings make the space seem bigger and brighter than it is.

He leads us to a spot that overlooks the rooftop seating. Being this late in the season, it's too cold to sit outside.

"The kitchen has your order, and if you need anything, just shout. Otherwise, enjoy your evening."

"Thank you."

"Wow. You pulled out all the stops for this." Carter is in awe as he takes a seat, blue eyes sweeping the view in front of us. Downtown is all lit up, like it's giving us our own personal show.

"It's why I like this place. It's hard to go out in this city, especially when we're winning."

Dropping his napkin in his lap, he turns to face me.

"It must be hard being in the spotlight."

"It is. But I love what I do."

It also means I make huge sacrifices in my private life. That conversation with Tommy all those weeks ago still weighs heavy on my mind.

Because now that things are more serious with Carter, I owe him. I owe him that conversation. Especially after knowing his past issues.

"Beer?" He offers me a glass, a soft smile on his face.

I take the glass and hold mine out for a toast. "To you and me."

"You and me."

We sip the beer as plates of food are brought out.

"This smells delicious." The waiter slinks off as quickly as he came.

"The garlic dip is my favorite."

"Wow. I guess you really don't want to be kissing me tonight," Carter says, dunking a piece of pita bread in the thick spread.

I grab his hand, taking a bite. "Not if we both taste the same."

"Not if you don't let me eat," he grumbles.

We catch up on the days we missed being together, with updates on Carter's students' project and how I think the season is going.

It's easy. Fun. Light.

Everything I want this to be.

Being in a safe place like this—one of the few I have in Denver—makes this easy to believe it's my reality with Carter.

That people wouldn't care that I like men.

But I know better. It's what keeps me in these places because I want to have my cake and eat it too. Carter and football.

Is that too much to ask for?

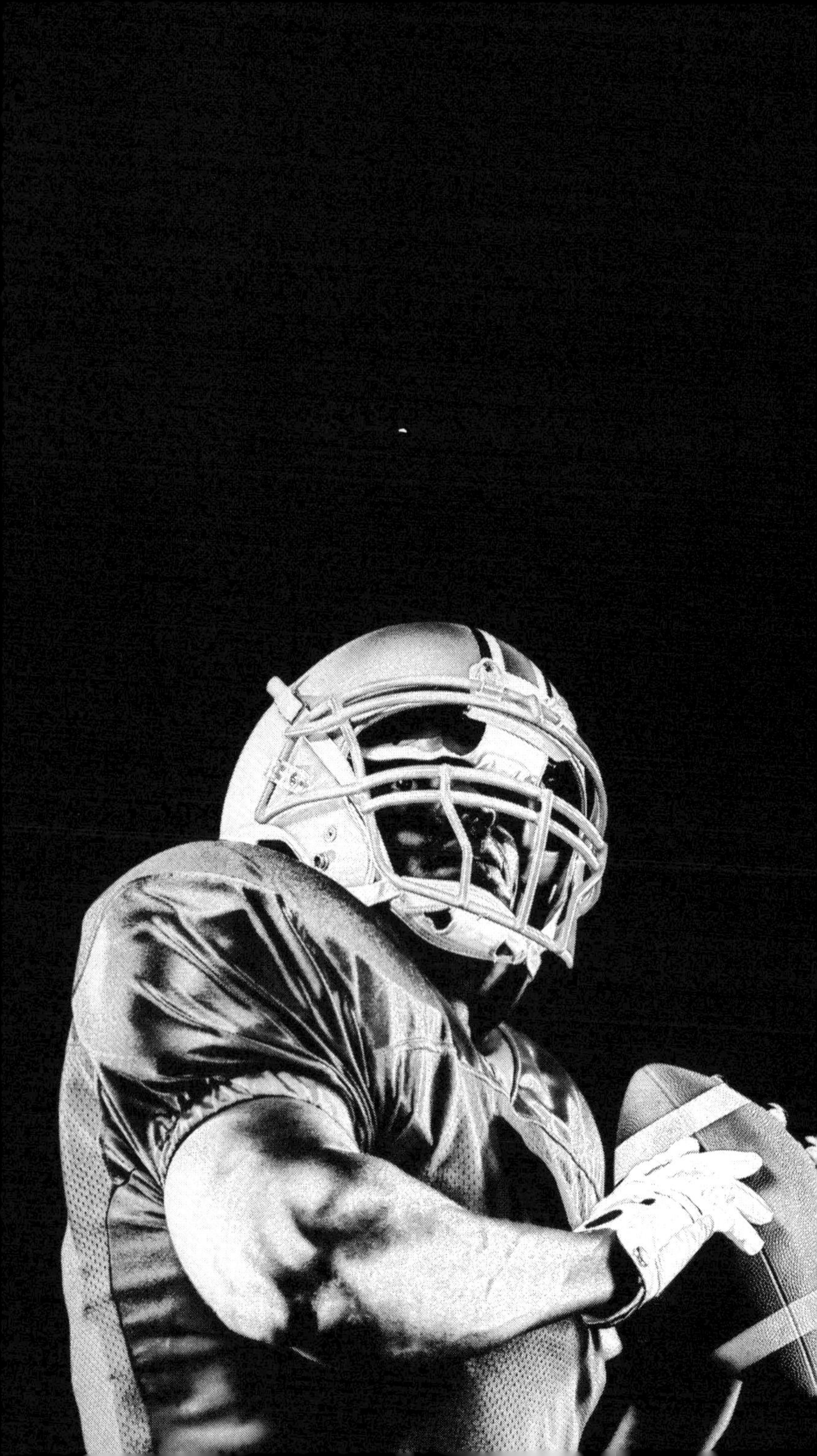

Chapter Twenty-Two

ALEX

"Black forty-two! Set, hike!" I call the play, watching as players snap into motion. Sheets of rain are soaking the field.

Seeing my guard get tripped, I scramble. Indy's defender—a beast of a man—is barreling toward me, and it's all I can do to find a receiver downfield to avoid a sack.

My feet don't move fast enough. Releasing the ball, the linebacker wraps his arms around me in a bone-crushing tackle as we hit the grass.

"Fuck!" I try to push the defender off me, feeling pain radiate out from my side.

"Shit, man. Are you okay?" He reaches out a hand to help me up. I wave it away.

Fighting a grimace, I hiss out a breath as I stand. The rain is coming down harder now than at the start of the game, if that's even possible. "I'm fine. Just give me a minute."

The trainers rush out onto the field, but I wave them away. There's still one more down and I'm not sitting this one out. The score is tied with only a few minutes left in the game and we need this win.

The Mountain Lions are sitting in a good spot to make the playoffs this year. With a win today, we'll be in first place. If Vegas loses today, then we can secure a first round bye. And that would mean home field advantage throughout the playoffs.

I know it's driving Vegas and their fans crazy, because Hollins has been tweeting up a storm this week, trying to unnerve us. It's hard on a good week to block out the noise, but even harder when it's coming from another player. Especially one that's such a dick like Hollins.

"Alright boys, time for a running play. Winchester, you ready?"

I can feel the excitement coming off of Logan. With our starting running back out, Logan has stepped up his game.

"Let's fucking go!" he roars, pumping up the offense. He's more than proven himself, but the whole line feeds off his energy.

"Red Heat Marlins on three."

Getting into position behind my center, pain flashes through my side as I take the handoff and slide it off into Logan's hands. With the slick conditions on the field, a defender misses an easy tackle and Logan darts into the open field for a touchdown.

The crowd explodes as I jog to the sidelines. Normally I'd go congratulate him, but fuck, does my side hurt.

"Can we look now?" the trainer grumbles.

"Wait until after the game. There's not much time left."

Swigging some Gatorade, I take my seat on the bench to watch Jackson kick the extra point.

Sideline Infraction

"Bring it home, Fisher!" I shout to Knox as the defense gets ready to take the field.

It's been a tough game. Indianapolis isn't a pushover of a team, and they've kept us on our feet the whole game.

But with a new quarterback, the holes in their lineup are easy to take advantage of. One that our defense picks up on allows Knox to force a fumble, sealing our victory.

Congratulating them, I get pulled over to the sideline reporters after the game.

"Alex, that was a hard-fought victory today. What do you think it took to overcome and win in these conditions?" Tracey, the sideline reporter asks.

"It was a team effort. Offense, defense, special teams. Everyone played their part. Indy is a good team, but we were able to edge them out today."

"Will you be watching the Vegas game later today to see if the Mountain Lions can clinch the top spot in the playoffs?"

I nod, smiling at the thought of Vegas losing. Not that it's something I can say in this interview. "As long as we're playing our game, that's all we can control. It'll be a good game to watch between two division rivals."

"That hit you took on that last series was brutal. How are you feeling?"

I brush it off like it doesn't matter. "All part of the game."

"Go celebrate the win." She waves me off as I jog into the locker room to the cheers from the fans.

Home field wins are one of my favorite parts of the game. The energy from the crowd always is on our side and makes it hard for other teams to come and play here. The black and yellow that fills the stands always amps me up and helped propel us to the win today.

Flinging my wristbands into the stands, I find relief

from the rain in the locker room. Adrenaline is flowing as all the guys are pumped from the win.

"Alright. Before everyone goes crazy, I've got a game ball to give out." Coach quiets everyone down.

"Alex. Game ball is for you. You brought us back in the fourth quarter, and now we're in a great position for the playoffs. But we can't back off yet. Everyone will be gunning for us, so let's keep the pedal to the metal. Great job, boys!"

Coach tosses me the ball, and I grab it, quieting everyone down. "This was more than just me out there today. We all fought hard for sixty minutes. But there's one star of the game. Starting in his first game—Winchester, this one is for you!"

Logan is as red as a tomato as the offense shoves him into the center of the locker room. "Thanks, man."

"Amazing play at the end. Keep doing that, and you'll be a starter in no time." I clap him on the shoulder and send him on his way. By the time I get back to my cubby, the trainers are glaring at me.

Shucking my jersey and pads, I follow them to the training room. As soon as my shirt comes off, the bruises are evident.

"We're going to do an X-ray just to be sure you didn't crack anything."

"It doesn't hurt that badly."

Paige, the team's longtime trainer, pierces me with a no bullshit look. She's not one you want to mess with. "Do you want me to poke around and find out?"

I wince. "Please don't."

After sitting through a round of X-rays, where thankfully nothing is found to be broken, I'm sent on my way with instructions to rest the next few days of practice.

Sideline Infraction

This deep into the season…that's going to be hard. Like Coach said, we can't back off now.

Frustration burns through me as I make my way back to my locker. Grabbing my phone, I see a slew of messages from people. But my eyes narrow in on the one from Carter.

> **CARTER**
> Want to go out tonight? Celebrate the big win – first place!

A smile graces my face before disappearing just as quickly. I don't know how much longer I'm going to be able to keep this thing going with Carter if we only stay inside my house. I want to be with him, but the thought of coming out makes me sick.

> What about ordering takeout?
>
> **CARTER**
> Don't you ever get stir-crazy staying inside your house?
>
> That hit was a lot harder than it looked. I'd rather soak in the hot tub and not have to deal with fans tonight.
>
> **CARTER**
> I'll grab Thai on my way over

I blow out a frustrated breath and stuff my phone back into my locker before hitting the showers. Cranking the water up to hot, I let it run over my battered muscles.

Having gone to the training room, I'm one of the last few stragglers in the shower.

I've taken hits like this before, but with each passing year, the aches and pains from the game get harder to brush aside.

And now, with Carter in my life, it's getting harder and harder to hide who I really am. I keep thinking back to that conversation with my brother. I'm not being fair to him.

I can't keep stringing him along.

I should tell him.

I need to tell him.

Maybe it won't be as bad as I'm making it out to be. Sure, Carter will probably be upset, but maybe it won't be the end of us.

Except you've lied to him from day one.

"Fuck!" I shout into the void. "Fuck, fuck, fuck!"

I want to hit something. Punch the tiled wall just to feel better. But that wouldn't help my situation.

The thing I love most is interfering with the man that I'm quickly coming to love.

Why can't life ever be easy?

"You look terrible."

"Nice to see you too." I close the door behind Carter and shuffle into the living room. Highlights from the game play in the background as I drop down onto the sofa. I turned on the fireplace the minute I got home. It's hard to shake the chill from the game.

He loses the hard stare. I know he's upset that I

Sideline Infraction

wouldn't go out with him tonight. I'm surprised I'm still standing with the guilt eating away at every part of me. "Sorry. Are you okay? That was a hard hit you took."

"It didn't feel good, that's for sure."

"What can I do to help?" Carter sits on the coffee table in front of me. Worry and care swirl together in his soulful eyes. "Do you need an ice pack or something? Ibuprofen?"

Carter is too good for me. I want to shout from the rooftops that I'm with this man.

I want to tell him. It's been at the front of my mind all afternoon.

"Carter. There's something I need to tell you."

"What's wrong?" Worry colors his face.

"I'm—"

The words are on the tip of my tongue, but the sportscasters' voices are louder.

"Breaking news out of Atlanta. Recent photos have come to light showing Atlanta Rising Football Club midfielder Mahoney Holmes embracing another man."

"Holy shit. I met him this summer when they played in Denver." I grab the remote next to Carter and turn up the volume.

"While no statement has been made yet by the team, it casts new light on Holmes's sexuality. Many in the sports world have come to his defense, but others are casting judgment. Derek Hollins of the Vegas Storm shared the following tweet:

VgsStarHollins22: Might be able to get away with that in "fútbol"…but real men play football and we don't have room for fairies…

FUCK.

Fuck. Fuck. Fuck.

"Did you know about this?" Carter asks.

I'm too stunned to respond.

This is exactly what I was afraid of. This—this reaction by Hollins—is my greatest fear.

He's a dick. Always has been. But it doesn't make it any easier to see it written out like that.

Whatever I was going to tell Carter dies on my tongue. What little courage I wrangled up to confess my lie to Carter is gone.

Any hopes of coming up with a plan together will never happen.

All because of an asshole in Vegas with a phone.

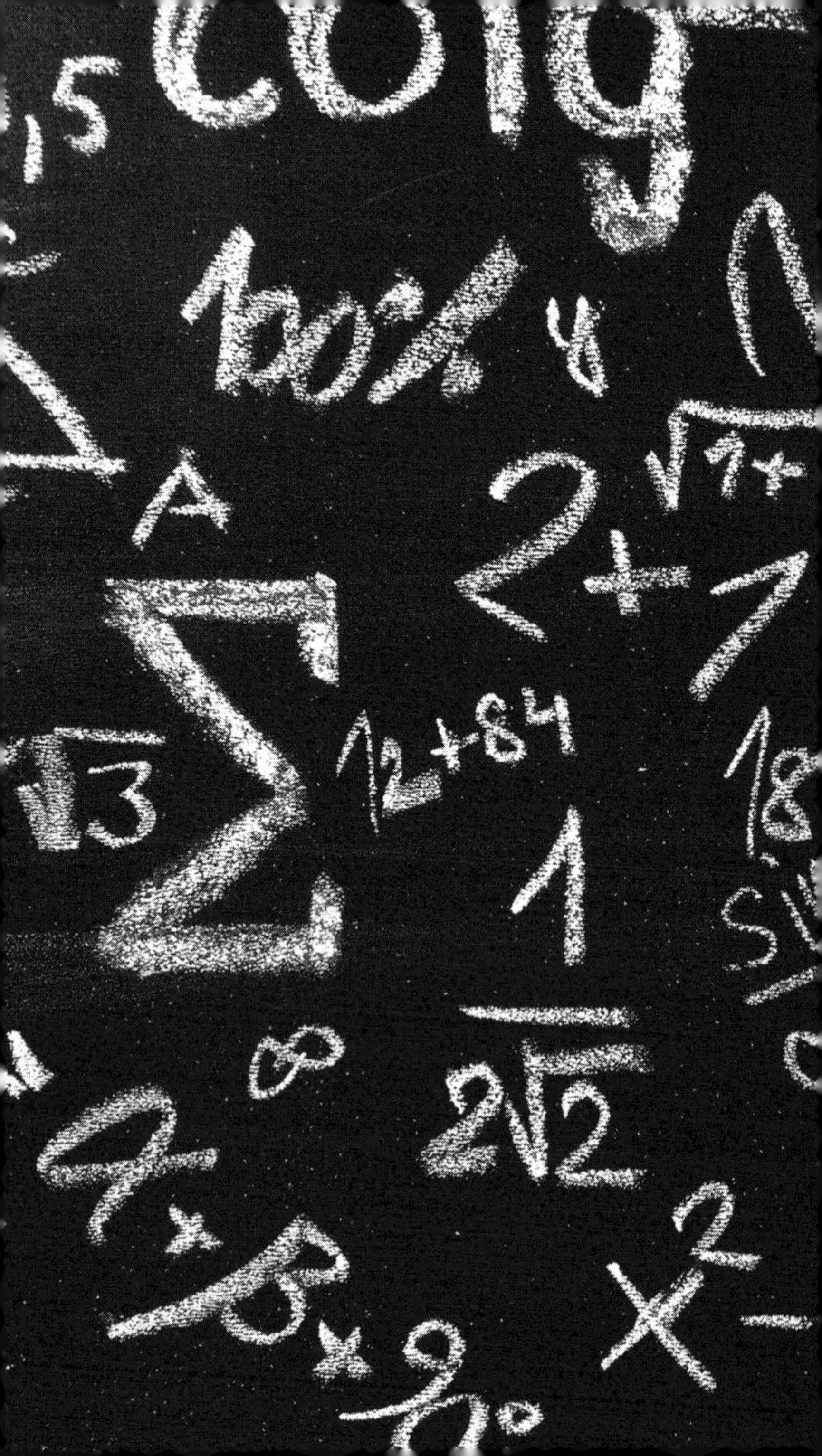

Chapter Twenty-Three
CARTER

"Do you really have to go into work today?" Alex groans as the alarm echoes through the quiet room.

"I'm not like you and get a rest day after a win."

He wraps an arm around me, pulling me close. "Maybe I can write a note for you. Get you excused from class."

Alex rubs his stubble against my back.

"It doesn't quite work like that." I make no move to get up, covering his hand with my own. Ever since he took that hit yesterday, he's been off.

I can't put my finger on it, but he feels clingy. Like if he's not touching me, he's worried I'll disappear.

"I wish it did. I'd like to spend my morning with you."

I close my eyes. The sun still isn't up, making it even harder to leave Alex in this warm bed.

"What would you do?" I turn, lining my body up perfectly with his. Sleepy brown eyes meet my own. Those eyes make it hard to think about anything else.

"Lots of things. Maybe start with a blowjob then let you take my ass in the shower."

I groan, biting down into his shoulder. "You should not be telling me these things when I already need to be out of bed."

"Why do you have to be such a good person and teach the future of the world?"

"Maybe we can do all those things this weekend." I kiss a trail from his shoulder up to his ear. "You're home this weekend, right?"

He nods against me.

"Then let's go out Friday."

I can see the argument on his lips before it even escapes. Covering his mouth with my hand, I plead my case.

"The parents of the students gave me a gift card as a thank you for chaperoning the dance."

"What?" Alex mumbles against my hand. "Isn't that part of your job?"

"Yes, but these were the students who got busted with alcohol."

"Ah."

"I know you don't like going out—"

"Why would I when I like having you here all to myself?" Alex whispers, kissing up and down my neck.

"Don't you ever get sick of the walls of your house?" I hate to complain because I love any time I get with Alex. Things are getting more serious, and I want to be out with him and show him off to everyone.

Alex shakes his head. "That's why I painted them a color I like."

I push him back. "I'm serious. I'd like to take you out. You've done so much for me, and I know yesterday was a hard day for you. Maybe getting out and blowing off some steam will help."

"Okay," he sighs.

A victorious smile spreads across my face. "I promise. You'll love it." Giving him a loud smack on the lips, I hop out of bed. "Now, if you hurry up, there may be enough time for a quick hand job before I leave for work."

He's up and out of bed before I can even finish my sentence.

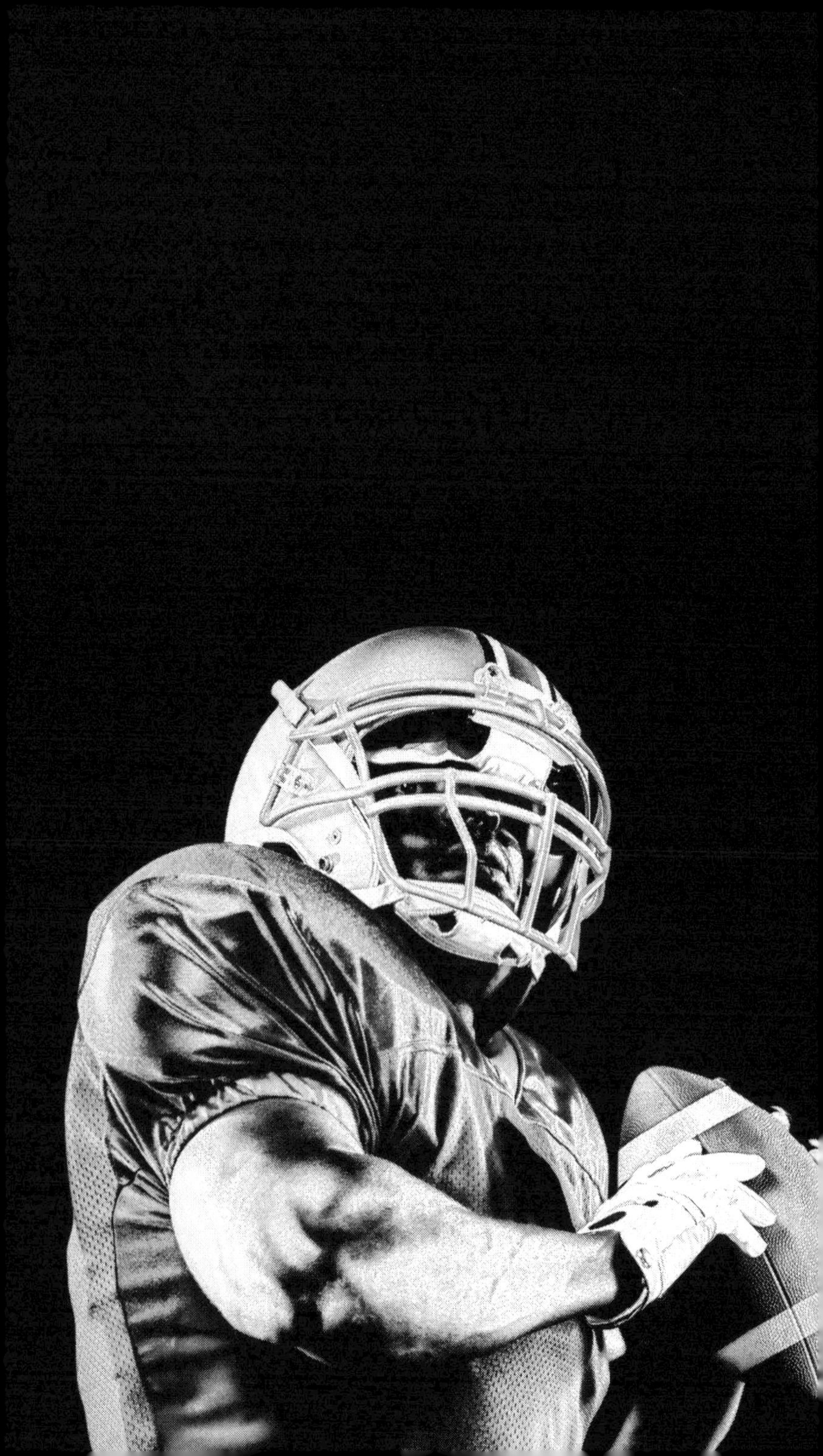

Chapter Twenty-Four

ALEX

You can do this. You can do this.
Maybe if I say it enough times to myself, it'll make it true. But the closer Carter and I get to the Punchbowl, the bigger my case of nerves gets.

Every bone in my body was shouting at me to say no to Carter. To not come out with him. But I ignored the dread that sat in my stomach and said yes anyway.

Because how can I say no to the man that I'm in love with?

"Everything okay?" Carter asks as he pulls into a parking spot behind the building.

I nod my head. "Sorry, long day at practice."

"What a hard-ass of a coach you have."

"Maybe you can talk to him." I unlatch my seatbelt and twist to look at him. "Tell him how hard we've worked to maybe get off early one day."

Carter's laugh does little in the way to calm my nerves. "Yes, because I'm sure a professional football coach would take the advice of a math teacher."

I poke him in the shoulder as we get out of the car.

"Our offensive coordinator was impressed with your students. Designed a few plays that have worked well with distracting opposing defenses."

"I'm still surprised by that."

I shake my head as I hold open the door. "Aren't you always telling me statistics can explain everything?"

"I'm glad you're actually listening." Carter pats my chest on the way in.

I'm surprised he didn't feel the rapid tattoo of my heart against my chest.

Calm down, Alex. You can do this.

Following behind Carter, we find an empty table behind the bar. With exposed brick walls and low lighting, I don't feel as on display as I thought I would. Arcade games are loud, as the sound of bowling balls striking pins cracks through the air. It's not as crowded as I thought it would be—the after work crowds haven't yet descended on the bar.

"Welcome to Punchbowl. Can I get you guys anything to drink?" The bartender wastes no time coming over. If the guy recognizes me, he doesn't show it.

"Two beers." Carter orders for both of us.

"Pretty bold of you to assume I'd like beer." I lean back in the chair, crossing my arms.

"Considering that in the few months we've been seeing one another, I haven't seen you drink anything else, I'm fairly confident in my choice."

It makes me inordinately happy that he knows this. "Okay."

Our server drops off two beers, and I try to hide my smile in the glass, but I can't. I can feel Carter's eyes on me.

"How are you feeling for the game this weekend?"

I shrug a shoulder, dragging a finger around the rim of

the glass. "I'm more worried about Vegas in a few weeks. It's always a tough game, but now there's so many more layers. Hollins taking out Colin last season being one of them."

"Is he a dirty player?" Carter asks, sipping on his drink.

"You tell me." I pull up his latest tweet, talking about how the hit I took against Indy will be nothing compared to what he does.

Carter visibly winces across the table. "You've never taken a hit like that before, have you? The league should suspend him."

"Should I be worried you're asking and don't know the answer? Besides, it's all talk. Can't do much about it."

"I wish I could help. I hate it that he's such a dick and I can't do anything to help the cute quarterback he's gunning for."

"You think I'm cute, huh?"

Carter rolls his eyes as he takes a long drink of his beer. "God, I never should've opened my mouth."

"You know I like it when you do."

A blush creeps up Carter's cheeks. For as commanding as he is in the bedroom, anything like this outside makes him shrink into himself. And I don't know why I like making him blush so much.

"Keep your dirty ideas to yourself. They're going to get you in trouble."

"Are you going to punish me then?" I quirk a brow at him.

He chokes on the sip he just took. "How do I keep setting myself up for this?"

"I'm surprised you don't hear it. You teach high schoolers."

Carter shakes his head, a lock of sandy-blond hair

falling into his eyes. I have to sit on my hands to not reach across the table and tuck it back into place.

"I've become immune to them. There are some things I can never unhear after hearing them."

"I think I had to bleach my ears after chaperoning that dance. Were we like that in high school?"

"I know I wasn't. But I'm sure high school was much different for you than it was for me."

I laugh, gulping down more beer. "As much as you think I was cool in high school, I was still awkward. I just didn't get beat up for it because I was quarterback of the team. That held some weight."

Carter's eyes move over me, studying me. "I highly doubt you were ever that awkward. And even if you were, I'd be totally into you."

"Even though you didn't like jocks in high school?"

He nods his head. "Oh, absolutely. You'd be the exception to every rule I have, Alex Young."

Before I can say anything, my attention is pulled away.

"Hey man! You're Alex Young!" Two guys stop in front of our table.

Whatever good feelings I had dissipate. It's just Carter and me here. Nothing about our posture says we're two guys here on a date. We're just hanging out. Every brain cell is telling me to abandon this conversation as fast as possible because it won't end well.

"Hey guys. Mountain Lions fans?" I ask, shaking their hands.

"Yeah! You looked great last week. With a few more games like that, we'll be heading to the Super Bowl for sure."

"My offensive line has been playing great. They get a lot of the credit for making me look good."

"He never takes any of the credit for himself." Carter

drops a hand on my forearm, giving me a squeeze. All it does is incite a riot of panic inside me. "He's been playing great."

My face heats as I look back at the guys, slowly sliding my arm out from under Carter's hold. I drop my hands under the table and hold tight to my knees.

They don't notice a thing.

Carter does.

"Oh my God." It takes him about two seconds to put everything together. He stands suddenly, knocking into the table and spilling his drink. "I have to go."

"Wait!" His retreating back doesn't stop.

"Listen guys, I should probably get this cleaned up. It was great meeting you."

"Yeah man." One claps me on the back, holding up his phone. "Quick pic before you go?"

The life of an athlete. "Sure thing."

As soon as the camera clicks, I slap them each on the back and try to find Carter. The bar's filled up since we arrived. People crowd around tables, blocking my view.

Dread settles in because I can't let Carter leave without talking to him. I finally spot him, slipping between two people holding the front door of the bar open.

"Carter!" I shout after him, but either he doesn't hear me or he doesn't care.

The second option has my heart stuttering in my chest. With one conversation, my entire world is coming crashing down around me.

Faster than I ever gave him credit for, I have to run after him, following him to the back parking lot.

"Carter, wait!" I grab his door handle before he can open it to get inside.

"Why?" The venom in his tone hits me square in the

chest. I don't think I've ever seen him so mad before. "I don't even know what there is to say to you right now!"

"I can explain."

Carter crosses his arms, leaning back against the car. "Oh really? You can explain how for the last few months that we've been dating, you've been lying to me?"

"I wasn't lying."

"Not lying? And here I thought I've been dating this guy who was out and proud because he pursued me, but now I find out that everything I've meant to him has been a lie."

"Just because I'm not out doesn't mean everything has been a lie."

Carter shakes his head.

Pain.

Anger.

Disappointment.

It's all radiating off him in waves.

And I wish I could say I don't deserve it, but I do.

"God, I'm such an idiot!" Carter smacks himself on the head. "You knew about my history with that jackass from high school and you did the same thing! Everything makes so much sense now!"

Fuck.

Fuck.

I can see him playing back every moment we've been together in a new light. Whatever we have—had—is crashing down around me because I didn't tell him the truth.

"Please, Carter. I love—"

"No!" he shouts, shoving a finger in my face. "You do not get to say that to me right now. Not when you've been lying. How could I have been so stupid? Everything we did was so your secret wouldn't get out. I never really thought

Sideline Infraction

about it because I didn't pay much attention to football before, but that's why we never went out. This entire relationship was on your terms, and you took me along for the ride."

"Just let me explain," I plead.

Carter ignores me, his fury palpable. "This is why I hate athletes. Everything is all about you with no regard for anyone else's feelings. I can't believe I let myself get taken in again." Shoving off the car, Carter goes for the door again.

"Please don't leave like this." The panic in my voice is real. "I was going to tell you."

"When? On your deathbed?"

I wince. "I was."

Carter pins me with a glare I've never seen from him before. "You know, I'm surprised you can be seen talking to me like this. Aren't you afraid someone might snap a picture and expose your dirty little secret?"

I fall back, as if he slapped me. "That's not fair."

"And what you're doing to me isn't fair either. Ever since that football player in high school broke my heart, I told myself I would never go back into the closet for anyone. And that's exactly what you made me do." Carter shakes his head at me. "And what's even worse was I didn't know you were doing it to me. God, I'm so stupid."

"I'm sorry..." I try to find the right words, but I can't.

"Sorry for what exactly? For all the lying? Making me believe that this was a real relationship? I'm sorry, Alex, but I can't. I can't be with someone who isn't honest about who he is with himself. I just...can't."

"Please, Carter. Let's just talk about this."

But this time, when Carter swings the door shut, I know I've lost him. He peels out of the parking lot without a look back.

Fuck.

In a matter of minutes, I lost the one person that meant more to me than anything else.

I want to scream and rage. But I have no one to blame but myself.

In my effort to never let the world see the real me, I let go of the one man I was most myself with.

With no hope of getting him back.

All I had was football.

It's all I'll ever have.

Because I just let the best thing that's ever happened to me go.

$\cot g$

$\sqrt{3}$

$\sqrt{1+}$

$2x+1$

$12+84$

1

$2\sqrt{2}$

Chapter Twenty-Five

CARTER

"Alright, hand in your homework."

Grumbles hit my ears as I stand at the front of the classroom, waiting to collect papers.

"Are we going to review these again? Because I still don't understand data-based predictions," Lucy asks, dropping her homework in the stack. "It's almost fifty percent of our football project, so I want to make sure I understand it."

The mention of the project has my heart stuttering in my chest. "Sure. We can review it again."

It's been two weeks. Two miserably long weeks since I left Alex in that damn parking lot. The cold of December slipped in, doing nothing to help my mood. The stupid organ in my chest can't decide whether to be angry or sad.

My brain is a different story. He's angry.

I can't believe how stupid I was. I let down every wall I had to be with Alex. He knew my history with football players.

And I still managed to let him break my heart.

Fucking football players.

While half the class has managed to turn in their homework, another group of students are looking at something on a phone.

"Ben. Phone away."

Except he doesn't hear me. Bags and papers are being shuffled around as class gets started.

"Ben. Don't make me ask again. Cell phone away, or it's mine until the end of the day."

"Geez, Mr. Brooks needs to get laid," he mutters, but not quietly enough for me not to hear him.

"Okay. Pop quiz time. Books away."

Everyone groans as I drop the stack of papers on my desk and walk to the board to put down some equations.

I drown out their complaints.

"Thirty minutes then we'll work on reviewing where we are with the project."

I slump down into my desk and start grading homework. It's a summary of where everyone is with their project. And I hate it.

I take a breath. Because if I don't, I'm going to slash red pen over each paper that's not worthy of it.

The last two weeks have felt endless. You can't escape the Mountain Lions in Denver. With their winning record, they're everywhere.

I can't escape Alex.

Every time I see his face, I think about what I would have done in his shoes.

Would I have lied to someone to date them? Could I be that selfish?

But then I think about playing in the NFL and wonder —was it really selfish of him? While I never spoke to Ryan again after he broke my heart in high school, I can't imagine being gay and trying to play football. It's a boys' club. It's part of the reason I've hated it all these years.

Sideline Infraction

So can I really blame him?

Except he lied.

Fuck. Why is this so hard?

And there's that ever-present ache when I think about Alex making a bad joke about what I'm thinking.

"Mr. Brooks, are you okay?" Lucy asks quietly from her spot in the front row.

"Why?" I adjust my glasses as other students look my way.

"You're laughing."

I'm losing it. I'm well and truly losing it.

All because I couldn't follow my own damn rule and not fall for the player.

"Were you nicer at school today?" Marley asks, dropping down onto the barstool next to me.

"Just because the students aren't paying attention, doesn't mean I'm being mean."

"So that's a no." She grabs a carrot and pops it in her mouth. "What's with the attitude?"

"Marley—"

"Let your brother have some space. He's obviously dealing with a broken heart," Mom says, coming into the kitchen. The smell of pizza accompanies her into the kitchen. She drops a kiss on my head as she walks over to the island.

"The mysterious man didn't work out?" Marley questions. "I thought you had major heart eyes for him."

I scoff. "Turns out he was lying."

"About what?" Mom asks.

Grabbing a slice of pizza, I stuff it in my mouth. "About being out."

"Can you please not talk with your mouth full? I raised you better than that." Mom rolls her eyes as she hands each of us a plate.

I swallow the bite and take a swig of beer. "He can't be out because of his job."

"In this day and age? Please." Marley's tone is harsh.

"Being me is still illegal in some parts of the world. So I understand why he can't." This is so not the discussion I wanted to get into tonight.

Mom called us to come over and watch the game since Denver is playing in Washington tonight. My no was promptly ignored and I was told to be over after school.

"So instead of talking it over with him, you broke up with him?" Mom asks.

"Ugh. I don't want to talk about this." I'm acting like one of my high schoolers. I know this, but it doesn't mean I want the attention on me.

"But if you understand why he's not out, why did you break up with him?"

I hate how logical my mom is. It's how I usually am. At least, when I don't have a broken heart.

"He lied to me about it, okay? That's the problem."

"Isn't that why you broke up with that guy in high school? What was his name?" Mom snaps her fingers, trying to remember.

"Ryan. The football player. How could you forget? Carter said he would never date a player after that. I've never seen him so heartbroken. Except..." Marley's eyes widen as she rakes her gaze over me. "Oh shit. Is he a football player?" She drops her voice another octave.

I gulp my beer down, trying to cool the instant heat that floods my face. I've always been a terrible liar.

"It's totally a football player!" Marley gasps.

"Marley, would you leave your brother alone? He doesn't need you making this situation worse."

"Fine." She stalks out of the kitchen and I hear the game turn on in the other room.

"Next time I'm staying at home," I mutter.

"What happened?" Mom asks, sitting down next to me.

"Marley just told you." I take another bite of pizza, needing something to do with my hands.

"What's the actual story? Your sister, God love her, has a tendency to exaggerate the truth."

"I fell in love with him and he lied about being out."

"How'd he lie?"

"He didn't tell me he wasn't out."

"Did he say he was out, or did you assume he was?" Mom asks, logically.

"I mean, we were dating. Why wouldn't I?"

"Plenty of people are still in the closet and date people. Maybe it's hard for him." She gives me a side-eye. "Is what your sister said true? Is he a football player?"

"Yeah." Dropping an elbow on the counter, I rest my head in my hand and turn to face her. "I get why he has to hide, but why couldn't he have told me? He knows about my history."

Mom grabs my free hand and holds it between hers. "Sometimes it's not that simple. Trusting someone with a secret like that can be hard."

"He tried saying I love you to get me to stay. You should be able to trust someone if you're at the point of saying those words."

"Just like you have a past, maybe he does too."

It dawns on me. I was too consumed with my own

anger and heartache to realize it. "Oh my God. The safety from Vegas."

"What'd he do?" Mom furrows her brow.

"Someone from a soccer team was outed and he tweeted some dumbass comment about it. He's kind of an ass to the team on a good day, but this was particularly harsh."

"I hate Twitter. It's a cesspool," she says, taking a sip of her drink.

I want to smack my head on the counter. "He said he was going to tell me, but I didn't believe him. I thought he was just saying it so I didn't leave."

Hindsight is twenty-twenty.

Alex was shifty that day. He didn't want to go out—the reason all the more clear now—but he was still on edge. I'd come to know him well enough to be sure something was up.

"He was going to tell me but then the news broke about that soccer player, and all the analysts did was read the negative reactions about it. Fuck."

I shove my hands into my hair, gripping tight. Tears well in my eyes.

"Just because you're thirty years old doesn't mean I'll let you get away with saying the f-word."

"Sorry, Mom."

"What are you going to do?" Mom starts rubbing my back. It always had a way of soothing me as a kid, and it still does to this day. I spent many days of my childhood, and much of my teen years, being soothed by my mother. Usually with milk and cookies.

I guess the adult equivalent is pizza and beer.

"Game's getting ready to kick off!" Marley shouts from the other room.

"Be there in a minute."

"It doesn't change the fact that he lied to me. And after what Ryan did to me, I told myself I would never go back into the closet for anyone."

And that's the crux of the matter. I love Alex. I do. God, do I ever love that muscly, outdoorsy, boy band-loving man. But I don't know if I could be with him in the way he would need.

It figures I'd meet exactly the right person for me at the wrong time.

Why is love so hard?

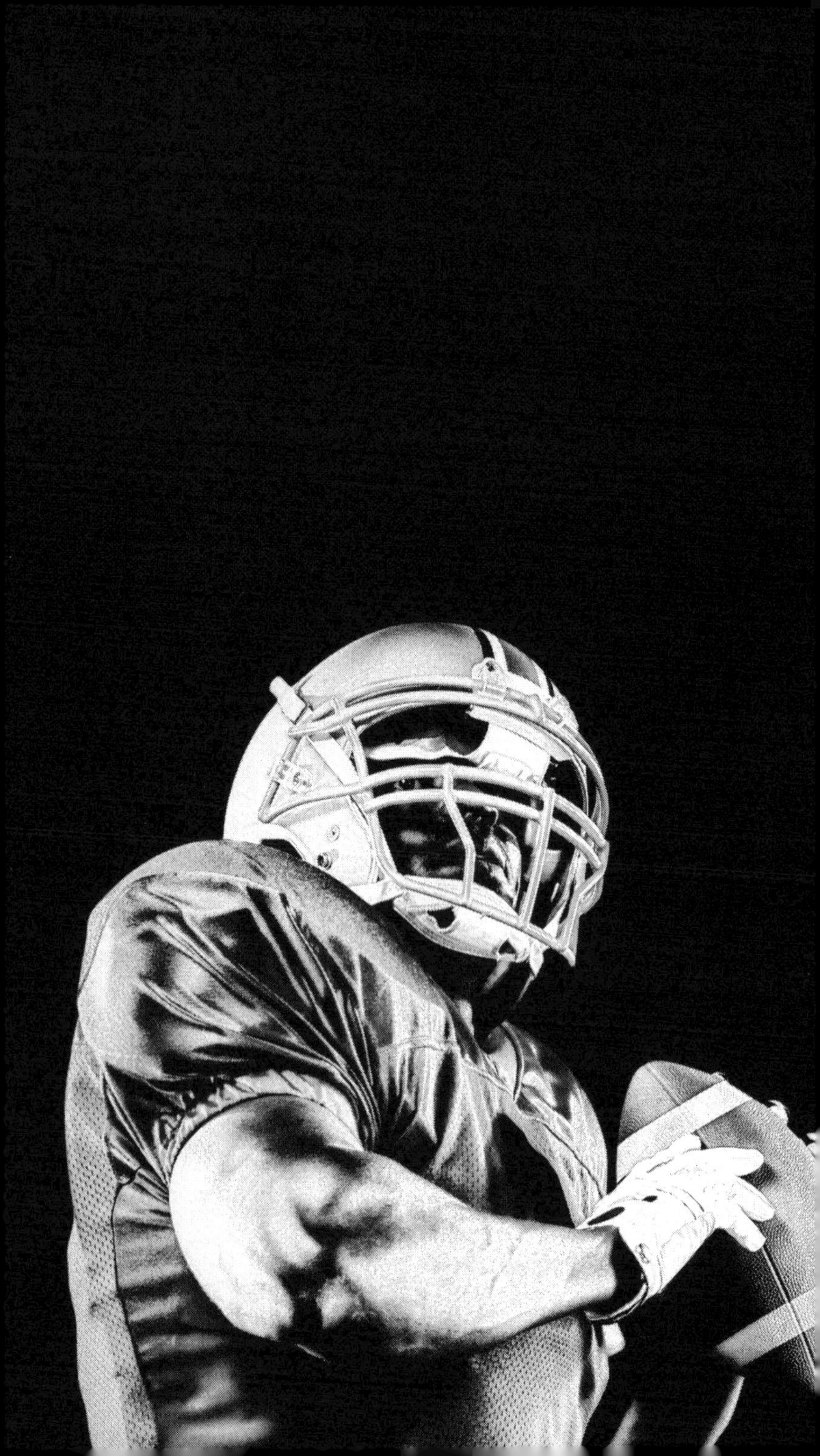

Chapter Twenty-Six

ALEX

"What's got you so grumpy today?" Knox whips a towel in my direction.

"I'm fine."

"Everyone knows when someone says they're 'fine' they're not actually 'fine,'" Logan states matter-of-factly.

"Is it too much to ask you guys to shut the hell up? We've got a big game today and I'm trying to focus." I run a hand through my ragged hair.

"Oh shit. Something really did crawl up your ass." Colin's eyes drift to the other three crowding around my locker.

The tension in the locker room is high. Everyone is getting pumped for the game today. Especially since it's against Vegas. They're gunning for us today since we're leading the division.

But the tension sitting in my shoulders is for an entirely different reason. It's been a long few weeks.

Long, agonizing weeks without Carter.

I've never had anyone in my life like him before. Even

that brief shining glimpse of him was more than I could handle.

Practice drained me of what little energy I have. It's like I'm moving through a swamp without him.

And every time I look at the coach? It's like I'm looking at Carter in twenty years and everything I'll have missed out on in life. All because I'm letting the fear win.

"As long as his head is in the game, let him be," Jackson pipes up as he tugs his jersey on over his pads. "Alex knows what this game means."

Fuck.

As if anyone needed to add any more pressure to the weight on my shoulders.

I grab the eighteen jersey out of my locker, tracing the captain patch. In the last two weeks, I've felt like anything but a captain.

Snapping at anyone who dropped a pass or missed a block.

Fuck, Knox is right.

Except I'm way more than grumpy.

"Listen up, everyone." Coach's voice echoes around the locker room. The Mountain Lions logo on the floor beneath him looks like it's ready to swallow him whole.

"It's going to be a tough game out there today. Conditions are less than ideal. But we're used to the weather—it's nothing new. Plus we have home field advantage. So play your game and the rest will take care of itself."

I barely hear Knox's speech when he takes over from Coach before everyone empties out of the locker room. The noise of the crowd as we run out onto the field doesn't seem as loud as usual.

It's like everything is dull.

But not the icy rain. It's cutting as it soaks through the long-sleeved shirt underneath my pads.

Sideline Infraction

Winter came early as my breaths are easy to see in the low light of the late afternoon. The stadium lights block out most of the crowd as we walk out to midfield for the coin toss.

Hollins is out there for Vegas. His cocky grin as he shakes Colin's hand has me wanting to throw punches out here.

Bastard.

"Hopefully you're prepared to lose," he says, giving my hand an extra tight squeeze.

"Only losers here are you," Colin cuts in before I can.

"Gentlemen. We don't want to kick you out before the game." The ref eyes all of us. The game hasn't even started yet and they're out for blood. "Let's make it a good clean game."

Vegas wins the toss and defers to the second half.

"Your head in the game, Young?" Coach asks as I grab my helmet.

"Yes sir." I don't maintain eye contact, instead watching as our special teams returns the ball to the fifteen-yard line. Not great starting position in these conditions.

"Gutter Away Houston. Got it?" Williams, our offensive coordinator, pops up next to me.

I nod, running out onto the field.

"Good strong start, got it?" I eye each of my linemen and receivers.

"Let's shut them up!" Colin yells, pounding the pads of the closest player to him.

"Gutter Away Houston, on three. Break."

Everyone moves into position as I get behind my center. My eyes track the defense, not settling on any one player to give the play away.

Calling it, the center hikes the ball as I drop back,

watching everything unfold before me. One of the linebackers gets around our tackle and I scramble. Backing up a few steps, I find Colin and throw the ball toward him.

The split-second delay allows him to only get six yards down the field before sliding out of bounds.

The weather isn't going to do us any favors as the next two plays don't gain us any yards.

Three and out. Worst possible way to start the game.

"Gonna be a long day for you, QB. A lot more where that came from," Hollins shouts as the lines switch up on the field. "Just you wait."

It takes everything I have to jog back to the sideline. All the tension inside of me is looking for a release. What I wouldn't give to be able to take it out on that dick.

But I can't do anything to jeopardize the game for my team.

"You're taking too many steps when you drop back into the pocket, Young." I haven't even taken off my helmet before Williams is in my face.

"Maybe if our tackles would block better…" I mumble.

"Care to say that to our faces?" Kelly, our center, gets in my face. "You think we're just letting them walk all over you?"

"Well, we're on the sideline now and not on the field. Someone's not doing their job."

He points a finger in my face. "Ever think it might be you? Worry about yourself, Young. You're not the only one out on the field."

His eyes are boring into me as he backs away.

"Pissing off your blockers isn't going to help anyone. Take a breath and I'll draw up some running plays for the next drive." The offensive coordinator claps me on the shoulder and is gone.

Sideline Infraction

For the first time in a long time, no one drops down next to me on the bench. It's like my aggression is radiating out from me and keeping everyone at bay.

But the nerves keep me from sitting still.

I pace on the sidelines as our defense tries to stop Vegas's offense from charging down the field. Instead, they steamroll right over us, easily taking the ball into the end zone.

Fuck. Vegas is off to a strong start, our fans voicing their distaste with boos.

"Alright boys. Time to get our heads in the game. Let's tie this up."

I get a few skeptical looks from the guys—because clearly it's my issue that's causing the team to flounder.

But it's only the first quarter. We can get those points back.

Rushing back onto the field, Vegas's D-line stops us on the first play.

Shit. Getting the guys back into the right headspace is going to be harder than I thought. Heads are hanging as they come back into the huddle.

"Alright. Let's shake it off. Charlie Blue Thirty on two." Everyone claps their hands, getting into position for the running play. It's going to be a fight to get every yard in this game with the rain coming down.

Snapping the ball, I complete an easy handoff to Logan, but not before Hollins comes at me. He pulls up a split second before plowing into me. The sneer on his face tells me he did it on purpose.

I should leave it. I should get back to the line and call a quick play to catch Vegas off guard. But I'm too on edge and have to poke the bear today.

"Play the damn ball, Hollins," I yell.

"Maybe if you were, you wouldn't be losing right now. Fucking fairy."

"What'd you say to me?" I'm in Hollins's face before I know what I'm doing. All I see is red.

"You heard me. Maybe if you weren't such a fairy you'd have an easier time staying on your feet."

"What the hell is your problem?" Kelly is right up next to me.

"Aww. Have to have your boyfriend defend you? Fucking queer," Hollins spits at me.

What tenuous grip I had on my sanity snaps and I'm punching Hollins to the ground.

Whistles and flags are being thrown as someone tries to pull me off him. Every ounce of pent-up sadness and anger is flying out of my fists. My helmet gets knocked off as Hollins swings a punch.

"You can do better than that," I egg him on. His knuckles crack my jaw.

"Fuck off, Young!"

"Aww, and here I thought you'd be a top." I give him my smarmiest smile.

"Get the fuck off me, you faggot!" This time, Hollins shoves me hard enough to knock me back off him, straight into the ref.

He's hauling me up while Hollins staggers to their sidelines. The crowd is booing all around me.

"...as a result, number eighteen of Denver and number twenty-two of Las Vegas have both been ejected from the game."

Kelly is shouting at the ref about what Hollins was saying, but I push him back to our side of the field. "We need you out there, man. Don't get kicked out too."

"You heard what he said to you, right? That can't slide!"

Sideline Infraction

The anger that's clouding my brain starts to clear.

Fuck.

I just got kicked out of the game.

I've always been the levelheaded one on the field. I'm one of the captains of the team.

And with one jab from Hollins, I put everything I've worked my entire life for on the line.

Fuck.

By the time I make it back to the sideline, Coach is waiting for me, his face hard.

"You'll be waiting for me in my office when the game is over."

One of the team assistants escorts me back to the locker room. Whipping off my pads, they make a sickening crunch as they land in my locker, knocking everything out of place.

"Calm down, Young. Don't make this any worse." His words are harsh. I've earned them.

I can't remember ever feeling like this. I hit the showers, letting the water wash out every bitter thought I'm having.

Fucking fairy.

Fucking faggot.

Ejected from the game.

God, if Carter could see me now…except, he doesn't want to. And why would he want to see me like this?

This isn't who I am. I don't get tossed out of games. I don't fight words with fists.

I don't know who was on that field, but it definitely wasn't me.

Shutting the water off, I wrap a towel around my waist and head back to the locker room. I waste no time in getting dressed and then stomping off to the coach's office. I don't want to be in there when the team comes back in.

The looks on their faces will be too much to bear.

"IN ALL MY YEARS OF COACHING,"–COACH'S voice startles me from my slumped spot in a chair—"I have never seen anyone act like that on the field. Give me one good reason why I shouldn't bench you for the season."

Fuck. This is worse than I thought.

I give it to him straight. "He called me a faggot."

His face hardens. It's as if he's aged ten years right in front of me. "That's quite the accusation, Alex."

I shake my head. "Not an accusation, coach. Called me a fairy and a faggot. And I know I should be the bigger person, but I snapped. Hollins is a dick, Coach. We all know it."

"Dick or not, it doesn't mean you can go around unleashing your feelings on the players of this league."

"Right."

"Is there any reason that you would take these words to heart?"

Coach doesn't say anything else. He sits there with an assessing look in his eyes.

It sets my teeth on edge. It's like he can see straight through me.

Does he know I'm gay?

Does he know I broke his son's heart?

Sitting in front of this man, every reason I have for keeping my secret—my truth—to myself starts to whittle away.

What if I told him?

I study the man I've come to know in front of me. He's

never guided me wrong. He never wavers in the face of insurmountable odds.

So tell him.

Wiping my hands on my pants, the tight ball of emotion bursts out of me.

"I'm gay."

"I see."

"And who I love shouldn't be an issue. But I'm not naive enough to believe that there won't be more people like Hollins in the league who won't accept me for me. It doesn't matter because what happened today was that Hollins was a dick and his behavior shouldn't be tolerated."

"But your reaction to him wasn't appropriate either."

I stand, pacing the small room. It's only now that I hear the guys in the locker room. Instead of the boisterous tone of a win, it's somber. "We lost, didn't we?"

He nods his head. "Hard to come back when we lose our starting quarterback."

"Fuck!" I'm ready to punch the wall, but Coach comes around his desk, grabbing my shoulders and stopping me.

"Son, I'm going to give you a little advice."

I suck in a breath, waiting to hear his words.

"I'm going to tell you what I told my son when he came out to me. Life is hard, but who you choose to love shouldn't be. Choose your hard, Alex. Whether you choose to continue living in this closet you've built around yourself, or stepping out into the light, it's going to be hard either way. But wouldn't the hard be easier if you were happy?"

Every single emotion that I've been holding in for the last two weeks—hell, since I made the decision not to come out—comes flooding out. The dam bursts open, and I can't fight the tears as they come.

Coach pulls me in for a hug and I cling to him for dear life.

The number of people who know my sexuality? Four. My parents, Tommy, and Carter.

Now five.

Telling Coach was different. Carter knew. My parents and Tommy also knew. It wasn't hard coming out to them because they knew.

But Coach didn't. He's the first person I've made the conscious decision to tell.

A weight I always knew I was carrying lifts off me. I feel a hundred pounds lighter.

From telling one person.

Imagine what it will feel like if I come out to the world.

"You okay?" Coach pulls back.

I take a minute to wipe the tears and steady my breath. "I think so."

"Good. Anyone you can go home to?"

A furious blush creeps up my cheeks. "That ship has sailed."

The last thing I want to do is tell Coach that I've been sleeping with his son. Not that it matters anyway. We're not together.

"I'm sorry to hear that. Now, go home and don't talk to anyone until you hear from me. I'll talk with the team and try and get this sorted out."

I just hope it doesn't end with me getting my walking papers.

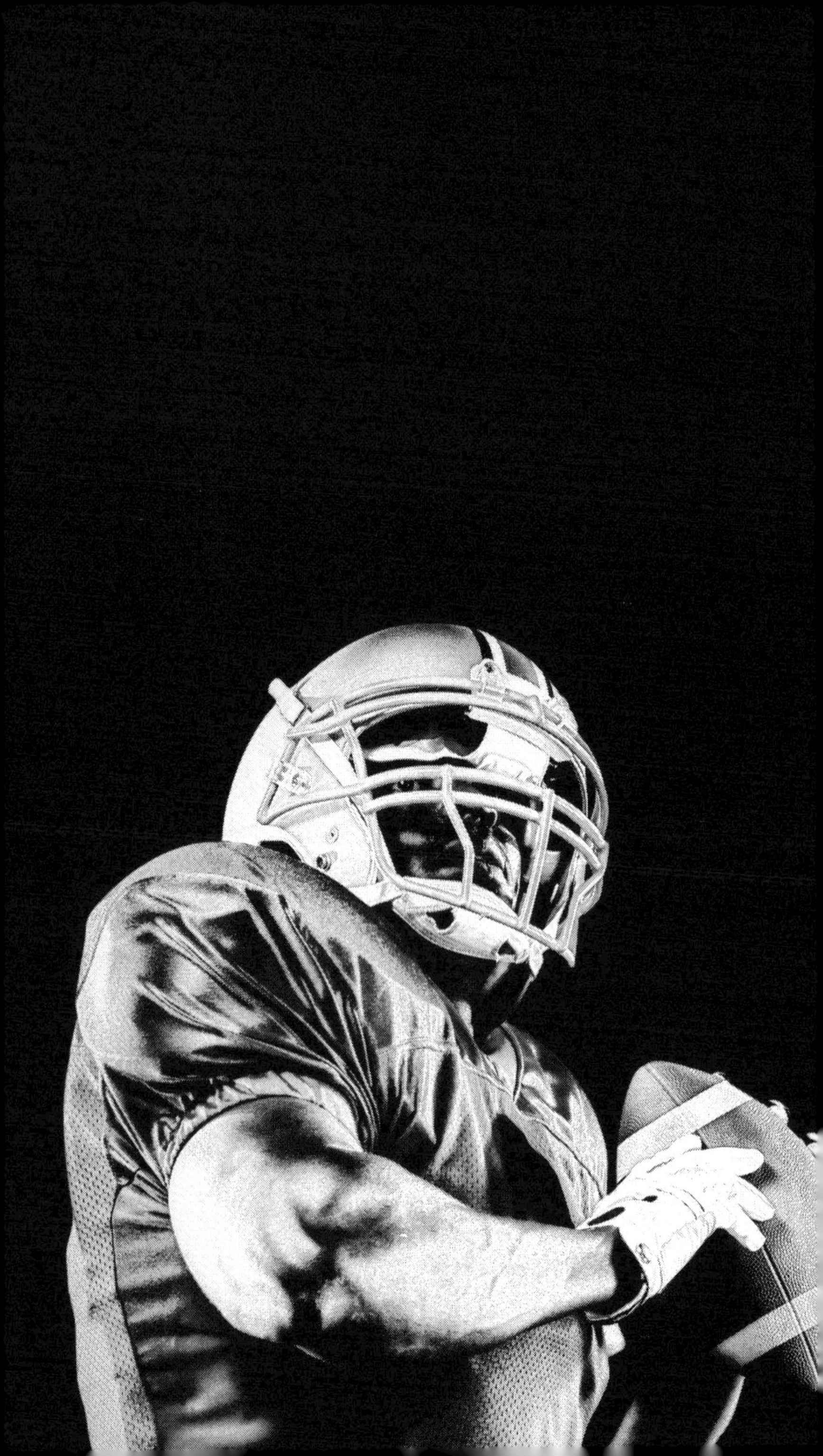

Chapter Twenty-Seven

ALEX

"What in the actual fuck is wrong with you?"

I glance up from where I'm sitting on the couch, icing my face. Tommy doesn't stop in the living room, instead going straight for the kitchen to grab a beer.

"That was a real question I was asking you." He cracks the lid and takes a swig. "Because never in my life have I seen that kind of behavior from you."

It's all the sports analysts have been talking about all afternoon. After leaving Coach's office with strict instructions not to pick up the phone for anyone except him or team management, I came straight home and parked my ass on the couch. If I didn't see a single person for the next week, it'd be too soon.

And my brother was disrupting that peace.

"Do you not think I know that?" I pause the TV on my face. My face is red as Hollins is shouting at me as I'm escorted off the field.

Definitely not one of my finer moments.

"Then what in the hell were you thinking jeopardizing your career like that?"

Tommy flops down onto the couch opposite me.

"He called me a faggot."

He chokes on his beer. "Way to bury the lede. Are you fucking for real?"

I only nod, finishing the rest of my own beer.

"Fuck. How are you still dealing with this kind of shit?"

Shaking my head, I need to burn off the excess adrenaline that is still pounding through me. I grab another beer.

"You know this is exactly why I'm not out. Because of people like him."

Standing, Tommy walks into the kitchen. It reminds me of the mornings spent here with Carter. The tiny shards of my heart ache remembering the look on his face.

"Do you really think everyone is going to be like him though?"

I scrub a hand down my face, catching on the newly grown beard covering my face. I haven't bothered shaving the last few weeks. It's taken every ounce of energy I have to get out of bed and practice, so why bother?

"It's not a chance I'm willing to take." I guzzle half of my beer in one swallow.

"Okay, you getting drunk isn't going to help anything." Tommy grabs the beer from my hand.

"Isn't going to hurt at this point."

"What'd your coach say about all of this?"

"I'm supposed to sit tight and wait until I hear from them."

"No way. You're going to go stir-crazy if you keep watching that." He points to the TV. "Which, bro, I don't think I've ever seen you look so angry before."

He throws his hands up in defense at my glower. "You know, no one invited you over here."

Tommy laughs, clapping me on the shoulder. "The joy

Sideline Infraction

of being your older brother. I get to stop by whenever I please."

"I really wish you hadn't moved out here."

"Oh no, you actually love me being here. Don't lie."

As much as I want to give him shit for being here for work—a weak excuse in my book—I'm actually glad he's here.

The last two weeks have been a hell of my own making. Sleep has been elusive. Every time I close my eyes, I see the utter dejection on Carter's face. And it makes me want the ground to swallow me whole.

"Let's get out of here." Tommy grabs his keys and pulls me toward the door.

"Do you really think that's a good idea? I really don't want people yelling at me tonight."

He waves me off like it isn't a big deal. "Don't worry. I found a place where people probably won't give two shits about you."

"Again, really great to have you here, bro."

He grins like a fool and walks out the door.

"Dude, you're putting way too much force behind it. You're going to break it."

"Don't care." I keep swinging anyway. All of my aggression is going into whacking these tiny moles that keep popping up. They're as good of a place as any for it.

"Okay, but I would like a turn too." Tommy side checks me out of the way as the timer goes off.

"Think you can beat my score?"

"I plan to." He grins an evil grin, one that I'm used to after years of being on the receiving end. "Loser buys the next round."

"Hope you're okay paying then."

The game starts up, the annoying laughs echoing in the din of the building.

When Tommy suggested this place, I was skeptical. I didn't want to be out anywhere where people would take notice. But with a hoodie and a baseball hat, I blend in quite easily.

Arcade games and penny machines line all the walls. Every game I loved as a kid is in here—from Whac-a-Mole to Pac-Man. Tickets shoot out the games for prizes to be claimed.

"I should make you pay. You're making those big quarterback bucks."

"For now," I huff.

"You really should get laid. It'd help you relax."

I nearly choke on my beer.

"What? I'm just saying. You're too wound up if you're fighting on the field."

"That's kind of the problem…"

Tommy stops, dropping the padded mallet of the game. "What do you mean that's the problem?"

"You know you're buying if you lose."

"Fuck that. What do you mean that's the problem?" He crosses his arms, pinning me with his best big-brother stare. When we were little, it used to scare the shit out of me. Now? Now it's mildly irksome.

"That *someone* I mentioned when you moved here became *my someone*, but now…"

"Jesus, Alex. What did you do?"

"Only broke the heart of the only man I've ever loved.

And will probably ever love. And now I'm destined to die alone."

"Okay, pity party for one." Grabbing my shoulder, Tommy steers me over to a high-top table. "Tell me. Now."

"I fell in love with the coach's son."

"Wait, like the coach of your team? Of the Mountain Lions?"

I roll my eyes. "What other coach would I have?"

"Fine. Whatever. How did you two meet?"

I rehash the events of the last few months, right up until Carter realized I'm not actually out of the closet.

"I told him too."

"Told who what?" Tommy asks.

"Coach. I told him I'm gay."

"Are you serious?"

I glance up at eyes that match my own, nodding.

"Alex. That's huge. How'd he take it?"

"About as great as I could have hoped for."

Awareness washes over Tommy's face. "Which makes all the sense in the world because his own son is gay. Of course."

I swallow down the rest of my beer. "It felt good telling him."

"I'm not saying it'll be easy, but have you thought about coming out? Like really coming out. I know it's all you ever think about, but maybe this is a sign. Maybe Hollins being a dick is the sign you need to change your life."

"The universe has a funny way of doing things if Hollins is the one to make me come out."

"He'll get what's coming to him," Tommy says. "I can't believe he said that to you."

"He's a dick. He deserved to get punched for saying that."

"I know you punched him because you're heartbroken, but you can't go around hitting people for being dicks."

I shrug, resting my elbow on the table and dropping my head into my hand, my focus now back on the earlier game. "Fucking sucks."

"You can't just be miserable the rest of your life."

Frustration boils over. "Fine. Let's say I come out. What happens when more people like Hollins start talking trash? I can't keep letting that shit roll off my back. It's not okay."

"I'm not saying it is. But if you keep losing your head like you did out there today, you're not going to get anywhere in life." He points at me. "Except maybe if you did, you'd be cut and no team would want you, so you could come out."

"God, you're such an asshole."

"Takes one to know one." Tommy gives me his best grin, and it goes a long way to ease the tightening in my chest.

My phone buzzes in my pocket. Pulling it out, there's an awaiting text from Coach.

> **COACH BROOKS**
> My office. 7am tomorrow. Do not be late.

"OH SHIT." I hold my phone up so Tommy can see.

"Guess it's time for you to face the music."

"And what if I'm cut?"

"Then I'll be there to help you figure out your next move."

Brothers. I guess they're good for something.

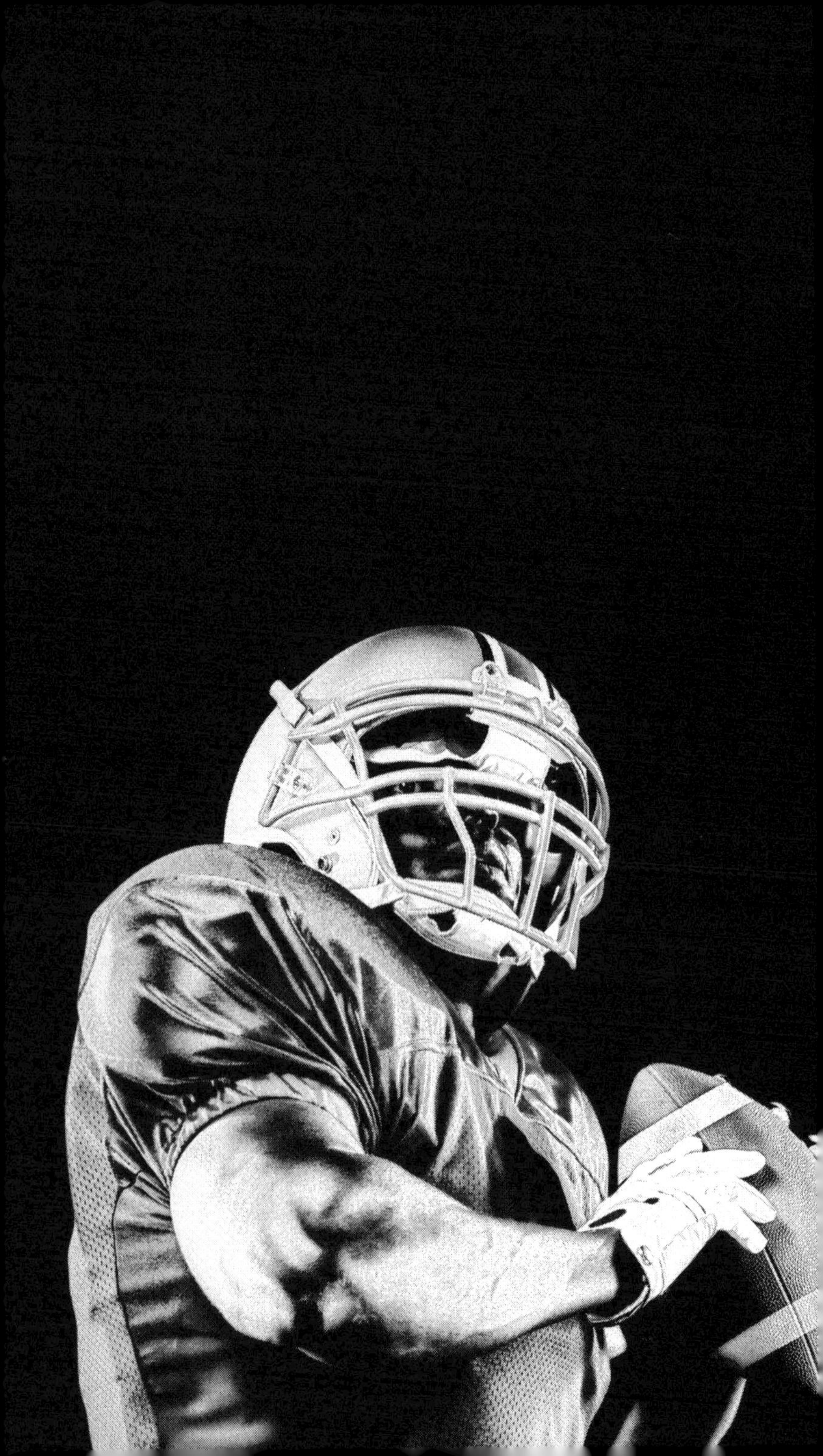

Chapter Twenty-Eight

ALEX

"Alex. Thanks for meeting me so early."

"Didn't really have an option, Coach," I say with a stilted laugh, trying to dispel some of the nerves that are threatening to explode out of me. "Am I benched?"

Coach clasps his hands in front of him. Whatever happens, I'll deal with it. I respect this man too much—as my coach and the father of the man whose heart I broke—to argue. I made my bed and now I have to lie in it.

"No. But management has asked me if you would be willing to give a talk on how the kind of language that Hollins used shouldn't be tolerated in the league."

"Wait…what?"

"I know you're not out and it's a big ask, but I was hoping you would consider it."

I shake my head, still not quite getting it. "I'm not benched."

Coach smiles at me. "No, you're not."

"I'm not suspended, am I?"

Coach shakes his head. "Again, no."

"No fines, nothing?"

"If you really want me to, I'm sure I could come up with something."

"Sorry, I just expected this to go a completely different way today."

Except the look Coach gives me doesn't exactly calm my nerves.

It does the exact opposite, in fact.

"What Hollins said is on video. It's grainy because of the noise of the game, but it's there. He's been suspended for four games without pay. The league is worried you'll take legal action against them."

I scrub a hand down my face. "Honestly, Coach? The only thing that mattered was I let my team down."

"It's why you're a better man than most of us, son."

"Other than talking to the league, I'm not in trouble?"

I feel like a five-year-old kid, pleading not to get grounded.

"No, you're not. You're free to go."

His attention shifts back to his desk, but I don't make a move to leave. Because now that the league has video footage of what happened, it suddenly feels important to tell my side of the story.

So important, I just blurt it out.

"What would happen if I came out?"

Coach leans back in his chair, crossing his arms. The look he gives me reminds me so much of Carter, it solidifies my decision. "While I can't speak for the team—and I have no doubt they would support you—you have my unwavering support. If you want to come out, I will be right behind you. Whatever you need, I'm here for you. We're a family, and we always have each other's backs."

His words cause tears to well up in my eyes. "I'm in love with Carter."

This time, a shocked look crosses his face. "Carter? As

Sideline Infraction

in, Carter Brooks? The son of my mine who has been moping around for the last few weeks?"

"I'm afraid that was because of me."

He whistles. "Can't say I saw that coming, but it makes so much sense. You were both so happy and then you weren't."

"I have to say, you're very observant of what's going on with all of your players."

"Alex, if you ever have the opportunity to coach, you'll find you're a part-time therapist. So yes, I keep an eye on my players." He leans forward. "You want to do this? You want to come out? There's no taking it back once you do."

I smile, the first real smile I've felt in weeks. Hell, the last however many years. Because finally, the pressure is off. "I'm choosing my hard, Coach."

MY KNOCK on the door seems to echo violently around the hall. Like everyone in the office space is going to know exactly why I'm here right now.

"It's open." I shove the door open, and Peyton's smiling face greets me. As does Colin's.

Fuck.

I was prepared to talk to her. Not him.

But if I don't do this now, I'm going to chicken out. Shutting the door behind me, I step into her small office. A Mountain Lions flag stretches out along the back wall, taking up what little space there is. Pictures of the team and of her and Colin line her desk.

"Hey man." Colin nods his head toward me as he shovels the rest of a bagel into his mouth. "You going to be ready for practice later?"

I cross my arms, trying to settle my nerves. Since we lost yesterday, we don't have today off. We'll be watching film all day to get ready for this next week.

It doesn't take a genius to know where we went wrong. Losing your starting quarterback tends to have a negative effect on the team.

I wave him off. "I'll be fine."

"Did you need something?" Peyton interrupts.

"I was wondering if you had a minute to talk."

She gives me a warm smile. It tells me I can do this.

I know in this exact moment that my entire life is going to change. Hell, it changed the moment I decided to do this. Hopefully it will all be for the better.

"What's up?" Peyton rests her arms on her desk, leaning closer to me.

"There's no easy way to tell you this." I rub a hand over the back of my neck.

"Dude, are you okay?" Colin leans forward, his face no longer smiling. "Did something happen to cause you to go off the rails?"

"I'm fine."

"Then why do you look like someone kicked your dog?"

"Would you let him talk?" Peyton chastises him.

"I'm gay," I blurt out. So much for tact.

Peyton's expression softens ever so slightly, while Colin's jaw drops to the floor.

"You're what?" Colin shakes his head, but I fix my gaze back to Peyton.

"Is there a reason you're coming to me with this now?"

The quiet calm in her voice settles the racing of my pulse. "Because I'm tired of hiding."

"Is that all?"

Colin's eyes are bouncing back and forth between the

Sideline Infraction

two of us.

It's weird how calm Peyton is. It's a much different reaction than when I came out to my family. It's almost as if...

"Did you know?"

Peyton stands up, rounding her desk. "I had an inkling."

"Wait, you knew?" Colin sounds gobsmacked, moving to stand next to Peyton. "Why didn't you tell me?"

"Because it's not my news to share." Her attention shifts back to me. "So what's the real reason?"

I scrub a hand down my face, leaning against the wall for support. Carter's face when he left me in the parking lot comes to mind. The utter devastation when he realized I wasn't actually out.

"I broke someone's heart because I'm not out. And in turn, broke my own heart."

Peyton wraps a hand around my bicep. "You know you shouldn't come out for someone else."

I swallow back the emotion that is threatening to overwhelm me. "I know. I'm not doing this for him. Well, not entirely for him. I kind of had a bad reaction to something Hollins said."

"Hollins is a dick. You should know better than to react," Colin interrupts.

I nod. "I know. But if he hadn't said what he did, I wouldn't have come out to Coach. The moment I told him, I felt lighter. And when I talked to my brother about it, the thought of telling more people, while terrifying, also feels like the right thing to do."

"How did I miss this?" Colin mutters to himself.

Peyton ignores him, pulling me in for a hug. "In case no one has told you, I think you're really brave. And that you can inspire people out there too."

"What, that's it?" Colin's voice has me pulling back. "Alex says he's gay and we're moving on?"

Colin's reaction is exactly what I was worried about. "You don't have to accept me for who I am—"

"Who said anything about not accepting you?" Colin holds up a hand, interrupting me.

"You. Based on your reaction just now."

This time, he looks offended. "You're a dick. I don't care if you're gay. Honestly, I'm more upset that you felt you had to keep it from us. Did you think we wouldn't have your back?"

Ever since Carter walked out on me, shame has been crawling all over my skin.

"You saw how Hollins reacted when Mahoney Holmes came out. He's been gunning for me all season. And then how he acted Sunday? It's hard to ask people to put themselves in the line of fire for me."

Carter huffs. "Hollins is a dick. He wouldn't know how to be a good person if Santa Claus promised him all the toys in the world."

I laugh. It's the first time in days, and it feels like my muscles are finally unclenching. "But it's part of the reason why. The league is a boys' club. People don't like people that are different."

Colin shakes his head. "You're right. And if I've done anything to make you feel like you couldn't come out to me, I'm sorry."

I'm shaking my head now. "No. Trust me, I wanted to tell you guys a hundred times. But I was scared."

My head drops. Tears wet my eyes. These last few weeks have been some of the hardest of my life. But once I made the decision to come out, I decided to go full steam ahead. Because if I back out now, when will I ever do this?

And I'm ready.

"Do you want me there when you tell the guys?" Colin asks.

"I haven't quite worked that out yet."

Clasping my shoulders, Colin pulls my attention up to him. "Listen, Alex. You're like a brother to me. I don't know how I would've gotten through the last few years without you. Whatever you need, I'm here for you."

I choke out a muffled thanks before pulling him in for a hug. I know not everyone is going to have this kind of reaction. It's going to get a lot worse before it gets better if the news around Mahoney is any indication.

But Colin accepting me for who I am? It's too much for me to take right now as tears start leaking out of my eyes.

"I should've known better," I tell Colin, wiping the tears off my cheeks as I pull back.

"I'm always here for you. And if anyone has anything to say about you being gay, then they can talk to me."

"Okay, I don't need you getting clocked in the head again," Peyton chimes in. "How are you thinking you want to do this, Alex?"

Peyton's tone says all business, but the wetness in her eyes tells me she's just as moved by Colin's reaction. It's all I hoped for.

"Umm, I guess I hadn't thought that far ahead."

Peyton rolls her eyes at me. "That's never good when she does that," Colin whispers to me, his arm still wrapped around my shoulders.

"She's never done that to me. How do I undo it?"

"I know how I do it, but that won't work for you."

I bark out a laugh.

"I can hear you both, you know that, right?" Peyton quirks a brow in our direction.

"Sorry, Rocky. Go ahead."

Peyton stares at Colin before turning back to me. "I

know a good reporter. How about a sit-down? A little bit more than just the team releasing a statement, but not putting you on the spot in a live TV interview."

"Do you think that's a good idea?"

She nods. "It puts the narrative in your hands. You can speak your truth and say whatever you want."

"After Sunday, I don't want to see my face on TV anymore."

Peyton shakes her head. "Oh, they'll be showing your face, but it'll be on our terms. I have a guy in mind who would be perfect for the job."

"Can't I just sit down and talk to you?" I laugh. The thought of telling my story to a nameless reporter has my nerves ratcheting up again.

"It'd be a quick interview if it were me. Trust me, this guy will tell your story exactly how it should be."

I blow out a breath. "If it's what you think is best, let's do it."

Peyton steps over, wrapping her arms around my waist. The three of us are standing in a group hug in the middle of her office.

"It's okay to be scared, Alex. But we'll be by your side the entire time."

I drop a kiss to the top of Peyton's head. "Thank you. And thank you for being so cool about all of this."

"Psh. Cool is my middle name," Colin jokes.

"Is this really what you have to put up with all of the time?" I ask Peyton.

"Eh, he's worth it." Peyton snakes an arm around Colin, pulling him closer.

Colin claps me on the back. "For real though. Whatever you need, the both of us are here for you. And who knows? Maybe you'll get your man back."

If only.

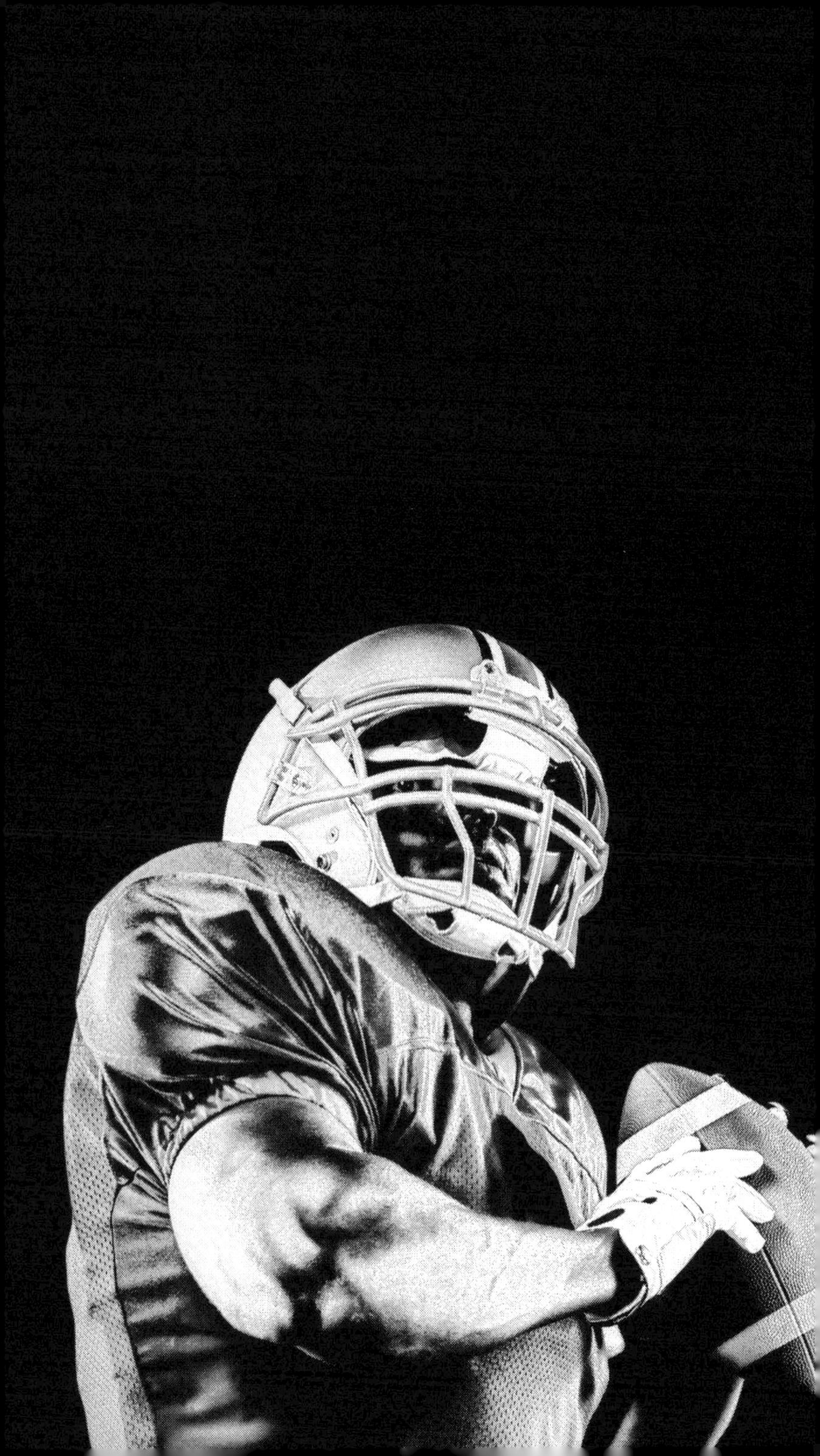

Chapter Twenty-Nine

ALEX

"You all set?" Colin asks.

"Stop asking. I'm fine." I grind my teeth together. When I asked Peyton to get this rolling, I didn't think she'd turn it around in a few days.

But I can't deny it's helped improve my mindset. Maybe that and winning the game on Sunday.

"You don't look fine," Tommy says.

"Why did I bring you two here? You're just making me more anxious."

"We're supposed to make you more comfortable. I mean, you are putting everything on the line." Tommy's face is stoic. When I told him the decision I made, he was there to support me, again, in whatever I did. Everyone has told me it's okay if I don't come out, that they didn't want to pressure me one way or another. Except it's time.

I'm ready.

"Have you met the reporter yet?" Colin asks from my side.

He follows me through the halls of the practice building. Peyton said it'd be low-key this way, but also put me on familiar ground. Walking in and seeing the Mountain Lions emblem does set my mind at ease.

At least, as much as it can since I'm about to tell the world I'm gay.

I shake my head. "Have you?"

"No, but I haven't seen Peyton much this week."

"Sorry if this kept her busy."

Colin pats me on the back as we walk onto the practice field. "Nah, I'm good. I don't want you backing out on this now that you're doing it."

"So I shouldn't ask you to drive the getaway car?" I laugh.

"No one is driving any getaway cars." Peyton steps up between us. People are milling about, setting everything up. "Trust me, you'll like Finn."

I blow out a breath. "Then he'd be the first reporter I like."

Having hidden who I am ever since I started playing in college, it's been hard to open up to anybody. What if I looked at someone the wrong way and I got outed? These people could make or break me, so I was always wary around them.

"Don't worry, I didn't like him at first either."

I spin on my heel, taking in the two men standing on the other side of the food table. Both are tall. While one has dark brown, floppy hair, the other is more polished with blond hair and glasses.

The glasses remind me of Carter and that ever-present pain in my chest that I broke his heart.

"I'm sorry, who are you?" I glance between the two men.

"Wes Cooper. I'm this guy's husband." He thumbs to the blond standing next to him.

"I apologize for him. Sometimes he has no filter. I'm Finn Anderson. I'll be doing your interview today."

I take his extended hand. "Nice to meet you."

"Don't worry if you don't like reporters. Finn will do a good job with you." Wes wraps his arm around Finn, and seeing the easy affection these two have calms my nerves.

"Sorry about that comment. This is just..." I can't find the right words to describe my mental state right now.

"Overwhelming?" Wes finishes for me.

I point at him. "Yeah, that."

"Peyton invited me to tag along because I was wary about having someone tell my story as well."

I lock eyes with Peyton and she gives me a knowing smile. I'm glad I have someone like her in my corner. I don't know if I could do this without her.

"Was it hard?"

Wes shrugs a shoulder. "Mine was different. I was coming back from an injury and didn't have to expose myself the way you are."

"Just tell your story. Don't try and be someone you're not," Finn jumps in.

"Did you ever have to come out like this?" I ask Wes.

He shakes his head. "No. But I'm a diver, and being in a sport that only gets recognition every few years, it wasn't as big of a deal. I was always out."

Scrubbing a hand down my face, I turn and look at the Mountain Lion staring back at me.

It's a simple thing, but it's been my home for my entire professional career. And I'm afraid that with this article, I could lose it all.

What if no one wants to be in the locker room with me?

What if Denver drops me because I'm too big of a liability?

What if no other team picks me up?

What if.

What if.

What if.

It's the same scenario that has been playing in my head the last few days, and it's hard to break the cycle.

Coach and the team have thrown their support behind me, but it doesn't make it any easier. Because I have no idea what the backlash could be.

"Finn. We're ready when you are," one of the assistants calls over.

"Knock 'em dead." Wes slaps him on the ass as Finn nods to the assistant.

Finn rolls his eyes, but the smile on his face gives him away. "I really am sorry about him. Sometimes he forgets we're not in the locker room."

"Hey! I resent that."

"Whenever you're ready, Alex. Take all the time you need." Finn claps me on the shoulder as he heads over to where the chairs are set up.

"You ready?" Peyton asks, adjusting my tie. Colin and Tommy are standing behind her, giving me encouraging looks.

"Am I doing the right thing? What if this all blows up in my face?"

"Can I answer that?" Wes chirps.

I nod at him.

"You're doing the right thing. I know it seems scary now, but just think of all the people you can inspire. Think about the kids who are struggling with their sexuality right now, thinking about how there are no gay football players. You can pave the way for inclusivity in the sport. And the more people who come out, the better it's going to be."

Sideline Infraction

Wes's words give me the vote of confidence I need to walk out and tell Finn my story. And I find that it's a lot easier to tell it than I ever thought.

Now I just hope the backlash isn't what I think it'll be.

EVERY SINGLE BONE in my body is exhausted. Finn didn't shy away from asking the tough questions. He stripped me down and I'm raw. All I want is a drink and to sleep for the next week.

But when I go into the locker room, I'm met with most of the team. Knox, Jackson, and Colin are all standing to the side, arms crossed, like they're waiting to lay into me.

"What are you guys doing here? Practice was over an hour ago."

"We wanted to be here to support you."

"Support me?" I ask like it's the dumbest question in the world.

"Word got out about what you were doing."

Of course. Gossip and news run rampant in locker rooms. It shouldn't surprise me.

"And you're all still here?" The offensive line's presence takes up a good part of the locker room. Five guys at three hundred pounds would take up most space in a room. It makes me want to run in the other direction and hide. They're intimidating on a good day, let alone on one where my nerves are frayed.

"Where else would we be?" one of the guys pipes up.

"It's my ass, right? It's a really good ass." Kelly, our center, shows said ass to everyone.

"That'd scare anyone straight," Williams yells.

"You don't care that I'm gay?" I blurt out.

Williams approaches, clasping me on the shoulder. "The only thing we care about is you lying to us. Why wouldn't you tell us?"

"You saw how Hollins reacted when that soccer player came out. I figured that's what everyone's reaction would be."

"Hollins is a dick," Knox says, everyone shaking their heads in agreement.

"You're the captain of this team for a reason," Logan agrees. "You're one of the best men here, so why wouldn't we support you?"

Their words of encouragement have emotion clogging my throat. I try to clear it, but it doesn't work.

"We've got your back. Whatever happens, we're here for you," Jackson states.

Everyone converges on me, wrapping me in a hug. I can't fight back the tears any longer. All the emotions come rushing out of my eyes. You'd think with how often this has happened the last few weeks, I'd be drained. Turns out, I'm not.

"Thanks, guys," I choke out, clapping everyone on the back as they start to disperse.

Except for the four guys now nodding toward the field for me to follow them.

It's cold. Darkness has settled over the field, with only a few lights from the building illuminating us. Our breaths puff out above us.

"So, anything big happen today, boys?" Knox asks.

"You're a dick," I laugh, accepting the glass of bourbon he hands me.

"Nah. I have half a mind to call you one, but you look dead on your feet."

"It's been a long day. Hell, a long few weeks." I sigh,

knocking back the entire glass in one gulp.

"Do you feel better?" Jackson asks.

"To be determined. I'm still worried about the backlash the team could get."

Colin wraps an arm around my shoulders, pulling me into him. "We've all got your back. If they want to fight you, they have to fight all of us."

"Which, Peyton told me to remind you—don't get hit in the head." I laugh, looking around at this group of guys. These men have become a second family to me. "I really don't know what to say."

"I know the toasts are usually your thing, but can I say something?" Colin clears his throat.

"Go for it."

"Wait, he needs more to drink!" Logan cuts him off, sloshing another two fingers of brown liquid into my glass.

"Am I going to need it?" I give him a wary look.

"Shut up and let me talk, will ya?" Colin glares at me.

Holding up my hands in surrender, I let him speak.

"What you did today was probably one of the bravest things I've ever witnessed. I don't know what it's like to be in your shoes, but it couldn't have been easy. I speak for everyone here and in that locker room that you are one of the best men we know."

I swallow down the now ever-present emotion that won't seem to leave.

"Whatever happens, will happen. We'll have your back. On the field and off. We love you, man. To Alex!"

"To Alex!" they echo.

I sip on my drink, relishing the burn as it goes down. "I really don't know what to say. I don't know if I'd still be standing right now if it weren't for you guys and the team. Thank you."

"No need to thank us, man. We're here for you and

that is never going to change." Jackson tips his head in my direction.

"I have to ask…is there a special someone?" Colin cocks one eyebrow at me.

Finishing my drink, I hold the glass out, needing more. "How much time do you have?"

2019

$\sqrt{1+}$

$\sum$

$2+$

$\sqrt{3}$

$12+84$

$\sum$

1

$2\sqrt{2}$

Chapter Thirty

CARTER

"Holy shit. Did you see this?"

High schoolers are never as quiet as they think they are.

"Ben, you're not supposed to have your phone out."

I swear, this kid doesn't want to keep his cell phone. I could retire if I had a dollar for every time I've taken it from him this year.

"Sorry, Mr. Brooks, but did you see this?"

Dropping my red pen onto my desk, I abandon the stack of quizzes I have to grade.

"See what?"

"This article on Alex Young. Did you know?"

"Know what?"

"He's gay."

"What?" I can't hide the shock in my voice. "Give me your phone."

"Am I in trouble?" He holds the phone closer to his chest.

"Just let me see the article."

Ben hands over his phone. It's open to *Sports News*

Weekly. And there, in big letters at the top are the words, "I'm gay."

Holy shit.

In this day and age, men and women coming out is becoming less newsworthy. Maybe it's because we're moving toward a more inclusive society, but many people don't even have to come out. But it's hard when you're in the public spotlight and everyone gets to have an opinion. Opinions that you neither wanted nor asked for.
When one of the biggest stars in football decides to come out, it makes headlines. Alex Young, quarterback for the Denver Mountain Lions, has made the decision to come out.
Now, hear as he tells his story exclusively to Sports News Weekly.

Finn Anderson: So why choose now to come out?
Alex Young: I was tired of hiding. As more and more of my friends partner off, I realized I was missing something in my life. Seeing other gay couples in public, holding hands and being in love, it made me realize how much I've been isolating myself.

FA: And how have you been isolating yourself?
AY: I've never had a long-term partner. Before this season, I've never let myself fall in love. No one knew the real me. I could go very few places without people recognizing me. It was safer to stay home in the bubble I created.

FA: Has being in the closet affected how you've played the game?
AY: If anything, it's helped my game. Since I didn't have a partner, my sole focus was on the game of football. It was a lonely life, but I studied more film and was better prepared than I would have been otherwise. That said, coming out isn't going to hurt the way I play—other players aren't negatively affected when they are in relationships, so there is no reason I would be any different.

Sideline Infraction

FA: How do you think others in the league will take this announcement?
AY: I'm not naive enough to think there won't be backlash, but I'm doing this anyway. There've been some vocal people against other sports stars coming out, so I know it'll happen. Football is a boys' club, and change will be hard. I just hope me coming out makes others out there feel like they can too.

FA: Do you think there are other gay football players out there?
AY: It would surprise me if there weren't.

FA: There's been a lot of discussion about recent events and how you were kicked out of the game against the Vegas Storm for starting a fight with Derek Hollins. He was suspended and you weren't. Care to shed any light on that?
AY: Words were said that I should've known better than to react to. Young people look to me as a role model, and it was not my best day. But those words are not words anyone should hear. It can have negative effects on young players and make it harder for the game to be more inclusive.

FA: Another popular sports star, Mahoney Holmes, midfielder for the Atlanta Rising Football Club, was recently outed. Have you had the opportunity to speak with him?
AY: I haven't. He has 100% of my support. I, thankfully, am able to come out on my own terms. I can't imagine having that choice taken away from you. I wish him all the best as their team is in the finals.

FA: Speaking of teams, how has your team taken your announcement?
AY: I haven't told them yet. I've told a few staff for the Mountain Lions and one of my co-captains, who is like a brother to me. They've all taken it in stride. It's the best I could have hoped for, so I'm only hoping the rest of the team takes it just as well.

FA: What happens if they don't?
AY: Then I have to figure out how to play the game I love with people who don't have my back. It's a team sport, and if you can't trust the people on your line, it's going to make it really hard. I don't think I'd be traded, but it's still a possibility.

FA: Would you consider retirement?
AY: It's not what I want, but if I'm cut and no one picks me up, maybe. I still have a lot of good years left in me. I still want to win a Super Bowl.

FA: Now the question everyone wants to know. Is there a special someone in your life?
AY: There was, but not anymore. I had something really good and because I was too scared to show the world who I am, I lost him.

FA: If you could say anything to him right now, what would it be?
AY: Even though we're not together anymore, I hope he's proud of me.

FA: What advice would you give to young players out there who might be feeling like you are now?
AY: I'd tell them that even though it's scary as f**k, I hope they have people in their life who can support them. The more of us who can come out and live our truth and be out players in this game, the better off we'll leave the sport.

FA: We might have to bleep that out.
AY: Sorry about that. I hope to be an ally for anyone who might need one. Because I love this game and I want it to be accepting of people like me.

Holy shit.
"Uh, Mr. Brooks. Can I have my phone back please?"

"What?" I glance down at the phone, squeezing it in a death grip. "Oh, sorry. Put that away."

He shoves it in his pocket as the final bell of the day rings.

"Don't forget to study for your quiz tomorrow!" I shout at their retreating backs.

The second the last student is out of the room, I close the door and pull out my own phone.

Alex came out. I keep rereading those last lines.

Is there someone special in your life? There was, but not anymore.

My mind is spinning. I want to call him. To reach out and tell him that I am proud of him, but like he said, we're not together anymore.

My phone lights up, and Marley's face is on my screen.

"Hey sis."

"It was Alex," she states by way of greeting. "The football player you're in love with?"

There's no way I can lie to her now. "Pretty easy to figure out now."

"Holy shit. I can't believe the guy you're in love with is Alex Young."

"Say it a little louder." I roll my eyes at her.

"It's not like you need to hide it anymore."

"Huh. I guess not."

For so long, I was protective of my relationship with him because I didn't want to move too fast or jinx it. But now, there's nothing holding me back from saying I was in love with him.

Except for the fact that you kicked him to the curb.

"Alex came out." I still can't believe it. Maybe if I say it enough times, it'll start to sink in.

"What are you going to do?" she asks.

Isn't that the million-dollar question?

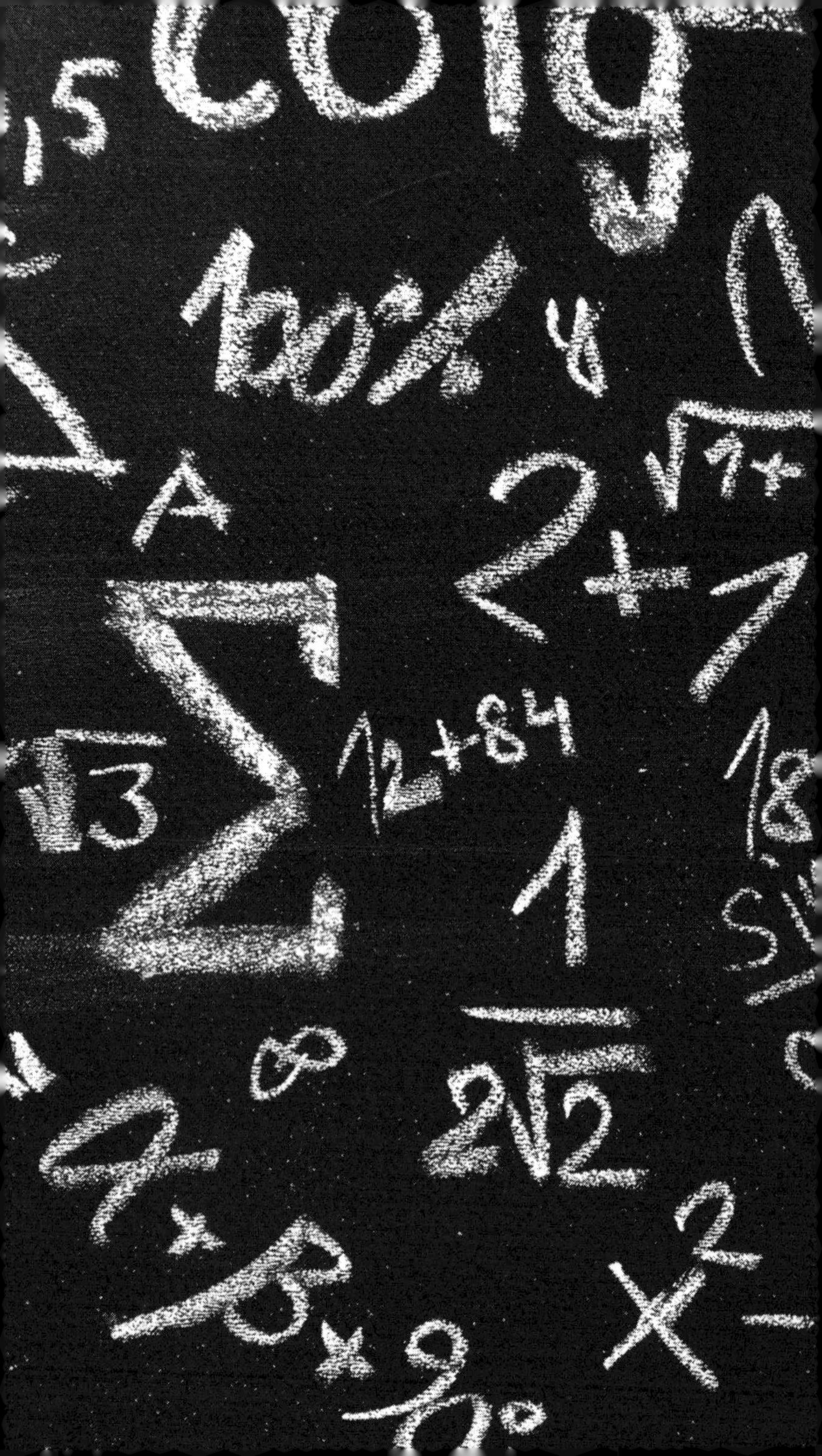

Chapter Thirty-One
CARTER

"How are you even sure he wants to see me?" I whisper into my phone.

I've been sitting in front of Alex's house for the last twenty minutes. I was surprised I was able to get into his gated community. Alex always called to approve me before. I'm even more shocked that no one has called security on me.

"Why wouldn't he? He loves you. He came out for you," Marley says.

"We don't know that." I shake my head.

"Then why would he come out now?" I can hear the eye roll through the phone. "It has to mean something."

I sigh. "But what if I'm making this into something it's not?"

"You wouldn't be as heartbroken as you are if it wasn't something," Marley states matter-of-factly.

It's my biggest worry. Before Alex and I even got involved, my brain was telling me that I was going to get hurt. That he was just another playboy football guy who couldn't care less about me.

So when I learned Alex wasn't actually out? It hurt. Rip my heart out and stomp on it hurt. A hurt I've never felt and don't think I can stomach feeling ever again.

"Carter, just go inside. You're going to drive yourself crazy if you just sit out there and analyze everything."

I don't get the chance to say goodbye before she hangs up the phone.

You can do this. It's Alex. You love him.

Giving myself a mental pep talk, I open the car door and make my way toward Alex's front door. I don't even have time to knock before he's pulling it open.

"I was wondering how long you'd be out there." The smile he gives me is a sad one. He's still the same Alex I've always known, but there's something different about him.

"Oh God. Did someone call security on me?" I turn to look behind me, but my car is barely visible from his front door.

"Security called to ask if I was expecting someone. Wanted to make sure no one was loitering when they shouldn't be."

"Great," I mutter. "Just what I need. People thinking I'm some sort of stalker."

"How about you come inside?" Alex swings the door open. Shoving my hands into my pockets so I don't do something stupid—like reach out for him—I walk into his house.

Shutting the door, Alex brushes by me as he heads into the living room. His cologne is soft, lightly lingering in the air. His gray T-shirt stretches across his shoulders in a mouth-watering way. And the way his joggers hug his thighs? I'm ready to say screw it and take him to bed.

But that won't solve any of our problems.

"So you came out."

Alex stops. Those same shoulders I was just admiring

are now bunched with tension. "Going straight for it, huh?"

"Would you like more small talk? How are you doing? I'm not doing so great. You looked like shit on Sunday," I deadpan. "Now you go."

Alex spins to face me, quirking a brow in my direction. "I really looked like shit?"

"That's what you're focused on right now?" Athletes. They're always worried about how they're playing.

"Right. Sorry." Resting his hands on his hips, I can see the measured breaths he's taking. "I came out."

"You came out."

Alex's brown eyes are a torrent of emotion. It's every emotion that I've been feeling these last few weeks. But neither one of us is saying anything.

I want nothing more than to pull him into my arms and tell him everything will be okay, but we're in this weird in-between place. One I don't like being in with him.

"Why now?" I whisper, almost as if disturbing the energy in the room will make it not real. That I'm not here with Alex.

Alex looks down, breaking the connection. "I didn't do it for you."

His words are like a knife to the heart. I wish they weren't, but they are. "Guess I should probably go then, huh?"

"No," Alex answers immediately. He closes the remaining distance between us, taking my hand in his. "Don't you think I would have called you before now if I came out for you?"

"So why did you then?"

Alex squeezes my hand before starting. "Hollins called me a faggot."

"Vegas really is the worst team, aren't they?"

He laughs, squeezing my hand. "I unloaded on him."

"I saw."

"After I got kicked out of the game, I had a heart to heart with your dad."

That stops me. "You did?"

"It's like everything piled on top of me at once and I couldn't take it anymore. I snapped. I had to tell someone."

I squeeze his hand. "That must have been really hard."

He nods, swallowing. "It was. I didn't want to do it for you because I didn't want to pressure you into coming back to me. It would've been another shitty decision on top of a shit sandwich I put you in. I was terrible to you."

His voice breaks and I don't think before pulling him into my arms. He sags into me. It's a relief to finally feel him again.

"As much as I love you, I knew it was a decision I had to make for me." Alex's breath is hot on my neck.

"I know it couldn't have been easy." I squeeze him tighter to me. Backing us up into the living room, I sit us down on the couch, not breaking the connection.

"It was actually kind of terrifying." Alex's hand plays with the buttons on my shirt. His voice is gravelly with emotion.

"How'd everyone on the team take it?" My own hands roam over his chest. God, I've missed the feel of him.

"About how I expected. Colin and Peyton have been great. Peyton set up the interview with the reporter—"

"And here I thought you didn't like any reporters," I interrupt.

"Only because I was scared of them finding out who I really am."

"And now that you're out?"

"Finn was great. Peyton wants him to do another story

in a few months to see how the league has responded, but he made it easy to tell my story."

"Has there been any backlash?"

I'm not naive enough to think that it would be all smooth sailing. I can't imagine how some people around the league are taking his news. It's part of the reason Alex wasn't out.

"About what you'd expect. Some are much worse than others."

"Let me guess…Hollins?"

"He's probably the worst of them all. But the team has been great. And I've been ignoring the news. If I need to know anything, Peyton fills me in."

I shift on the couch so I'm now facing Alex. His eyes are glassy. "I knew they would be. Did you think they would treat you any differently?"

Alex shrugs a shoulder and goes back to playing with the buttons on my shirt. "Yeah. It's one thing to say you're okay with it, but a completely other thing when it's one of your teammates."

"If anyone says anything bad about you, I'll…"

"You'll what?" A smile plays on Alex's lips. "Beat them up for me?"

"I mean, I could try."

"I think it's sweet you want to try, but they would snap you like a twig."

"Hey!" I swat him in the chest. "I'm slightly offended you think I couldn't take any of them."

"Okay, Carter. You can take a three-hundred-pound linebacker, no problem."

"If it means they hurt the man I love, yeah."

"The man you love?" Alex asks.

This time, it's my eyes dropping. I play with the V of

Alex's T-shirt. "Just because you broke my heart doesn't mean I stopped loving you."

"But I hurt you. And I'll never forgive myself for that."

"I won't lie, you did. Even now it still hurts."

"Then why are you here?" Alex grasps my chin, forcing my eyes to his. "You came over just to tell me how much it hurts that I broke your heart?"

"No. I came over to see if you were okay."

"And that's it?"

Pushing Alex back, I sit up straighter. The intoxicating scent of him is too overwhelming to be having this conversation so close.

"You just came out, Alex. Are you even in the right headspace to be in a relationship?"

Alex shakes his head, and it's like a lead balloon settling in my gut. Did I come here under the guise of checking to make sure he was okay, but also to see where we stood? Yes. But with one shake of his head, it's like he's decimated my heart again.

"I'm not saying no to you, Carter." Fisting a hand in my shirt, Alex pulls me toward him. "I couldn't be in a relationship with anyone else but you. There's just a lot going on right now and for once, I want to be fair to you."

I cup Alex's warm, wet cheeks. "Then lean on me. If you're having a bad day, let me help. It's not always easy when you're in love. This is just the really hard part for us."

"You really want to be with me after everything I did to you?"

"You don't plan on going back in the closet any time soon, do you?"

Alex shakes his head. "Definitely not—even if that were possible."

"Then I'll be here for you every step of the way. It'll be

our new normal." I wave a finger between the two of us. "So you and me?"

Alex nods, moving closer to me. "If you'll have me."

"If I'll have you..." I roll my eyes and close the remaining distance between the two of us, crushing my lips to his.

Fuck, I've missed this. Missed *him*. The scrape of his stubble against my mouth has me moaning in delight. Strong hands pull me over his lap, his hard length pressing against my own.

It's like no time has passed at all between us, yet everything has changed. I know it'll be a shift for Alex to want to be out in public together, but I'll take it slow with him.

Because I want this with him. More than I've ever wanted anything in my life.

Alex pulls back first, his eyes hazy. "You have no idea how much I've missed you."

"I think I do." I wrap my arms around his neck, dropping my forehead to his. "I'm pretty sure I gave my students detention for any little thing."

"Ouch. Don't mess with Mr. Brooks."

"More like don't mess with Alex. Those hits you landed on Hollins? Yikes."

Alex winces. "Not one of my finer moments."

"If it's what brought you back to me right now, then I guess I'll allow it."

Pulling back, Alex cups the back of my neck, bringing me closer to him. "Can I tell you I love you for real now?"

I think back to that day when I shut him down. I didn't want to hear it then. Not when he was trying to keep me for the wrong reasons. Now? Now I want to hear it. "You may."

A heart-stopping grin spreads across his face. "I love you, Carter Brooks. I want to spend every night with you, wake up every morning and shower with you, and listen to boy bands while we argue about comic books and you tell me horror stories from school."

"I love you, Alex Young." My voice is thick with emotion. "I want to make dinner with you, and dance in the yard with you, and get into fights with comic book fans, and eat cheese fries at diners. I want it all with you."

"So have I changed your mind on football players?"

I kiss Alex, long and slow. A sweeping of tongues as we take each other in again.

"You most certainly have, Mr. Quarterback."

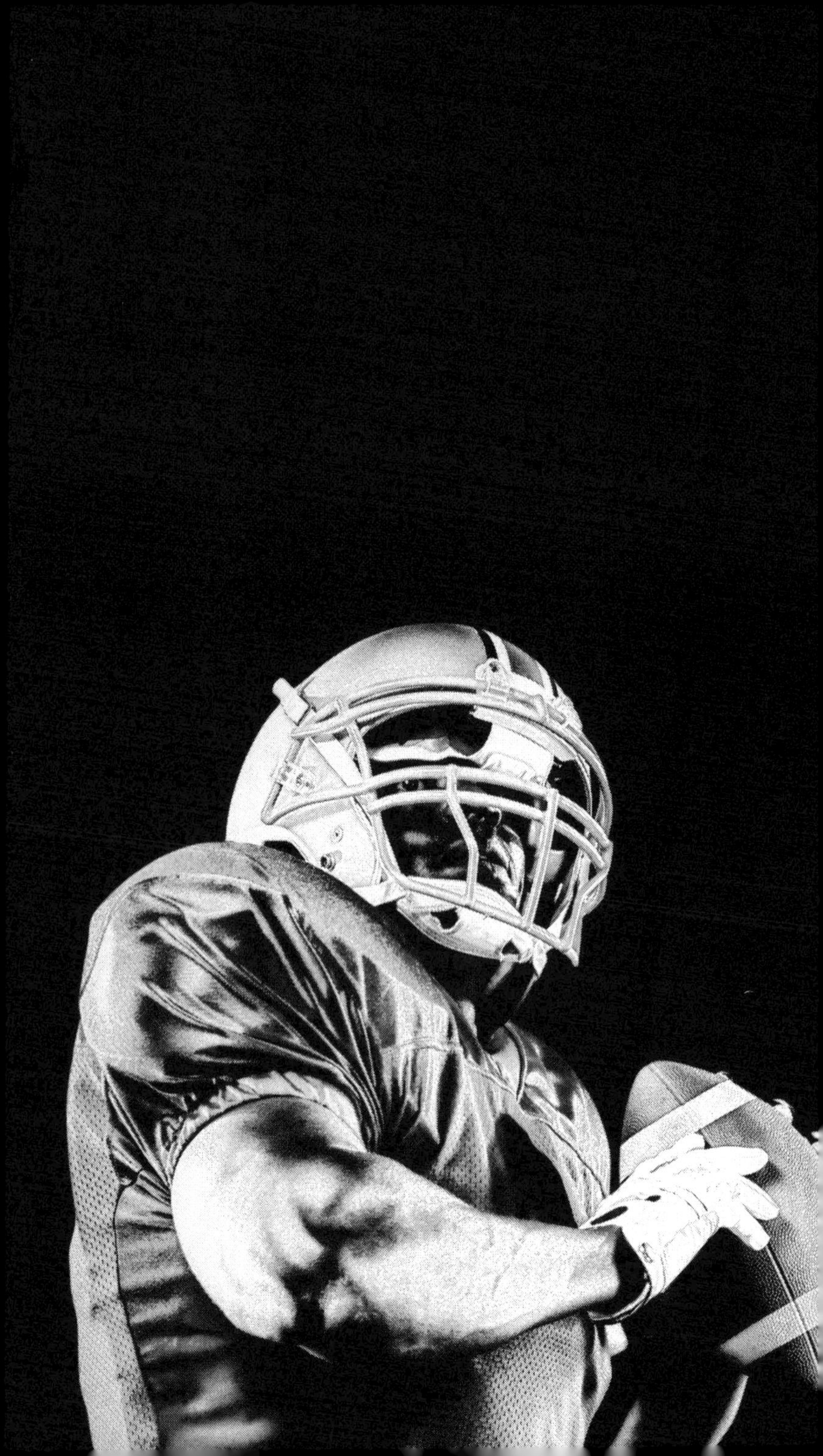

Chapter Thirty-Two

ALEX

"Are you boys ready?" Knox yells.

"Fuck yeah!" Shouts echo around the locker room.

It's finally here.

The AFC championship game.

The game before the Super Bowl.

And we're playing San Diego at home.

I'm practically crawling out of my skin with energy.

"Alright everyone, listen up!" Coach Brooks shouts.

Everyone quiets as he moves to the center of the locker room.

"One game. Focus on this game. Don't look forward. I want you to play your game today. San Diego is a tough team, but if we stick to our game plan, there's nothing we can't accomplish as a team."

Colin and Jackson flank me as I look around the entire locker room. Every single man in here has fought all season long. Despite the outside noise and pressure, we've stuck together. We're a winning team—always near the top of the conference, so we're used to it.

But when my news broke, the media circus around the team was too much. Instead of the focus being on the team and our record, it became about me.

I anticipated it, but it was hard for the guys.

Even with a loss to end the season, we're here.

One game away.

"Who are we?" Knox shouts, stepping into the center of the room.

"Mountain Lions!" we roar in response.

"Whose house is this?" Knox yells again.

"Our house!"

"Then let's go out there and protect it!"

No one is quiet as we all yell and scream at the top of our lungs as we leave the locker room. Everyone slaps the Mountain Lion logo before we gather to run onto the field as one team.

Our breaths create a fog around us in the late-January cold. A foot of snow was dumped on the city yesterday, but it didn't stop our fans. Playing in front of the home crowd is exactly what we wanted.

And there's one person I can't wait to be playing in front of.

Carter.

I let my mind wander to him during the pregame ceremony.

Jackson and Colin have always told me how much better they play when Tenley and Peyton are in the stands. How they want to make them proud.

I've never understood it until now.

With this being such a big game, I want to make Carter proud. I want him to shout, "That's my boyfriend!" from the stands.

It sounds silly, but ever since I came out, I love seeing him wearing my number to every home game.

And this one is no different.

Knox and Colin go out for the coin toss, and San Diego wins.

Putting on my helmet, I'm ready.

Ready for the biggest game of my career.

Let's fucking go.

CARTER

"I'M GOING TO BE SICK."

San Diego is celebrating on the sidelines. One lucky Hail Mary pass and Denver lost.

One game away from the Super Bowl.

"Come on. We can wait down in the family suite and see them," Mom says, wrapping an arm around me.

"They lost," I whisper, turning to look at her. "What happens now? What if I'm bad luck and he hates me?"

I feel like I'm five years old again, needing my mom. She's been through this with my dad. I know what happens now. But I don't know what I'll be walking into when I see Alex.

I've been there for him through some hard games, but nothing like this.

"You aren't bad luck, Carter. It just wasn't their day. Be there for him. Tell him you love him. That's all you can do." She kisses my cheek, and we follow Marley out of the suite and down the elevator.

The morose sound of seventy-six thousand fans leaving the stands weighs heavy as the elevator doors open in the basement.

Media are lingering in the concrete hall as players start heading to the locker room. When I see those sad, dejected eyes I love so much, I don't think.

"Alex!" I call out to him.

His head snaps to mine and he jogs over to me, wrapping his arms around me. I don't care that he's cold, sweaty, and covered in dirt. I wrap my arms around him and squeeze him as close to me as possible.

"We lost." His voice breaks, nearly breaking me. "We lost."

"I know," I whisper into his ear, my hands drifting into his hair.

Shutters click around us, but I don't care. The man in my arms is close to breaking.

And it's damn near breaking my heart.

"I just...I thought we had it."

"I know," I repeat. God, why can't I say anything to console Alex?

"We had it." This time, Alex breaks. Hot tears sting my neck and it takes everything I have not to lose it too.

I need to be strong for Alex.

Because as much as this is a game, it's what he lives for. His job.

And it means the world to him. And the fans.

To lose it, this close to the Super Bowl, will nag at him for a long time.

"I guess the football gods wanted San Diego to win more."

This earns me a laugh. "That doesn't make me feel any better."

Alex pulls back, his eyes wet and red. "I know. I'm terrible at this." I thumb away the stray tear. "You did everything you could. You fought so hard this season, and even though you didn't win—"

Alex interrupts, "Again, not helping."

I lean in and kiss him. "Then stop interrupting me."

"You were saying?" He drops his forehead to mine.

"Even though you didn't win, this season still means something. You came out. You were a role model before, and now, you're someone so many young kids can look up to. So yeah, you didn't win today, but I feel it in my bones that you'll be hoisting that trophy soon."

There's a fire in me now. I believe it. I absolutely believe that Alex and the Mountain Lions will win a Super Bowl.

"Maybe two or three in the next six years?" Alex laughs, wiping the last of his tears away.

"Oddly specific, but okay."

"That's what your student said."

I roll my eyes. "Now you're choosing to listen to high schoolers?"

"I mean, they did bring us together."

Alex closes the distance between us, his lips brushing mine in a tender kiss.

Alex of six months ago would never have done this. Hell, Alex of two months ago would have balked at the idea.

Now, here he is. Taking what he needs.

And I give it to him.

I put everything I'm feeling for him into this too-short kiss.

Shouts from around us pull us out of our bubble. Flashes are blinding as the present is forced back in our faces.

"I guess I probably should have thought about the crowd," Alex says, an embarrassed flush creeping up his face.

We've been out together since the article, but that

doesn't mean he's comfortable with PDA. Especially one as intimate as we just shared.

"I should probably get into the locker room." The sadness is back.

"I'll be waiting."

There's a quiver to Alex's lip and it wrecks me. I hate seeing him like this.

"Thank you."

I pull him in for another hug. "You never have to thank me for being here for you. I love you. That will never change. Whether you win or lose. I'm always on your side."

"You're going to make me cry again." Alex steps away. "I love you too."

Alex gets swallowed up by the rest of the team as he heads back to the locker room.

Any nerves I had about Alex freaking out right now are washed away.

Because the man I love held on to me for dear life just now. Like I was his anchor in the storm.

And there's no other place I'd rather be than tethered to my boy band and comic book loving quarterback.

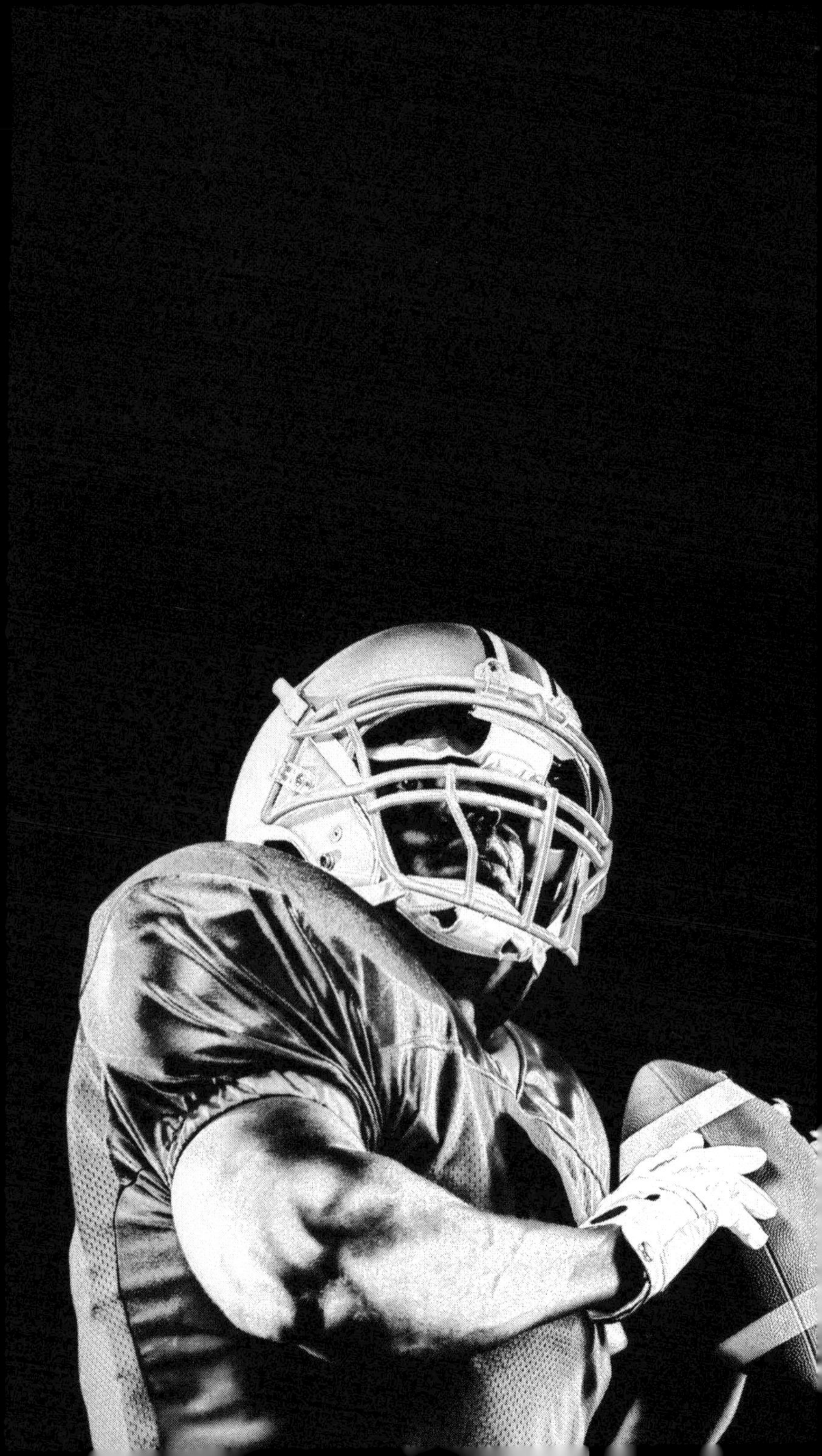

Epilogue

ALEX - TWO WEEKS LATER

"I could live here."

"Wouldn't you miss football?" Carter grabs my ankle and pulls my weightless body to him.

"I wouldn't be sore all the time, that's for sure."

The sun continues its descent toward the horizon. Gold and pinks reflect off the ocean. After a heartbreaking loss in the AFC championship game, Carter booked us a week in Mexico. He implemented a strict no-TV rule so I couldn't hear what the analysts were saying about the Mountain Lions' loss in the playoffs.

For the second year in a row.

"I can think of other ways you'd be sore."

"Oh yeah?" I push my sunglasses up my head as I wrap my legs around him. His skin is pink from a day spent in the sun.

"Maybe you could be a football coach down here and I could teach. Just you and me."

"Mmm. I like the sound of that." I pull Carter closer, pecking his lips with mine, tasting his piña colada.

"Too bad you'd go stir-crazy." Carter's hands drift

lower. It sends a shock through me. Even after all these months, I love that I still have this reaction to him.

And that I get to be with him like this.

I never thought that this could be my life. I thought I would be in the closet until well into my retirement. But I guess all it took was one man to change my perspective.

It hasn't always been easy, but Carter was by my side for all of it. The good and the bad.

The picture of the two of us after the game made headlines. I guess my boyfriend consoling me was breaking news.

"You're right," I sigh. "It's nice to dream though, right?"

Carter brushes a piece of hair behind my ear. His dark eyes are locked on mine. "Maybe we could come back here for the honeymoon."

I throw my head back on a laugh. "So is this you agreeing that last night was a real proposal?"

"I never thought that was how I'd get proposed to, but I'll relent."

"Yes!" I pump my fist in the air, alcohol buzzing through my veins. "See, I told you it was romantic."

"It was only romantic because it was coming from you." I know he wants to be more annoyed than he actually is.

"Excuse me, gentlemen. But your table is ready," one of the servers interrupts.

"Table?" I swing my gaze back to Carter.

"We'll be right there, thank you." Carter nods in his direction. "C'mon. We don't want to be rude and keep them waiting."

My legs drop from his hips as I follow him out of the pool.

Grabbing a towel, I dry myself off as best I can. "Are we even dressed appropriately for dinner?"

Carter tosses me my shirt. "We'll be fine. Now stop asking questions."

Linking my hand with his, I follow Carter out toward the beach. For being late January, it's relatively quiet here. The sand is still warm from the sun. And sitting under a pergola is a table set for two.

"What's all this?" I pull Carter to a stop in front of the table. Lights are wrapped around the poles as a bottle of champagne sits in an ice bucket. The waves are coming closer to shore as the tide comes in.

Carter shrugs a shoulder. "I wanted to do something special for you. I know the last few weeks haven't been easy, so, yeah…" Carter mumbles as he waves a hand around the setup.

"Just being here with you is special enough."

Carter pulls me into his arms. "I know. Between coming out, all the interviews and the playoffs, you've been going nonstop. So hopefully this entire trip is a good break for you."

I drop my face into Carter's neck, trying not to let my emotions get the best of me. He smells like the ocean and sunscreen. "Thank you. For being so wonderful and loving me like no one else could."

"You never have to thank me." Carter's breath is hot on my ear. "I love you, Alex. And I'll love you for as long as I can."

"That's going to be a really long time."

"Good. Because I plan on it."

His lips on my neck have my blood stirring. I trail a hot path of kisses up his neck, mirroring everything he is doing to me. I squeeze him tighter to me, not wanting to break the connection.

"As much as I'd love to keep doing this to you, I think it'd be rather inappropriate right here."

"Why do you have to be so sensible?" I groan.

"One of us has to be." Carter pushes me toward the table as he takes his own seat.

Everything smells incredible—at least three different kinds of meat, vegetables, salsas. A pitcher of margaritas in addition to the champagne.

"They outdid themselves."

Carter hands me a flute of champagne. "They did. And I didn't even tell them we were celebrating anything tonight."

"Well, I guess we need to make a toast since this is now an impromptu celebratory dinner."

"You're the one with the speeches, captain. Go right ahead." Carter rests his elbow on the table as he leans closer to me with his glass extended.

"To the man I love. I hope we never get bored with one another. That even when we're old and gray, we're still going to comic book conventions together. Going to diners after and maybe a few trips back here. And hopefully have a few kids running around to chase after."

Carter's eyes are glassy. "That sounds pretty fucking amazing."

I clink my glass to his. "To us. To you and me and the amazing life we're going to have together."

"To us." Carter sips his champagne, then sets it down. "But you did forget one thing."

"Oh yeah? What's that?" I quirk a brow in his direction.

"A championship ring."

I knock on the table immediately. "You're going to jinx it!"

"Nope. Like Austin said, the Mountain Lions are going

to win two Super Bowls in the next few years. Just you wait and see."

"As long as you're there by my side when I hoist that trophy."

"I'm not going anywhere, future husband of mine."

Damn. I love this football player.

THE END

Want to see that proposal scene? Keep reading...

Want to know more about Finn and Wes? Check out Off The Deep End today!

$\cot g$

15

100% 4

$\sqrt{1+}$

A 2

$2 + 1$

$\sqrt{13}$ $\sum$ $12 + 84$

1 18

S

8 $\dfrac{}{2\sqrt{2}}$

2

$x -$

Bonus Scene

CARTER

"Someone's feeling frisky."

"I can't help it if you look too good in nothing but swim trunks."

Alex is flush against my back, distracting me from the task of trying to get into our hotel room. Warm lips kiss up my neck.

"We really shouldn't be doing this right here."

I drop my neck to the side, giving him better access as the light flashes red again.

"Then open the door."

Alex reaches around, his fingers skirting the waistband of my shorts.

"Maybe if your hands weren't on me, I could concentrate." Two more flashes of red before green. "Thank god."

Shoving the door open, I turn, giving the muscled man behind me my full attention. My lips collide with his in a messy kiss, one where we're both fighting for control.

His lips taste like the piña colada he was drinking by

the pool earlier. My fingers drift down and over his abs, trailing over each ridge. "You know it's unfair that you are allowed to go shirtless like this."

Laughter shakes his body. "However would you like me to make it up to you?"

I step back, letting my eyes take him in. He's only been in my life for a short while, but I don't think I'll ever get my fill of the man in front of me.

It's been nothing short of a crazy few weeks together since he came out, but I'm glad we get this time alone together.

Especially with what I'm about to propose.

"Care for a little role playing?"

The air in the room shifts. Alex closes the distance between us, fisting my shirt in his hand to pull me close. "What do you have in mind?"

A smile tugs at the corner of my mouth as I back us into the room. "On the bed. Hands up by the headboard."

Alex follows my instructions without a word. Seeing him laid out for me like this has so many ideas on what I could do to him running through my mind. Grabbing my belt from the chair, I walk around the bed and make quick work of tying his hands to the slatted board behind the bed.

"I think I'm going to like this." Alex's voice is gravely.

"I have no doubt you will." I drop a quick kiss to his lips. "I'll be back in a minute."

I find what I need and head into the bathroom, letting the door shut behind me. As much as I wish we weren't here, I'm glad Alex we're together. I know he'd much rather be preparing for the Super Bowl, and seeing the dejection on his face was like a knife through the heart. He tries not to show how affected he is, but I know it. I can see it when he thinks I'm not looking.

Sideline Infraction

That's why I'm hoping this little outfit will be the perfect distraction for him.

Fixing my hair in the mirror one last time, I throw open the door and my eyes find Alex's immediately.

"Need someone to save you?" I quirk a brow his way as I watch his pupils widen as he takes me in.

"Holy shit."

I don't miss the way his cock tents his briefs. Or the way he's licking his lips.

Taking a step closer to the bed, I drag a finger up the defined muscles in his leg, watching as goosebumps break out in its trail.

"Like what you see?"

"Fuck, do I ever."

Alex hasn't taken his eyes off me. Dropping down onto the mattress, I yank his legs apart, moving between them.

"Enough to let me rescue you?"

"Yes. God yes. I'd let you do it to me every day of the rest of our lives if we were married."

"What?" His words stop me in my tracks.

"What what?" Alex is looking at me with a confused expression.

"Did you not hear what you just said?"

He licks his lips. "Something about letting you do this to me everyday…"

"If we were married," I finish for him.

"I didn't…." it dawns on him as he trails off. "Holy shit. Can you untie me? This is really not how I want to be having this conversation."

"Oh, yeah. Sorry." I scramble across the bed, undoing the ties.

Alex sits up, inching closer to me. "That was so not what I meant to say. Are you freaking out?"

I don't even get the chance to answer before he's

answering for me. "It's fine. You can forget I said anything and we can go back to what we were doing."

"You expect me to go back to what we were doing after you say that?"

"Umm, yes?" He asks, unsure.

My mind is whirring. We haven't been together that long. Hell, even shorter since Alex has been out.

But the words that I didn't want to hear?

You can forget I said anything.

Because now the thought of linking my life to Alex's - in a permanent way - has a whole new set of awareness buzzing through my veins.

"What if I don't want to forget it?"

"Are you serious?"

"I don't think this counts as a real proposal by any stretch, but the idea of you and me getting married?" I waggle a finger between the two of us. "I happen to love that idea."

"Duly noted." Alex links his hands behind my head, pulling me down over him. Our bodies line up perfectly - just like they always have. "So then what does count as a real proposal?"

"A little wining and dining wouldn't be the end of the world. Maybe play our song for me."

Alex leans up, taking my lips in a hot kiss. "Is this you telling me no?"

"This is me saying a yes will come when it's a real proposal. Are we really going to tell people that you said you wanted to be married to me on a whim when you were half naked and I was dressed up like Superman before sex?"

Alex laughs. "We don't have to tell people that's how it happened. Saying I proposed in Mexico works just fine."

Sideline Infraction

I push back, straddling his hips. His dick is still long and hard under me. "Then maybe you should work on your proposal again."

"Maybe I should hold out on you until you agree that it was a real proposal."

I smirk at the man below me. "Do you really want to test that theory?" I lean closer, my lips a breath away from his. "I know you don't like edging, and that would be it in the worst way."

"I hate you," he grumbles.

"Really, Alex. This is hands down the best proposal ever. Your best work."

Alex flips us around, my back now on the bed. "Which means you should just say yes to put me out of my misery."

Running a head down his chest, I grab a hold of his hips, pulling him closer to me. His hard length brushes against my own.

"I don't know if I'll put you out of your misery, but I'll definitely be doing something to you."

Alex stops me, his hand resting on my heart. "Joking aside, I love you. If you want a marching band through downtown Denver or me asking you after I finally win the Super Bowl, I'll give you whatever you want. Because you deserve everything."

I don't know how I thought I could ever live without this man. Even those few weeks were too many. "I love you, Alex. So damn much. I don't need a big embarrassing display of our love. I just need you."

"And you'll always have me."

He gives me a long, mind-melting kiss. Everything slows around us and it's just the two of us here together. The outside world isn't a distraction. There's no talk of how the Mountain Lions didn't make it to the Super Bowl or if Alex was more of hindrance to his team after coming out. It's all white noise as we're here together.

Alex breaks the kiss, his eyes hazy with need. Those swollen lips break into a smile that has me itching to kiss it away.

"Now, can we get back to you rescuing me?"

Acknowledgments

Book 10 is out in the world!

In the blink of an eye, I've written and published 10 books! TEN! I don't even know how that happened. This has been the craziest ride, and I for one hope it continues!

There are so many people to thank, and I hope I don't miss any! Thank you Jenny for beta reading this book and loving Alex! You helped make this book what it is and I'm so grateful for our friendship. To Claire, Suzanne and the Happily Editing Ann's…because without our writer's retreat, I have no idea where this book would have been! To Norma for always being by my side. To Tina for always being there and making me laugh with all the dog videos! To Katie for being the best girl you could ever turn to when you need anything at all! To LJ for being the best human I know. And for all the other amazing author friends who are too many to name…I love you all!

To my Street Team…thank you for being the biggest cheerleaders of my books! The fact that you love them so much keeps me going!

To all the readers, bookstagrammers and BookTokers…I LOVE your passion for reading and my books! So many of you have found my books and spread the love and I will be eternally grateful! THANK YOU!

<3 Emily

About the Author

After winning a Young Author's Award in second grade, Emily Silver was destined to be a writer. She loves writing strong heroines and the swoony men who fall for them.

A lover of all things romance, Emily started writing books set in her favorite places around the world. As an avid traveler, she's been to all seven continents and sailed around the globe.

When she's not writing, Emily can be found sipping cocktails on her porch, reading all the romance she can get her hands on and planning her next big adventure!

Find her on social media to stay up to date on all her adventures and upcoming releases!

Also by Emily Silver

The Denver Mountain Lions

Roughing The Kicker

Pass Interference

Sideline Infraction

Illegal Contact

The Big Game

Dixon Creek Ranch

Yours To Lose - newsletter bonus story

Yours to Take - coming March 23, 2023

Yours to Hold - coming June 29, 2023

Yours to Be - coming August 24, 2023

Yours to Forget - coming November 16, 2023

Off the Deep End — A standalone, MM sports romance

The Ainsworth Royals

Royal Reckoning

Reckless Royal

Royal Relations

Royal Roots

Royal Ties

The Love Abroad Series

An Icy Infatuation

A French Fling

A Sydney Surprise

Get all my titles now:

Made in the USA
Columbia, SC
22 July 2023